SOLOMON'S WELL

AJ BAILEY ADVENTURE SERIES - BOOK 5

NICHOLAS HARVEY

Printed in the United States of America

First Printing, 2020

ISBN-13: 979-8639438035 (Amazon only)
ISBN-13: 978-1-959627-05-0 (IngramSparks)

Cover sunset photograph by Drew McArthur

Map licensed through Shutterstock

Cover design by Wicked Good Book Covers

Author photograph by Lift Your Eyes Photography

DEDICATION

For Cheryl, my mermaid.
What a leap of faith we took, yet she never hesitated.
We risked everything, and she's never wavered.
Her belief in us has been relentless,
and my love for her is endless.

1

1794

Santiago Velázquez stood on the deck of the Burman, a three-masted merchantman sailing under the British colours, with an English captain and an English crew. If that alone wasn't enough to make the Spaniard hesitate, the captain, one Andrew Farnley, now consorted with his coxswain and glanced sternly in Santiago's direction. The moon occasionally broke through the heavy cloud enough to illuminate the coastline of the island they sailed quietly by. Surely they had far greater issues afoot than to worry about an Hispanic-looking man aboard their ship, he thought, as he tried to judge the ship's distance to the low cliffs of the southern shore. The Burman had been part of a fifty-nine-ship convoy out of Jamaica, bound for England, escorted by the frigate HMS Convert. Less than an hour earlier they'd watched the lead ships scatter before striking the reef on the east end of Grand Cayman island. Captain Farnley had chosen to veer south, along with a dozen or so other ships, safely clearing the treacherous shallows. It appeared Farnley was now comfortable with their position and heading, as his attention fell to Santiago.

The captain knew him as William Miller, an American businessman visiting the sugar cane plantations of Jamaica. The unfortunate fellow who had provided Santiago's papers would likely have been discovered floating near the docks by now, but getting word to a sailing convoy was near impossible. Santiago's English was perfect, having grown up and taken his education in Washington. Later, in 1779, he returned with his parents to their native Spain at the outbreak of the Anglo-Spanish war. His olive skin and curled dark hair could not be disguised so easily, and his explanation of descent from a Spanish grandmother did little to dissuade suspicion. Why the captain chose this moment to turn his focus to his paying passenger, Santiago could only guess, but the man was gathering several more seamen, so clearly time was of the essence. The Spaniard moved swiftly amongst the shadows of the sails and rigging to find the steps below.

His private cabin in the stern was no more than a cot with enough room to stand alongside, but it did have a small window that opened. Santiago peered down to the dark water far below, trying to recall how far the rudder protruded beyond the tail of the ship. He welcomed the breeze brushing his sweat-covered brow in the warm, humid night. His choices were limited. If he waited, they'd be clear of land. If he jumped, he'd be swimming for another island under British control. Turning, he sat on the bed and removed his boots. His fate aboard this ship was certain, he decided, and took off his jacket and vest. Reaching under the bed he retrieved the real reason for his visit to Jamaica. Wrapped in cloth and bound securely with twine, the heavy package was over a foot long and two thirds of that wide. Taking his broad leather belt he fastened the package to his chest. Footsteps echoed from the deck above. Santiago stood and checked the package was tightly secured. He was a small man, and the weight of his bounty alone would make swimming difficult, but he had no choice. Above him, feet fell heavily on the steps; there was no more time for contemplation. He made the sign of the crucifix, allowing himself a slight smile at the irony.

The drop was farther than he had anticipated, and the impact with the water considerably more forceful than he expected. For a second he thought he'd struck the rudder, despite having jumped towards the starboard side, but it was a combination of breaking the surface and the package being shoved up violently into his chin. Santiago kicked frantically for the surface, the air knocked from his lungs and the taste of blood in his mouth. He gasped desperately as his head broke free of the ocean, and as he settled he made sure his belt was still holding firm. To come all this way and lose the package now would be unthinkable. Voices rained down from the departing ship and he glanced back in the darkness, just able to make out the large silhouette against the sky. He quickly turned and spotted what he hoped was the land, and struck out with steady strokes. As though a million candles were lit at the same moment, the sky illuminated with a silvery glow, bathing the sea all around him. Santiago halted and looked up at the full, bright moon, now free of the clouds. God is lighting the way, he rejoiced. The small splash of water to his left confused him. Until the sound of the musket reached his ears. God is also lighting their target, he realised. With distance being his best ally, he reached and kicked with all his might, desperate to clear himself of the English muskets. Ignoring the barrage of nearby splashes, Santiago swam with all his might.

He noticed his right arm drop mid stroke before he felt any pain. He tried to thrust his hand forward again but the limb barely moved and the pain reached him in a searing wave. Often he'd wondered what it would be like to be shot – God knows he'd seen enough men drop from a lead ball, many at his own hand. Now his curiosity was answered and he surely wished he didn't know. The light evaporated as quickly as it had highlighted the stricken Spaniard and the splashes ceased as the marksmen lost their target. Santiago felt the front of his right shoulder and the warm, unmistakable flow of blood told him the ball had passed through him. He had to make the shore. Flipping over, he tried swimming on his back, using his one good arm to help as he kicked keenly with his legs. The considerable weight of the package sank him deeper into the water and he struggled for breaths without swallowing the warm, salty water. As he dragged himself through the softly ebbing sea, he prayed aloud between gulps of wet air. He prayed for the strength to make land. He prayed for the strength to live. Not for his own salvation – he was content for God to take his soul, but not before his mission was complete. For his mission was God's work, after all. Surely the All-Powerful One would shepherd him through this quest. These challenges were merely tests of his faith, tests of his love, tests of his relentless desire to serve his country, and his God. He kicked a little harder, occasionally rolling over to glimpse the land he sought.

The water that felt so warm just a short time ago began to chill Santiago's bones. He shivered and felt the strength in his one good arm slowly fade, becoming as weak as his wounded limb. His head began to swirl and spin as though he'd overindulged in the rum that flowed like water in Jamaica. He pulled up and tried to clear his head with long, even breaths. He touched a hand to his wound and felt the blood still flowing freely. He rested his weary legs and quickly slipped below the water, the package and his sodden clothes dragging him down. His head suddenly cleared as his feet touched the sea floor and the water stung his eyes. He was close to shore. Spluttering his thanks to the Lord, he set out with renewed energy, pulling firmly and kicking with all the strength he had left. A test he had faced and that test he would conquer, for his faith in God was unwavering, the mantra he recited over and over to himself.

"Test me further my Lord," Santiago coughed. "I will not fail you," he whispered softly in Spanish.

His sweeping hand dragged over sharp rock and Santiago cried out in a mixture of relief and pain. His knees struck the jagged dead coral known as ironshore and cuts opened swiftly, but he didn't notice or care. Hauling himself upon the ancient limestone, he curled up and tightly clutched his precious package as the shivers returned. Once more the moonlight found an opening in the clouds and Santiago's surroundings became clear. He lifted his head and forced his weary eyes to focus. He was at the foot of a small cliff, no more than fifteen feet high, and farther along the base of the cliffs was a wooden ladder, affixed to the face. The Spaniard blinked repeatedly as his mind felt heavy and he struggled to make sense of the images before him. Standing at the base of the ladder was a young African boy, a slave he surmised, perhaps in his early teens by his muscular form. The boy stared back but made no move towards him and his expression was hard to make out in the dim light. Santiago tried to prop himself up to a seated position but the ironshore tore at his skin and wet clothing, provoking more violent shivers. He collapsed back down. The water lapped against the shore and echoed serenely, almost musically, in his ears. His eyelids felt as though their only purpose left in this world was to close. He willed them open and looked at two dark-skinned feet, effortlessly standing on the razor-sharp rock without any shoes. Santiago tilted his head up.

"I am on God's mission," he uttered weakly in Spanish. "I would welcome your aid."

The boy tipped his head to one side and stared curiously back.

"Help," Santiago said, in English. "I need help."

The boy crouched down and leaned over the Spaniard, lightly moving his tattered shirt to reveal the bleeding wound in his shoulder. The boy's brow creased and their eyes met. Santiago smiled, or at least he intended too, but he wasn't certain his desire was met by the muscles in his face; he simply had no strength left.

"Solomon," the boy said quietly in English. "I am Solomon."

"My Lord is taking me Solomon," Santiago mumbled incoherently in Spanish. "I have failed you God, but please accept me…"

Thus Santiago Velázquez left this world, still desperately clutching the precious item that had paved the road to his demise.

2

TUESDAY MORNING

Mermaid Divers' thirty-six-foot Newton dive boat, Hazel's Odyssey, eased away from the buoy they'd been moored to for their first dive that morning. Annabelle Jayne Bailey, English owner and operator of the boat, coiled the rope she had just released in a neat circle on the bow deck in preparation for their next mooring. Her shoulder-length purple-streaked, blonde hair whipped in the wind, quickly drying in the hot Caribbean sun. After the dive, she'd peeled off her wetsuit down to her bathing suit and needed to get a long-sleeved tee-shirt on to cover her full sleeve tattoos from the UV. Having turned thirty the previous year, she was trying to be more responsible about her sun exposure, covering her toned figure more diligently. She walked back along the gunwale beside the partially enclosed cabin and joined the eight divers on deck, busy switching their gear to fresh tanks. At the helm, Thomas Bodden, her friend and first mate, piloted the boat towards Peppermint Reef, a shallow site for their second dive. A young Caymanian, Thomas was one of the only locals to work in the dive industry, despite diving's rich history on Grand Cayman island. AJ felt the boat slow and looked up to the fly-bridge, curious why Thomas had shut the throttle down.

"Better get to the bow, boss," he shouted down in his musically accented English.

AJ hurried back to the bow and scanned the ocean ahead. Just off the starboard side she could see something barely breaking the surface and moving.

"What is that?" she yelled up to Thomas. She thought it might be a big clump of sea grass but that would be strange where they were, over the deeper reef on the west side.

"I believe there's a turtle caught up in whatever that is," Thomas said, gently playing with the throttle to keep them close without running into the mess in the water.

"It's a damn net, Thomas, the turtle's caught in a net. Call Casey at the DOE and ask her to get out here quick," AJ shouted as she hustled back to the rear deck where the group were all peering around to see what the commotion was about. She slipped her buoyancy control device, or BCD, back on, with her old tank still attached, figuring she wouldn't need much air and it was still a third full anyway. Slipping her fins on her feet she pulled her mask on and stepped to the back of the boat.

"Stay on the boat guys, I'll shout if I need a hand," she said to the group, before giant-striding into the clear warm water.

She dived down about ten feet so she could approach with a clear view, and sure enough it was a hawksbill turtle. What surprised her was the amount of fishing net the poor creature was dragging with it: the nylon mesh trailed down at least thirty feet. How the turtle was managing to keep itself near the surface was a miracle. Turtles breathe air and can hold that breath for extraordinary lengths of time underwater, if they're not stressed. This hawksbill was severely stressed and needed all the air he could get.

She didn't have much time and it seemed like a mass of netting to get through just to reach the turtle; if she wasn't careful she'd be as snared as it was. She reached out, grabbed a piece of net and, unsheathing her titanium dive knife, she sliced at the nylon to see how easily she could cut through it. The plastic twine surrendered under the blade but it made the net spread out even more – if she kept wading her way from the outside in, she and the turtle would be in a forest of netting. At least now it was trailing in one long stream. She decided to approach on the surface and see if she could free the turtle's flippers. She surfaced and put some air in her BCD to keep her afloat. Turning back to the boat she removed her regulator and yelled up to Thomas.

"Did you get hold of Casey?"

Thomas gave her the okay sign back so at least she knew help was on the way. Thomas couldn't jump in with her as it would leave the boat unattended with eight customers on board. The turtle was opening and closing its beak and she could see the strands of nylon mesh caught in its mouth. It was not only held by its flippers, it also had netting snagged in the back of its beak. She had even less time than she thought. Putting her reg back in she started clawing her way across the top of the netting. Very little of it floated on the surface, but just a foot below was a wave of mesh that grabbed and snagged on every piece of equipment strapped to her body. She freed herself when she could, and dragged the parts she couldn't untangle with her. It was tough sledding and the ten or twelve feet between her and the stricken turtle felt more like a mile. Somehow, if she could cut it free she had to stop it from snaring itself again as it tried to paddle away over this sea of netting she was wading through.

AJ finally got within arm's reach and could see approaching any closer would just pull the netting that was wrapped around the turtle and drag it under. She carefully took out her knife and slowly extended her hand. The turtle immediately thrashed its flippers, certain a predator was taking advantage of its precarious position. She waited until it calmed a little before reaching all the way. The turtle watched her and chomped firmly with its beak but didn't thrash its flippers anymore. She slipped the blade between its left flipper and several strands and quickly severed the nylon. Edging forward she lined up and cut the next few strands and the turtle's beak slowed its biting, somehow sensing it wasn't being threatened. Three more cuts and the left flipper was freed, and all hell broke loose.

Feeling its limb break free, the turtle thrashed it wildly attempting to swim its way out. AJ got the knife clear just in time but took a swat to the head knocking her mask off her face and her reg from her mouth. She spluttered and gasped, luckily grabbing her mask before it disappeared underwater. She slid it back on, careful not to stab herself with her own knife as she did so and unhooked the reg from the net where it had instantly snared. The turtle's flipper snagged on another piece of netting and it calmed down again, apparently deciding it was back where it had started, which was fairly accurate.

Okay, AJ decided, cut it almost free, but not completely free until we're ready to go. Leaving the new strands holding the left flipper, she moved on to the beak which was going to be harder. The nylon was wrapped tightly around the turtle's face and neck and she was sure it wouldn't be pleased with the blade against its cheek. Moving very slowly she gently slid the blade under a few strands and cut them carefully. The turtle looked at her with its big dark eye and she could see its eyelid dropping. It had worn itself out completely, and if she didn't get it freed soon it would be gone. Moving a little faster she cut and sliced nylon strand after nylon strand. This close to the turtle she could now see the wounds around the base of its flippers where the net had sliced its leathery skin. AJ wanted to cry but there was no time for tears. She wanted to scream at the recklessness of the fishermen who'd lost their net, but that wouldn't help either. She reached farther and cut more nylon.

AJ heard the boat approach but didn't take the time to look up; she almost had his beak free.

"What can I do?" came Casey's voice from the DOE boat as she pulled up close. Casey and her husband had run a dive operation on the island for a long time and finally pulled the boats out when she was offered a job at the Department of Environment. It was a perfect fit, as she still got to play in the waters she knew so well and was happy to be rid of the stress of keeping her own business afloat.

AJ spat her reg out. "I've almost got him cut free, but somehow we have to get him away from the net. If he starts to swim he'll snare himself again." She gathered her breath as the water slapped her face. "We need to pull the net down and away from him, I think."

AJ managed to get her reg back in her mouth and hoped her air would last; she was sucking down lungful after lungful with all the exertion. She heard the boat motor away but paid no attention, as she knew Casey would figure something out to help. The hard part now was getting herself to the other side of the turtle to cut the right flipper free. She could feel she was caught up herself in the net, so rather than try going around she ducked under and started cutting from below. After several minutes she'd got most of the right flipper clear but knew it would try and thrash again if she cut the last few strands. Or maybe not, she wondered, sensing it was totally exhausted. As she was considering her options she heard a tapping sound and recognised it as someone signalling with metal against a dive tank. AJ looked down and through the maze of netting she could see Casey in full dive gear below her. She must have grabbed a kit off Hazel's Odyssey.

AJ waved and gave her a pull sign, hoping she could see her signal through the nylon screen. She turned back and severed the last few strands holding both flippers, and the turtle just floated there. For a moment she thought they might have lost it but it slowly started moving a flipper and gained momentum when it realised it wasn't trapped anymore. AJ felt herself being pulled down and for a second was confused. Then she realised she was now firmly snared in the net that Casey was pulling with all her might.

The turtle began to swim lethargically away as the path cleared and Casey must have seen him go as she stopped pulling the net down. AJ took a couple of deep breaths to fend off the urge to panic; now she was the one trapped and it seemed like the net was wrapped completely around her. She began to cut at the nylon and freed her left arm but the problem was her snared tank and BCD, which she couldn't reach behind her. She'd drifted down from the pull of the net, and at about thirty feet below the surface her regulator made a ghastly clunk as the tank ran out of air.

She could see Casey was making her way up but she was on the outside of the ball of netting and had no way to get to her. AJ wriggled her arms down and unbuckled the waist belt of her BCD, shaking her body and hoping the straps would drop off her shoulders. It worked: the netting stayed with the rig and she kicked her way free and glided up towards the surface, careful to exhale some compressed air from her lungs as she went. She broke the surface to cheers from the boat, but didn't have time to waste. With a long inhalation she dived back down and kicked towards the sinking net now weighted by her deflated BCD and tank. Casey was gathering armfuls of netting to slow the descent but was clearly going to need help. AJ swam down to the opposite side and took hold of two fistfuls of the nylon mesh. The two of them kicked for the surface and slowly dragged the netting with them. With great relief AJ broke the surface again to another round of cheers from Hazel's Odyssey.

"Didn't want to lose my gear," she spluttered as she tried to catch her breath and couldn't help laughing in between.

Casey spat her reg out. "I couldn't figure out why the net started sinking so fast until your tank went past me."

AJ waved a hand at her. "Ah, it was empty."

They both laughed as Thomas swung the stern of the Newton over so they could drag the net, AJ's gear and themselves aboard.

Once they'd managed to get the whole net on the swim step, Casey shed the borrowed BCD and tank and began to figure out how to transfer the mess to the DOE boat she'd arrived on. Her co-worker helped, and with the two boats stern to stern she shovelled the tangled pile of nylon across. She gave AJ a quick hug before stepping over her transom to leave.

"Any way to trace the net to a buyer or a particular fishing boat?" AJ thought to ask before they pulled away.

Casey shook her head. "Nope, and this is the second one this week we've found on the west side. I reckon they get too close and snag the wall out at the north-west corner. It's at night of course." She waved and the boat pulled away.

AJ sighed; never a dull moment, she thought.

"Why do they fish at night?" one of her customers asked.

"Because it's illegal," AJ answered. "Can't use a drag net inside Cayman waters – they're supposed to be outside the international mark, nowhere near the reefs. Seems someone is coming in during the night and trawling close to the island."

Thomas started the Newton's diesel back up and they finally headed towards their second dive of the morning. AJ grabbed a towel, dried herself off and pulled a shirt from her rucksack. She slipped it on and was about to head up to the fly-bridge when she heard her mobile ringing in her bag. She looked at the caller ID. Jonty Gladstone. That was someone she hadn't spoken to in a while. Their paths had first crossed when she'd saved him from himself in an expansive cave system he'd discovered on the north side of the island. She wondered what he could possibly want.

"Hey Jonty, how have you been?" she said as she held the mobile in one hand and scaled the ladder to the fly-bridge.

"Can we meet for lunch or a drink or something?" he said.

Jonty wasn't big on salutations, but this was abrupt even for him. "I guess. What's up? What do you need?"

"Can't talk over the phone, can you meet today?"

"Uh, I guess. We're out on the boat but we're not doing an afternoon. 1:30 at Greenhouse Cafe work?"

"See you there," he said and the line went dead. Never dull, she thought again.

3

TUESDAY LUNCHTIME

AJ spotted Jonty in the back corner of the Greenhouse Cafe, her favourite lunch spot at the edge of George Town. Jonty was in his late thirties and had been on Grand Cayman for the better part of thirteen years, having landed there after a misunderstanding with the Federales in the Yucatan peninsula of Mexico. At least that's how he preferred to explain his rapid departure and hastily organised relocation. He made his living as a dive guide and instructor, when anyone would hire him, but his passion was treasure hunting. The former kept the lights on and the latter had paid off in a few small finds, but usually cost him more than he discovered. Scruffy in appearance and gruff in his manner, his northern English straight-talking approach alienated many, but AJ found him amusing. She sat down and waved at Jen, the owner and chef, before turning to Jonty.

"So what's your latest escapade you couldn't talk about over the phone then?"

Jonty grinned and his weary eyes sparkled for a moment through what was most likely a lingering hangover.

"I think I'm on to something pretty big, but I need some help."

Jonty leaned back as Jen approached their table. She swooped in and hugged AJ. "Hey girl, what are you up to with this trouble-maker?" Jen nodded towards Jonty as she straightened up.

AJ laughed. "He offered to buy me lunch, so I figured I'd get a free meal while he asks me to do something for him."

"I didn't say I was buying," Jonty grumbled.

"I should probably make you pay up front in case you do a runner," Jen retorted, unable to keep from laughing.

Jonty shook his head and frowned. "You always treat your customers like this?"

"Just the ones that don't pay their bills." Jen waggled her finger at him, and AJ sat back, enjoying the show.

Jonty looked down at the table. "One bloody time, I forgot I hadn't settled the bill. One time, and I came back and squared up."

"Yeah." Jen rolled her eyes. "A week later."

"Bugger me, will you just take our order and leave us alone, we got business to talk over." He groaned.

Jen turned to AJ. "Hear that, dear, you've got business to discuss, best I hurry along and get the man some food." The two women laughed while Jonty folded his arms and scowled at them.

"What'll you have then?" Jen finally settled down enough to ask AJ.

They both ordered and Jen made her way towards the kitchen, leaving AJ to dubiously return to Jonty's big find.

"You were saying?"

He looked around the room to make sure no one could overhear before continuing, "Ever hear of the Cross of Potosí?"

AJ thought for a moment. "No, can't say I have. Kinda sounds Italian."

"Bolivian," Jonty corrected her quietly. "Well, today Potosí is in Bolivia, but in the mid-1500s it was a small Incan hamlet considered to be within Peruvian borders. It would have stayed a small hamlet and been ignored by the Spanish conquistadors, if they hadn't discovered something valuable in the mountain that overlooked the village."

Jonty checked around their table again for anyone listening.

Content they were not being overheard, he continued. "Silver. The mountain was full of silver, and the Spanish had just discovered this new way of separating the silver from the ore. It was called the mercury amalgamation process. Horribly poisonous as you'd gather from the name, but they didn't know that at the time. The place went crazy, and the Spanish brought slaves from Africa and Peruvian workers from hundreds of miles away to work in the mines. The hamlet was quickly transformed into a city. In its heyday it was bigger than London of the same period. High up in the Andes mountain range, at over 13,000 feet, the danger of working in the mines, which was already treacherous, was even more lethal at that altitude. But the Spanish didn't care, they were greedy for the wealth and slaves arrived every week to replace the dead. They moulded the silver into bars, then shipped the bars to the first Spanish colonial mint in the Americas. There they were minted into pieces of eight before being shipped to Spain or the Spanish colonies throughout the world. Potosí silver funded much of Spain's continuing wars, exploration and enormous wealth."

"So you're looking for pieces of eight?" AJ interrupted, wondering where this interesting, but long, story was going.

"Nothing that simple," Jonty answered keenly. "Stay with me here, it's taken nearly five hundred years for a lot to happen. I'll shorten the story as best I can. So, by the early 1600s Potosí was a powerful city and with it came violence, infighting amongst the wealthy, gang wars amongst the workers, and huge numbers of deaths in the mines. That was in addition to several disasters when dams broke, floods, and so on. But the Spanish mining boss, Domingo Beltran, thought he was all that and a bag of chips. He reckoned he was one of the most influential people in the world at the time, and to prove his power and stature he had his artists mould an ornate silver cross. Not stopping there, he had them inlay forty incredible, and large, Columbian emerald's. His plan was to send the cross to the King of Spain as a gift from himself and the city of Potosí. He sent four of his best soldiers, charged with delivering the cross into the hands of the King. There's no record of what happened to those men but what we do know is La Cruz de Potosí, as the Spanish called it, never reached the homeland."

AJ had found herself transfixed to the tale and now sat back in her chair and was about to ask a question when Jen returned with their food.

"Here you go," Jen said, smiling, as she placed their meals in front of them. "I put a little something special in his, so don't be surprised if he chokes a bit," she added, winking at AJ then scowling at Jonty.

"Bugger off, you evil woman," Jonty retorted, but he managed a grin and Jen left laughing.

Jonty didn't touch his food and before AJ could ask anything he launched back into his story. "Not a word exists for nearly two hundred years about the cross, until the late 1700s. Spain was ruled by King Charles IV, who would rather go hunting than deal with affairs of state. Apparently he wasn't the sharpest knife in the drawer, and the country was better off with him out of the way. His wife, Maria Luisa, who according to historians was a switched-on lady, essentially ran the country for him. In 1792 there's record of her sending agents of the crown on a mission to find the Cross of Potosí. We can only imagine it was based on some information she'd obtained, but there's no history of what that may have been. What we do know is one of those men was a bloke called Santiago Velázquez."

AJ held up a hand. "Wait, you're saying 'we' like more than just you know about it?"

"Yeah, yeah, I mean it's not common knowledge you can Google, but in the treasure world this part is known. I'll get to the bit that's not known soon, I promise."

AJ took the opportunity to have a bite of her sandwich and Jonty continued, "What we know about Velázquez is he sent a message back to Spain, from Jamaica, that he'd had success, and would be returning. That was in late 1793, and the message reached Maria Luisa in the spring of 1794. As you can imagine, it took a while to sail around in those days. And then they heard nothing more. Neither the cross nor Velázquez ever reached Spain."

Jonty finally took a swig of his drink and looked at his sandwich with distrust.

"She's kidding with you, you know that, right?" AJ said with a grin.

Jonty looked at her blankly. "I'm not so sure." He took a small bite anyway and chewed cautiously.

Not falling over or choking violently, he apparently decided it was safe to continue. "So here's where it gets interesting."

AJ thought it had all been interesting so far so she ate her sandwich and listened intently.

"Two things happen in early 1794." Jonty hesitated, thinking a moment.

AJ helped him out. "The Wreck of the Ten Sail?"

"Well yeah, so technically, I guess three things happened. Obviously everyone on this island, and lots of people that visit here, know about the Wreck of the Ten Sail, where a flotilla of boats led by the frigate HMS Convert mistakenly thought they'd cleared Grand Cayman in the middle of the night, and made the north-west turn towards the far end of Cuba. They clobbered the East End reef, taking out ten of the sailing ships. What most people don't realise is there were fifty-nine ships in that convoy, so forty-nine of them scattered, regrouped and continued on their way."

Jonty took another bite, risking death for more of Jen's flavourful sandwich.

"So what's the other two things you've found out?" AJ asked, now eager to know the whole story.

Jonty chewed quickly. "Alright, I'm getting there. First is, an American bloke named William Miller, who was in the sugar cane plantation business, turns up dead in Jamaica, the day after his ship sails from port. His ship just happened to be the Burman, which was part of the fifty-nine-ship convoy. Funny thing was, they sailed with a William Miller on board, but the captain reported in his log that he became suspicious of this Miller as he looked incredibly Hispanic although he spoke perfect English. He was preparing to question the man when the apparent impostor leapt from the ship and swam for the shore. They fired at the man in the water and the captain noted he thought they'd wounded him. That's where the trail stops. There's no record of William Miller on Grand Cayman or a Santiago Velázquez for that matter. It's the night of the Wreck of the Ten Sail so there are numerous accounts of the survivors, which was almost everyone on the ten ships, but they were all at East End. The Burman had sailed south of the island and this incident was noted in the captain's log about an hour after the ships went aground. The Burman would have been halfway along the southern coast."

He sat back and took another bite, this time chewing slowly and looking at AJ expectantly.

"So that's it? You think Velázquez drowned somewhere off the southern coast and maybe had the cross with him? Talk about a needle in a haystack," AJ responded.

Jonty grinned and reached into his pocket, pulling out a folded piece of paper. He unfurled it, flattened it out with the palm of his hand, and slid it across the table. He kept his hand over the paper and looked around the room again.

"Read it to yourself, not out loud."

AJ took the piece of paper once Jonty slipped his hand away. It was a photocopy of what appeared to be an old handwritten poem. The lettering was shaky, almost juvenile, and the parchment stained and marked. She carefully read it in silence.

The Well, by Cudjo

My Papa dug that well.
Steps of stone, two men deep,
with axe and spade
for o'er two weeks.
Oaken pail, filled to burst,
for dark and light

it quenched a thirst.

My Papa dug that well.
Been baptised, water poured
my own path set
to meet the Lord.
For two score, water flowed,
my Papa passed
well still don't slow.

My Papa dug that well.
Devil's ocean crashing,
cool fresh water
ruined to brackish.
Abandoned, and forgot,
the shrubs took root
and hid the plot.

My Papa dug that well.
Master's soul, laid to rest,
his hateful son
put all to test.
Secret since, Papa tell,
my jewelled faith
went down that well.

AJ looked at Jonty. "You're thinking 'jewelled faith' might be the cross? Seems a bit of a stretch, mate."

Jonty grinned. "Cudjo was a slave on the Ferguson plantation, a smaller cotton plantation east of Pedro St James. Cudjo's father, Solomon, was one of the first slaves bought by Stedman Ferguson when he purchased the land and opened the plantation in 1793. I've got their names on the first census on the island from 1802, and then another from a few years later."

AJ looked back at the paper. "Secret since, papa tell," she whispered.

"Exactly," Jonty said firmly.

"Boy, that's a long time for something that valuable to be lying around at the bottom of a hole," AJ said. "I'd be surprised if it's still there."

"Why?" Jonty replied quickly. "Where else is it? No one's ever seen or heard of it again. Even in the 1800s it would be worth far more intact than melted down for the silver and separating the emeralds."

AJ pondered that a moment. "I suppose. But how are you going to find a well covered over from the 1700s?"

"1800s actually, when it was covered over, but anyway," he replied, grinning again, "I found the well. It's long since filled in and buried – it would take an excavation to see what's under there. Problem is, it's on private land."

"You know full well if you find it, you have to report it to the authorities and show them the site. You know the law," AJ cautioned, making sure Jonty wasn't on a cowboy mission.

"Of course," he replied quickly. "Nothing to tell right now, all I have is a theory."

"Okay, so if you can't get to the well, what can you do?" AJ thought for a second before adding, "And what do you need me for?"

"I think I've found another way in," Jonty whispered. "From the water."

"Oh, a cave, or a tunnel?" AJ asked, leaning in.

"Of course," Jonty said with a smirk.

4

1814 (20 YEARS LATER)

Solomon leaned against the doorway of his wattle-and-daub, thatched roof dwelling. It was small, as were the other four slave quarters built in a half circle, a hundred yards from the plantation owner's single-storey wood-framed house. Far enough away to not be bothered by the comings and goings of the slaves, but close enough to keep an eye on them, and for help to be hailed when needed. The sun was low in the western sky, casting long shadows from the huts towards Stedman Ferguson's house. A baby murmured and fussed from inside and Solomon turned and smiled at his wife, Polly, holding their first living baby. Children had come late to the family. Polly was now twenty-six, and after their first was stillborn a year before, they were sure a family wasn't in the Lord's plan for them. Now, with a miracle named Pegg held in her arms, Polly looked up and smiled back at the strong, muscular figure of her husband.

"Go on now, take care of his bidding before it gets dark," she said softly.

Solomon nodded and, still smiling, turned and started the walk across the clearing. His own hands had helped fell most of the mahogany trees that had once covered the land from the low bluffs on his right, to the extent of Ferguson's 50 acres to his left. The money made from the valuable wood helped fund the cotton plantation that first thrived, and now survived, as the American plantations boomed and drove the prices down. He still took great pride in the work he and the other men and women of the plantation put forth each day to keep the place alive. Mr. Ferguson had been fair to them all, and as Solomon had grown and become a leader amongst the families, Mr. Ferguson relied upon him more and more. The Englishman never said as much, but Solomon felt a level of respect and caring not usually afforded a slave. Taken from the Gold Coast in western Africa at age eleven, his memories of home were thinning after twenty-two years on the plantation. His mother had died on the gruelling journey by sea, and his father had been sold to someone else in Jamaica, before Solomon, along with five others, had been shipped to Grand Cayman and delivered to Mr. Ferguson. For several years he'd been angry and defiant, but as time rolled by and his strength grew, his focus shifted to the work at hand, and he found himself invested in the outcome of each crop. To his credit, Mr. Ferguson had been firm but patient with his young slave. He'd never taken a whip or a stick to him and when the man had shown concern for a slave girl that fell ill, even summoning the white doctor to attend to her, Solomon found he'd begun to accept his new life. The girl survived – her name was Polly.

Solomon quietly walked around the back of the stone house and found the shutter Mr. Ferguson had asked him to repair. He figured they'd be having their supper about this time and he didn't want to disturb them, especially with Mary, Mr. Ferguson's wife, being pregnant and nearly ready to have their own child. Mrs. Ferguson was an American woman, from Georgia. The daughter of wealthy plantation owners, she did not share what she considered her husband's languid handling of his slaves. She mainly ignored 'those people' and barked orders at the two women she allowed in her home to clean and prepare food. Her pregnancy had been a welcome surprise to everyone, hoping she may soften with the joy of finally growing their family, at age thirty-seven. But it appeared the opposite had been true and she lashed out more frequently and venomously than before. Mr. Ferguson seemed oblivious, or content to allow her tirades, as he slipped into melancholy, uncharacteristic of the man.

The wood had dried and split along the top rail and Solomon noted the tools and nails he'd need to make the repair. He would patch it up for now and keep an eye open for a suitable piece of wood to replace the top rail. He turned to leave when he heard Mr. Ferguson's voice raised from inside the house. He'd never heard the man shout in anger before. He heard quickening footsteps on the wooden floor and saw the cook beating a hasty exit, heading for the slave huts without looking back. Solomon froze, unsure what was best to do. If he bolted as well, he could be seen, and as of that moment they didn't know he was there. He'd prefer it to stay that way, at least where Mrs. Ferguson was concerned.

"Damn you woman, damn you all to hell!" came the plantation owner's voice from inside. Solomon was stunned; he'd never heard the man lose his temper, let alone scream almost uncontrollably.

"Deny it, I dare you, deny it to my face!" he bellowed. "Tell me our child is a gift from God himself."

Solomon carefully crouched low and tried not to move for fear of creaking a board on the veranda that encircled the house.

"If you were a man, this wouldn't have happened!" Mary Ferguson's voice echoed from the walls, a voice he, and everyone else on the plantation, had heard raised before. "You, who's happy to let this place fruitlessly drift along, as impotent as the fool I married. You dragged me to this godforsaken island, away from my family, away from the life and wealth I deserve." She yelled in a constant stream of well-aimed blows, using words that Solomon didn't fully understand. His English had come a long way since landing, when he had spoken nothing but his native Akan tongue, but much of the language still eluded him.

"I should have left you years ago when it was clear you would amount to nothing. Fifth biggest landowner on this piece of sand in the ocean is the equivalent of a grounds keeper in Georgia! My father wouldn't hire you to clean the mud off his boots."

"Then go to them, damn you, take the first sail from here and be gone with you!" The man's voice was cracking, his pain ringing through his angry words. Solomon couldn't understand the breadth of the circumstances but his owner's anguish was plain to hear. "Or go to him, why don't you? I'm sure he'll cast aside his wife and three children to open his home to you. You're nothing but a piece of flesh to that man; he'll tar you as a hussy and a fabricator if you dare suggest he coveted you."

"To hell with you, Stedman Ferguson, to hell where you'll burn for eternity," Mary shouted, but the gusto had left her voice.

"You've brought shame upon this home, shame upon yourself, and now you carry a devil inside you. My place with the Lord may be uncertain, for I am not a man free of sin, but you, along with your child, have earned your place in purgatory."

The house fell silent and Solomon finally breathed again. Confused and dismayed, he edged towards the steps down from the veranda. Once he set foot on the ground, he ran. He ran back to his hovel made of dirt and twigs and sat with his wife as she fed the baby from her breast. He softly caressed her hair and considered how lucky he may indeed be, despite his circumstances.

Mr. Ferguson remained in his melancholy state for two more weeks. Mary Ferguson continued to fuss, shout and throw things at the women sent to help her. It was an especially hot and humid night when Mary went into labour. The doctor was sent for but by the time he arrived it was to no avail. The newborn baby cried in the arms of a slave woman, and Mary Ferguson lay dead in the bed in which she'd given birth to the boy. Solomon waited outside the house, sitting on the front steps leading from the veranda, his intent to pass on the joyful news of the birth to the rest of the workers in the half circle of huts. Mr. Ferguson walked out and surprised Solomon by sitting next to him on the steps. Solomon went to stand, assuming he should leave, but the man put a hand on his arm.

"Stay," he said solemnly.

They sat in silence for a few moments and Solomon hesitated to speak, unsure if it would be polite to do so, or rude to enquire. Mr. Ferguson finally spoke in a low, solemn voice.

"The Lord has seen fit to provide a boy. He appears healthy, though somewhat small."

"Praise the Lord, sir – and your wife? Mrs. Ferguson is well too, sir?"

The man neither replied or moved, he sat on the step and stared off into the dark night. Solomon wondered if he'd even been heard, but eventually Mr. Ferguson turned and looked at his slave.

"I believe I've instilled in you, your family, and your fellow workers, the importance of faith, Solomon. Do you take that to be the case?"

Solomon nodded. "Yes sir, you taught us right, sir, we all believe in the wonders of the Lord."

Mr. Ferguson looked back out across the land. "Then know that the good Lord has chosen to both bless this house, and lay a burden upon it."

"Sir?" Solomon said quietly.

"I believe you, and hopefully you alone, have an understanding which is the blessing, and which is the burden, Solomon." The man stood and turned to go back into the house. "Please tell everyone we will put Mrs. Ferguson in the ground tomorrow morning, before the heat gets the better of us."

Solomon rose quickly, unable to conjure any words to say, and watched his owner walk slowly back into the house. Apparently he'd not made it away completely unnoticed a few weeks back.

5

—————

TUESDAY AFTERNOON

AJ walked down the dock she shared with her friend and mentor, Reg Moore. When AJ's family came to Grand Cayman on holiday when she was a young teenager, it was Reg who took them diving. The young girl had been hooked. They'd all stayed in touch and when AJ surprised her parents with her desire to become a dive instructor, rather than go to university, it was Reg her father turned to for guidance. After AJ learned the trade for a few years in the Florida Keys, Reg gave her a job on one of his growing fleet of boats, and eventually helped her get set up with her own operation. The dock was actually his, and he ran his three boats from the jetty when they dived the west side, but he leased a spot to AJ to use as well. Of course, he'd never told her how much that lease was or billed her a penny for it.

The boats were tied to buoys overnight in the shallow sandy area a few hundred feet from shore, and then brought in to load gear and customers. Reg's last boat was being tied up at its overnight mooring and he waited for his captain to paddle back in. A broad-shouldered Londoner with a mop of salt and pepper hair and a scruffy grey beard, Reg looked the part of an old tar, as indeed he was. A former hard hat Navy diver and salvage man, he was an imposing figure with a gruff demeanour, barely hiding a heart of gold.

Reg's dog Coop met AJ halfway down, and ran excited circles around her feet. Coop, named after English boxing legend Henry Cooper, was still a puppy but fast becoming a well-trained boat dog and never left Reg's side. He was pure mutt, or Cayman Brown Hound as the locals called them.

"Here you go," AJ said, handing Reg a cold bottle of Strongbow cider before reaching down and making a fuss of Coop.

"Hey, cheers," he grunted, grinning at his puppy rolling on his back to get his stomach scratched.

"I saw Casey this morning," AJ said, Coop reminding her of the turtle rescue. Casey also helped with Canine Friends Cayman, the island's volunteer dog rescue that Coop had been adopted through.

"She better not be buttering up Pearl to rescue another bloody dog, this one's enough." Coop nudged Reg's hand and the big man leaned down and scratched his ear.

"No, we had to cut a turtle out of a fishing net, right out there near the point." AJ pointed towards the north-west horizon. "Casey arrived just in time to save my bacon: I got the turtle out, then I snared myself as bad as he'd been."

"You talking about a trawling net?" Reg asked.

"Oh yeah, the thing was huge, Casey took it away." AJ went to drink her cider but continued instead, still mad about the situation, "There's no way the turtle dragged it in from international waters, and it wouldn't have drifted that far. Someone was trawling near the island. Casey said it's the second time they've found a net off the west side recently."

"Idiots, must be getting too close to the wall and snagging the reef. Those nets are expensive – you wouldn't dump it overboard unless it was caught up so bad you couldn't free it," Reg growled.

"Unless..." AJ pondered a moment. "Unless they dumped it because they thought they were about to get busted."

Reg took a long, easy swig of his cider and considered the idea.

"Surely the marine police or DOE would know if they came up on someone acting suspiciously."

"True. Casey would have mentioned that I guess." They sat down on the end of the dock as Reg's captain arrived back and pulled the kayak from the water. The sun was getting low in the western sky before them, and they sat quietly enjoying the sunset, as they often did.

AJ shared everything with Reg and his wife Pearl; they were her island parents and while they couldn't replace her actual mum and dad, they were much more than just friends. But she knew what she was about to say wouldn't be received gladly.

"You'll never guess who I had lunch with today," she said breezily.

He stared at the sunset and didn't change his expression. "Jonty Gladstone."

"Damn, is there anything that happens on this island you don't know about?" she said, smacking him on his beefy arm.

He smirked, briefly. "What the hell you wasting a lunch on that fool for?"

"He asked, and I didn't have a good reason to say no."

"He's the damn fool that nearly got you killed a few years back, that's good reason in my book," he scoffed. "He's a drunk, that's another good one, he has crap taste in music… should I go on?"

Pearl performed at the Fox and Hare pub in West Bay a few Friday evenings a month and Jonty had made the error of criticising her music one night, after overindulging in spirits. Reg had dragged him outside and adjusted his review of the performance by pinning him to the wall by his throat. When Reg had released his grip enough for the Yorkshireman to speak, Jonty amended his critique to say Pearl was an outstanding singer, which she was indeed, just not his cup of tea.

AJ laughed. "No, you make a valid point, but anyway, I had lunch with him," she replied, still trying to figure out how to present Jonty's potential discovery.

"So, what's his latest harebrained scheme he's roping you into?" Reg asked.

"Treasure, of course," AJ admitted, "We'll see if there's really something to it but he's done a ton of research and it sounded plausible."

Reg finished his cider and set the bottle down beside him. "What's he need you for?"

"A boat. It's over past Pedro St. James castle, along the low bluffs; he asked if I could take him out there and have a look. Arthur's Odyssey would be perfect for it. Might go Saturday, on my day off."

AJ's original dive boat was a rigid inflatable, or RIB, she had acquired at auction when she first formed Mermaid Divers. These sported a rigid fibreglass hull with tough inflatable sides, hence the name. Incredibly hardy craft, used by coastguards and military special forces, they were known for their seaworthiness and speed. AJ still used hers for smaller groups, or when they needed to run two boats to accommodate more people.

Coop jumped up and trotted back along the dock as an English woman's voice reached them.

"Mind if I join you?"

AJ and Reg shuffled farther apart and made room for Pearl to sit between them. A diminutive woman with wavy blonde hair, a buxom figure and a warm smile, she handed them both a fresh, cold cider before taking a seat. She gave Reg a kiss and AJ a hug, while Coop fussed around everyone looking for some love.

"What's been happening today then?" she asked with a twinge of cockney accent. "I've been doing book work all bloody day, my eyes are tired of looking at numbers, I tell yer."

AJ jumped in quickly to steer the subject away from Jonty Gladstone before she took more grief. "Jackson will be here in a few days."

Reg grinned, clearly amused by AJ's redirection, and Pearl put her arm around her. "That's wonderful, how long can he stay?"

"I'm not sure. I talked to him last night and he said they were heading back to the US and would stop by the island on the way. He couldn't say where they were so I'm not sure how long it will take them to get here. They usually stay over for three or four days, but it'll depend on weather and whatnot for getting back to the States."

AJ's boyfriend, Jackson, worked as a volunteer on one of Sea Sentry's marine conservation boats. His boat, the Sword of the Sentry, patrolled mainly in South American waters, taking on illegal fishing and poaching issues such as shark finning. They'd met at a function Sea Sentry had put on while passing through Grand Cayman about a year ago and been dating since, albeit sporadically seeing each other.

"You have to be excited, how long has it been?" Pearl enthused.

"Too long." AJ grinned. "Months and months. I might not let him leave this time."

"Well if he's here long enough for you two to ever make it out of your little apartment, we'd love to take you both for dinner," Pearl said with a wry smile.

"Maybe you want to invite your other boyfriend along," Reg barbed, trying not to laugh.

"What's this? Another boyfriend?" Pearl asked, looking back and forth between them.

"Bugger you, Reg," AJ retorted. "He's being an arse. I had lunch with Jonty Gladstone and I knew I shouldn't have said anything about it."

"Lunch, like a date?" Pearl said in surprise.

"No! Of course not, he wanted to talk to me about taking him out with the RIB to scout a lead he has." AJ shook her head and made a face like she'd tasted something awful. "Ewww, a date with Gladstone, not in this lifetime."

"Good, I was worried you'd lost your marbles for a second," Pearl added.

Reg leaned forward and looked sternly past his wife at AJ. "Just make sure he doesn't get you into trouble. That bloke won't make old age, but he don't need to take you with him. He'll relieve the world of himself sooner than you think with the nonsense he gets up to."

He leaned back and they watched the sun fall beyond the horizon in a dramatic display of oranges and yellows. AJ knew Reg was right: Jonty was a loose cannon, but he was also a skilled diver, especially in flooded cave systems known as cenotes. Her curiosity in the story he'd told wouldn't let her drop it for now, although she did need to tread carefully. But she was sure Reg wouldn't let her forget that.

6

TUESDAY NIGHT

Jonty rocked back on the wooden dining chair, balancing it on the two back legs more precariously than he realised. He took a sip of rum from the glass in his hand before swishing the mostly melted ice around in the bottom of the tumbler. He let the chair drop back on all four legs and reached for the bottle on the table. It was empty. He sighed and glanced over at the clock on his bedside table, easily visible across the room of his tiny apartment above a garage in West Bay. It was 12:42am. He looked back at the table covered with notes, maps and a couple of history books. Jonty never claimed to be the organised type, but he knew every notation, location and name involved in his search by heart. He often shuffled the research around on his little table hoping a new thought or lead might jump out at him.

This project had been a casual interest for years, going nowhere in a hurry, until two weeks ago. A sometime girlfriend, who worked at the Cayman Islands National Museum in George Town, had texted him with an interesting find in their archives. Since then, the project had become his whole focus. He knew Jules had reached out because she couldn't help clinging to some hope they'd have a relationship, beyond the occasional roll in the hay, and the poem was simply an excuse to text him. He was sure she didn't see any meaning or value in it, and probably hadn't expected him to either. The date of the poem, 1835, had sparked a mild interest with Jonty. It was the year that emancipation was finally enforced on Grand Cayman. That was enough to encourage him to read the poem itself, which fanned the flames of his curiosity. The accompanying note, made by a member of the museum staff, sometime between 1979 when the museum opened and now, had set him ablaze. The note showed what few details they knew about Cudjo, son of Solomon, slave to the Ferguson plantation.

Jonty slid a large old, photocopied map across the table, from under a pile of notes. Maps of Grand Cayman, from the early days since its discovery by Christopher Columbus on his final voyage to the Americas in 1503, through the next few hundred years, concentrated on the reef systems surrounding the island. That's what sailors were concerned with at the time as the shallow reefs ended the careers of many fine sailors, along with their ships. Very few maps were drawn showing any details of the interior, the towns that began to grow, or the divisions of land holdings. The map Jonty had acquired, again through his friend Jules at the museum, showed the land owned by one William Eden, an early plantation owner whose estate was located at Savannah's Pedro bluff on the south coast. He built Pedro St. James, the sturdiest building on the island, often referred to as a castle although it was more accurately a larger house, built from stone, but far more imposing than any other dwelling at the time. The map showed the borders of Eden's property, and marked to the east, was a much smaller neighbouring plantation, owned by Stedman Ferguson.

Jonty pushed his empty tumbler and cheap rum bottle away from him and pulled his laptop computer closer. With a few clicks he opened a satellite map of Grand Cayman and zoomed in on the southern coast near Pedro St. James. The house had been rebuilt several times over the years after a series of fires, storms and lightning strikes, before finally being purchased by the Caymanian government in 1991 and restored as a historical site. Scrolling to the east of the tourist site, the coastline curved from facing south-west to directly south and several larger homes had big plots of land overlooking the low bluffs. He studied the coastline and compared it to the old map, laid across his table. A few details were different, likely erosion over the centuries, but the main features matched exactly. Especially a small inlet that cut into the low bluffs no more than a hundred feet. The satellite image would only zoom in so far, but the vee-shaped inlet formed a small cove with the ocean lapping at the base of the bluffs. Jonty was familiar with that cove.

A creaking noise pierced the silence of the night and Jonty sat up straight in his chair. It sounded like the rickety outdoor stairwell that led up to his door, across the kitchen from where he sat. He listened intently, but heard nothing more. He let out a tired sigh; his paranoia always peaked when he was close to a treasure haul, and the rum probably didn't help. He needed some sleep. His alarm promised to be painful at five-thirty in the morning, waking him to the hangover he knew he had coming. Same hangover he woke up to most mornings. He closed his laptop lid and cleared the tumbler and bottle from the table. He dropped the bottle in the rubbish bin where it loudly clanged against its brothers already stacked up, cushioned only by a few fast food wrappers. The tumbler he added to the numerous dirty plates and cutlery accumulating in the sink, before turning towards the bathroom. He toyed with the idea of skipping his evening teeth cleaning in favour of two minutes more sleep, but he needed to use the loo anyway, so he trudged into the bathroom and swung the door closed behind him. The bathroom light was on the same switch as the ancient extractor fan that whirred, whistled and groaned without seemingly moving any air anywhere. He made a mental note, for the fiftieth time, to discon-nect the fan from the switch. He glanced at his own stream as he stood over the loo. A deep golden yellow, he observed, dehydrated as usual. His strict regimen of coffee until noon, beer until five, and rum from then on, still wasn't giving his body the fluids it needed apparently, despite the water in the coffee and the ice cubes in the rum. He rinsed his hands and splashed some water over his face before squeezing the very last drop of toothpaste from the tube that he'd made work for two weeks' worth of last squeezes. He made another mental note to buy toothpaste. This would join the rest of the list that would have evaporated from his mind by morning. He gave his teeth a good thirty-two seconds of scrubbing and called it a bonus based on his preference to have skipped it altogether, swished some water around his mouth, dried his face, and left the bathroom, finally silencing the light along with the dilapidated fan.

He killed the kitchen light over the table and closed his laptop lid as he stepped towards his bed only a few feet away. Everything was only a few feet away in the open-plan studio apartment. Jonty stopped before he reached the bed. As a professional alcoholic he had an amazing ability to function and think to some degree while maintaining an alarming amount of cheap rum in his system. Hadn't he already closed his computer lid, he pondered? The sound of movement behind him made him swing around where he was met with a mighty blow to the side of the head. As he crumbled to the floor, half slumped against the foot of the bed, he was amazed he remained conscious after such a wallop. He looked up and struggled to focus his eyes. Standing over him was a large figure of a man in jeans, a black sweatshirt and some kind of dark bandanna wrapped around his face. The dim bedside light illuminated them enough for him to be fairly certain he didn't recognise the person. He was dark skinned, with hair in neat rows, tightly woven to his scalp, and in his hand was a small billy club. The man raised the billy club again and all Jonty could think of was cornrows – wasn't that the name for hair braided that way? He was pretty sure it was cornrows; then the club swung and his world went black.

7

1816 (2 YEARS LATER)

It had been two years since the birth of Francis Ferguson. Nursed and cared for by one of the slave women who took care of the house, he remained small for his age, but continued in good health. Solomon's daughter was just beginning to walk, making it much harder for Polly to keep up with her, especially as she was pregnant again. Solomon glanced back inside the hut and smiled at his growing family. More and more he found himself feeling happy and content. The anger that had burned inside as a young boy had lessened as he became a young man, and almost vanished with the birth of his first child.

Occasionally the word freedom came across his mind, but he wasn't sure what that even meant to him now. This was the land he knew, the family and community he knew, and the work he knew. As a free man, he'd get paid money and in turn would pay for a home, land, food, clothing, all of which he had now. In the village where he grew up as a young boy, no money changed hands, or even existed. Everybody worked within the village to support the people. He really didn't understand the concept of money or what its use might be. Mr. Ferguson treated him as a valued worker, he often sought his advice and thoughts on the crops and made sure the food they grew and he bought was fairly divided. When times were lean, Mr. Ferguson's own plate was a little lighter at supper time, as he asked the workers to ration their food.

Shortly before the harvest of each crop was always the hardest time. Much work was to be done but supplies were thinning. Mr. Ferguson would say the sale of the crop would get them by, and it always did. Solomon knew nothing of the cotton prices, shipping costs or market shifts. He made sure the crop was the best they could manage in the soil their land offered and trusted his boss, and owner, would keep them fed and sheltered. Mr. Ferguson's demeanour had slowly improved after the death of his wife and Solomon noticed he was back to his easy manner within a few months. The man took very little interest in Francis, which most attributed to the boy reminding him of his wife's passing. But Solomon had thought much about that night he'd overheard them argue, and the man's words on the steps after Francis was born. He shared his thoughts with no one, not even Polly, but after much contemplation he was confident he knew the man's plight. He couldn't do anything to help except keep this knowledge to himself, but he sensed Mr. Ferguson knew his secret was safe, which in turn grew their mutual respect.

Solomon gently closed the door and left his wife and child peacefully sleeping. Polly was due any day and sleep was a precious commodity, between her own discomfort and Pegg's needs. Pre-dawn light glowed the eastern sky in pale blues behind the plantation house as Solomon walked from the half circle of huts to the well, 50 yards to the west. He walked down the stone steps into the ground until he could scoop fresh water with his hand and take a drink. The water was cool and refreshing, filtered through the bedrock of the island. Four years ago, he and the other men had dug the well after the original one had dried up. The old well was nothing more than a hole in the ground big enough for a bucket to be dropped in and had never been dug deep enough. The new one was a step well, a curved stairwell of stone down into the earth almost twelve feet deep. They'd hit the water around nine feet down but kept going to keep a pool of fresh water in the base at all times.

Solomon liked to start his day at the well. Taking some water in the bucket he walked back up the steps and away from the well to wash his face. Two more men joined him and they politely murmured good morning to each other as they too washed themselves. The slaves were from several different regions in west Africa; only a few spoke Akan, and even they spoke different dialects. English had become their common language by default, and the only tongue Mrs. Ferguson had allowed. Of the twelve slaves on the plantation, there were four adult men. The eldest tended to the vegetable crops and fished most days, helping in the fields during the busy seasons. The other three worked the fields, attended to maintenance and anything else that required brawn or the skills they'd learnt over the years. Despite the other man's age, Solomon had become their leader and they all looked to him for direction. It had been a gradual evolution as his strength, abilities and relationship with Mr. Ferguson all grew.

Solomon took a last scoop of water as he returned the pail to the top of the steps, ready for the women to use. A voice rang out in the early morning stillness, and when Solomon heard his name, he knew it could only be one thing. He ran across the pasture and met the woman who'd shouted by the door to his hut.

"She started now, so you keep yourself nearby but outta the way." She smiled at him. "Be useful and fill a bucket with water, we'll be needing plenty."

The woman stepped into Solomon's hut and left him standing in the early morning light, paralysed by fear, joy, and every other emotion men feel while their wives are in labour. At thirty-five years old Solomon had led quite a life. He stood six foot tall, his body muscular, strong and lean from hard work, and his mind sharp and wise as the leader of the village. But once the screaming started and the labour began, he was the same hopeless fool that most fathers were reduced to. He stumbled back and forth with pails of water, most unneeded but the women knew to keep him busy. After three hours of labour, Polly gave birth to a baby boy. Solomon was finally allowed into the hut and knelt by the wooden platform with a straw-filled mattress that served as their bed. Polly was exhausted but smiling and holding their son on her chest. Light poured through the windows with the shutters lifted bringing with it the breeze off the ocean, a welcome respite from the rising heat. Solomon reached over and gently caressed his wife's face.

"You are well?" he asked, wiping the sweat from her forehead.

"I am fine. You have a son, I am blessed to give you a son," she replied, her face glowing with a mixture of fatigue and pride.

"The Lord has given us a great gift indeed, he's a handsome boy, my love," he whispered as he softly touched his baby.

Hearing a small commotion outside the hut, Solomon turned to see Mr. Ferguson standing in the doorway. He made to rise but the man waved him to stay where he was.

"I don't mean to disturb you but I heard the baby was with us. I see this to be the case." He smiled at them both.

"A son, sir, we have a son." Solomon beamed back.

"And how are you Polly? Do you or the baby need anything?" Mr. Ferguson asked.

"No sir, we're both fine, thank you, sir."

Solomon turned and stood. "We need a name for the boy, sir, how would you like him called, sir?"

When they first arrived, the slaves had been given names more acceptable and pronounceable in English. The handful of children born over the past twenty-four years had all been named by the Fergusons, including Solomon's first child, Pegg.

Mr. Ferguson thought for a moment before replying, "Do you have a name in mind?" He stepped inside the hut. "Tell me, what would be a name you would have chosen in your homeland?"

Solomon was speechless. He was eleven years old when his village was raided by African slave traders, black men from another region who sold them to the white men to be shipped across the sea. He remembered some of the traditions and customs but many he was too young to know, or had forgotten in the many years since. He thought about the names of the other children his age, and thought about his own given name for the first time in as long as he could remember. Cuffee, his name was Cuffee. It meant Friday and he was named so because he was born on a Friday.

"Cudjo, sir," he blurted out. "He'd be Cudjo. Today is Monday and our name for Monday is Cudjo. We most often name our children by the day they are born."

Mr. Ferguson nodded. "Cudjo huh? That's a fine name." He took a step further into the hut and reached a finger down to the baby. The boy wrapped his tiny hand around the man's finger and wriggled about on Polly's chest.

"Welcome, Cudjo," he said softly before straightening up and walking to the door.

Solomon watched him stop at the doorway and turn for another look. His gaze moved from Solomon, to Polly and the baby. His eyes held a mixture of pain and happiness.

"Thank you, sir, for coming to see us. I'll be in the fields shortly, sir."

Mr. Ferguson stared at the child, lost in his own thoughts. Finally he glanced at Solomon. "No rush, I'm sure you have the others working hard." With that he strode away towards the house where his bastard child was learning to walk, in the arms of a slave woman.

8

WEDNESDAY MORNING

AJ filled her stainless steel travel mug with coffee and screwed the lid on. She walked the few steps to her two-seat dining table, reached over and drew the curtains back. Outside it was still dark but the landscape lights in the garden revealed the palms between AJ's tiny apartment and the beach were gently waving in the breeze. She'd heard rain during the night, drumming on the steel roof, but the morning appeared clear and full of promise for another lovely Caribbean day. Grabbing her Mermaid Divers sweatshirt, she scooped up her keys, tucked her travel mug under her arm and stepped outside, locking the door behind her.

Her apartment was a guest cottage in the grounds of an expansive home overlooking the north end of Seven Mile Beach. Rent was cheap in exchange for keeping an eye on the family's holiday home, and taking them diving when they come over from Atlanta, Georgia. AJ owned a condo in West Bay but she preferred to rent that out and live in the apartment she'd called home for nearly ten years. It was a short walk through the garden to Boggy Sand Road where her fifteen-passenger van waited. She drove down Boggy Sand to the end where it sharply turned and met West Bay Road. Turning right she wound around to the Foster's market on the right-hand side, and parked in the almost empty car park as the dawn light spread across the island. It was 6:55am and the store opened at 7:00am. She optimistically wandered towards the front door; it was the islands, and opening early in the morning wasn't likely, so she was surprised when the doors slid open. She grabbed two bags of ice, a couple of mangoes and a pineapple, and headed towards the checkout. On the way she hesitated by the bakery, finally tossing two cinnamon rolls in a bag. At the checkout a slow-moving Caymanian lady was just logging in and setting up her register.

"Morning, miss AJ, how you doing today?"

"I need more coffee, but other than that it's a lovely morning," AJ replied sleepily.

The woman chuckled. "Don't know why folks get up in the dark, if God had meant for us to be doing things at 6am he'd a made it light by then, I reckon."

AJ handed her some cash. "A bit like daylight saving time really – what's the point these days, right?"

"What's that now?" the lady responded, and AJ remembered they sensibly didn't observe daylight saving in the Cayman Islands. She considered explaining the concept, then decided better of it; neither side of the conversation seemed quite ready for serious discussion this early.

"Oh, it's a silly time change thing they do some places." She took her change and picked up her supplies. "Have a lovely day, dear."

"You too, see you tomorrow. In the dark, Lord knows why," the lady mumbled.

The drive from Foster's to Reg's dock, next to the West Bay public dock, was half a mile, and she pulled into the car park to see Hazel's Odyssey already tied alongside the jetty. Thomas was an early bird, so he usually brought the boat in, while AJ picked up the daily supplies. He also had an irresistible quality of treating every morning like Christmas morning.

"Good morning, boss, it's another fine day for diving and being out on the water," he greeted her as she stepped aboard the boat, with arms laden. He smiled broadly and took the bags of ice from her, his lanky frame moving about the boat like an egret.

"Morning Thomas, it should be a fun day today, we only have four divers and it's the Campbells," she said, heaving her rucksack onto the cabin shelf under the front window. "Got us a treat for breakfast, they're in the paper bag," she added, holding up the bag.

"Hi there," came a voice from the dock, and AJ looked out to see a family of four moving past Reg's crew, who were starting to prep their boats for the day. The Campbells had been diving first with Reg and then with AJ, for years. They were one of the early clients Reg steered towards Mermaid Divers as she began building her client base. They returned at least once, often twice a year, and dived every morning of their stay.

"Welcome back," AJ greeted them and reached up to help them with their gear. "Blimey, the kids are so much taller than the last time you were here."

Joe and Wendy stepped aboard and dropped their gear on the deck so they could give AJ and Thomas a hug. The kids, Ashley and Kelby, followed suit and AJ noted Kelby, now 16 years old, towered over her 5' 4" frame by half a foot.

"We have to buy Kelby new clothes every three months, he's sprouting like a weed," Wendy said, laughing. "Can we rent a BCD for him? He tried his on before we left and it's too small for him now."

"Of course, we'll grab one from below before we shove off," AJ replied.

They hugged Thomas before milling about and setting up their gear while chattering about the weather in their home state of Connecticut, and how lovely it was to feel the warmth of the island. AJ and Thomas helped with their equipment and made sure everyone had what they needed before untying the mooring lines and easing the Newton away from the dock ahead of the crowd. AJ called down as she idled the diesel motor in the no-wake area near the shoreline.

"Are you guys up for a slightly adventurous dive this morning?"

Joe stepped halfway up the ladder so he could see AJ at the helm on the fly-bridge as both kids yelled back in the affirmative.

"What did you have in mind?"

AJ turned and knelt in the pilot chair, keeping one hand on the wheel. "How about a wall drift? If we catch it right with the rising tide this morning there should be some current coming out of the north and we can drift from the north-west corner back towards the west."

Joe grinned. "Let's do it, sounds exciting."

"Alright, might be a little lumpy off the corner so get suited up before we make the turn, okay?" AJ turned back to face the open water and gently pushed the throttle forward, bringing the boat up on plane.

Fifteen minutes later they'd made their way around the north-west corner of the island and headed straight into the seas coming out of the north. Hazel's Odyssey effortlessly climbed the three-foot rolling swells and eagerly powered down the troughs between. The dive tanks rattled in their racks and everyone held on tightly. Thomas had joined AJ on the fly-bridge and they fashioned a plan as they motored out.

After ten minutes of pounding in the heavy seas, AJ finally slowed and nosed up to a dive buoy. Thomas hooked the line from the buoy, secured their own line through the loop and tied it off on one of the bow cleats. Hazel's Odyssey rolled and bucked while the waves dragged her back west, until the line went taught, and she settled down to rise and fall with the swell washing beneath her hull. AJ shut the motor down and hurried down the ladder.

"Right then team, we're on Three Towers and as you can see the surface current at least is ripping westward; we'll see what we've got when we get down. Normally I'd follow you in, but in this case I'm going to splash first and check the current below before you follow me, okay?"

They all nodded from the benches where they wriggled into their BCDs strapped to tanks still held in the racks.

"If it looks good, Thomas will help you in one by one, and as soon as we're all in we'll descend together. It's really important to stay together on a drift dive; it's incredibly easy to lose the group if you stop to look at something without the group knowing, so make sure you get someone's attention. Let me know when you get to a half tank and we'll move shallower, then at a 1000psi we'll start coming up for our safety stop which will put us back on the boat with no less than 500psi. I have a bright orange inflatable surface marker buoy, which I'll deploy on our safety stop so Thomas can see where we are. He'll be tracking our bubbles the whole time so if anyone does get separated, keep drifting with the current but come up to fifteen feet, do your three-minute safety stop, then surface and he'll pick you up. If we see we've lost one we'll do the same and abort the dive at that point." She looked around the group who all looked eager to go, except Wendy who appeared a little nervous. AJ winked at her. "This will be a blast, believe me. Remember we're drifting so don't fight the current, surrender to it and cruise, this should be effortless. If you see something back upstream you want to check out, forget about it! You'll burn down your air swimming against the current."

AJ slipped into her BCD and walked to the swim step before pulling her fins on each foot. Timing the swells until the stern was down in the water, she took a giant stride into the ocean and kicked away from the boat. After a few yards she grabbed the tag line Thomas had tied off the back to keep them from drifting away before they descended. She dipped her head in the water and could see the reef sixty feet below her. Picking out a large sea fan she noted it was leaned west but not drastically laid over. She put some air in her BCD so she'd bob easily on the surface and looked back up at the boat, rising and falling five yards away.

"Looks good guys, get in as quick as you can, move away from the boat and grab the tag line."

The Campbells wasted no time shuffling to the swim step with

Thomas lending a steadying hand as he guided them into the water. With everyone bobbing on the tag line AJ nodded to Thomas who gave her the okay signal back.

"Alright guys start going down, I'll drop last in case anyone has trouble descending."

All experienced divers, the Campbells dropped below the surface and headed down towards the reef as a group. AJ followed and revelled in the silence underwater, after the raucous sounds above the surface. The deeper they descended the more the current lessened, and the surge from the waves dissipated completely at sixty feet. The current below was a gentle but steady pull of around one knot, as AJ gathered the group and rolled over the drop-off to drift along the wall at ninety feet. With visibility at over a hundred feet, it was easy to keep everyone in sight, and they settled in for a relaxing ride along the edge of the underwater mountain whose peak formed the island. Enormous tube sponges and black coral fans waved in the water column, grabbing their nutrients from the waters streaming by. Every indent in the reef housed a myriad of fish taking a break from swimming against the current. A shiny-shelled hawksbill turtle glided along the edge of the wall above them for several minutes, before stopping to feast on a sponge he couldn't resist. AJ tapped on her tank with the stainless steel carabiner she carried, pointing into the deep blue away from the wall where a pair of Caribbean reef sharks briefly checked out the divers before moving on in search of prey. She steadily brought the group up the wall so by the time Joe signalled his tank was at 1500psi they were already back to sixty feet where they could continue drifting along the top of the reef. After another ten minutes, as they finished admiring a colourful queen trigger fish, Joe and Kelby both signalled they had reached 1000psi and AJ led the group steadily up to fifteen feet for their safety stop where they could let their bodies dissipate some of the excess nitrogen in their tissues before surfacing. As they continued to drift she unravelled her surface marker buoy, or SMB, and after lightly inflating it, spooled it out from the reel clipped to her BCD until it reached the surface.

Turning to face the west AJ noticed the line from the reef to a dive buoy up ahead and tapped on her tank to get everyone's attention. Pointing to the line she signalled for the divers to grab hold as they approached. Thomas must have seen the SMB stop drifting near the dive buoy as the drone of the diesel motor echoed through the water and the hull appeared above them as he attempted the tricky manoeuvre of tying into the dive buoy singlehandedly.

Once back on the boat the Campbells enthused about the dive and their new love of drifting. AJ slipped out of her wetsuit, dried herself off and put on a long-sleeved tee-shirt to keep her tattooed arms from the hot morning sun. Thomas pointed at the buoy they were tied to and then way off in the distance to the north-east.

"You drifted well over a mile. You splashed in at Three Towers and now we're tied up to Valley of the Turtles, that's quite a distance."

"It was a perfect current," AJ replied, climbing the ladder to the fly-bridge. "Slow enough to see everything, and fast enough to cover some ground. These guys were expert drifters."

She continued up the ladder and paused when she reached the top. A boat was coming in from deep water, heading in the direction of North Sound. A boat she'd never seen before. It was a commercial fishing boat of some sort, around sixty feet long, with outriggers, a low cabin structure and a wheelhouse over the cabin. Something was piled on the aft deck and AJ watched a crewman notice her looking, and pull a tarpaulin over whatever it was. There were plenty of fancy sport fishing boats out of Cayman, some that length or more, but this wasn't fancy. The small local fishing boats were no more than twenty-five feet long. She'd never seen anything like this boat before.

"Lines clear," Thomas yelled from the bow and AJ stepped to the helm and started the diesel motor. As she eased the Newton away she took her mobile from the tray on the dashboard and clicked a photo of the fishing boat. It was probably half a mile away so it wasn't a great picture but she texted it to Casey at the DOE anyway.

9

———

WEDNESDAY MORNING

Jonty came to and immediately wished he hadn't. It felt like dumbbells were resting on his skull and the light streaming through the kitchen window pierced his eyes and burned like a plasma cutter boring into his brain. He was pretty sure he was going to be sick. He was still slumped awkwardly against the end of his bed and his neck screamed in pain from spending the night jacked at some weird angle to his body. Hangover and concussion, he thought, as he tried to carefully ease himself upright: that has to be the ultimate twofer. It occurred to him he was lucky to be waking up at all after a double helping of head blows from a billy club, but the way he felt at that very moment, he was leaning towards a preference for being dead and hoping there was a next time, or a really cool afterlife. Waves of nausea washed over him and he felt chilly and clammy hot at the same time. He needed some water but that was all the way over in the kitchen. It may as well have been in China with his current ability to move. Squinting against the vicious sunlight etching his brain, he realised the kitchen table had been cleared of all his paperwork, and his laptop.

Crawling on his hands and knees, Jonty slowly and painfully shuffled across the short distance to the kitchen, went around the table, and reached into the sink. Fumbling around, his fingers found the tumbler from the previous night, and he lifted himself up using the counter as a balance, until he could reach the tap and pour some water into the glass. The running water echoed around his head as though he stood beneath a raging waterfall. He sipped the water slowly, fearful he'd retch it up if he drank too quickly. He managed to get most of it down and it seemed to help. He hauled himself to his feet and waited for the room to stop spinning before moving again. Slowly turning, he checked the table now he was able to look down upon it. The only thing left were the stains that had accumulated in the wood over goodness knows how many years that table had been around. He wanted to swear, loudly, but stopped himself before he only made things worse. He looked over at the bedside clock and wondered why his mobile hadn't been screaming with calls as he was two hours late for work: it read 8:55am. He looked around the room trying to recall where he'd left his mobile. A sinking feeling joined the other sinking feelings as he remembered it had been on the table. Whoever it was that broke in last night must have taken it along with everything else.

He stumbled his way to the door and turned the handle, pulling it open. Hot, humid air wafted in and made Jonty feel nauseous all over again. He let his stomach settle, then looked at the outside handle, which appeared to be undamaged. He tried it a few times and it all seemed to be intact and functioning. He closed the door and bolted the lock, glad to be back in the cool air conditioning. The man must have picked the lock, he surmised, or he himself had forgotten to lock the door. He was usually habitual about locking it, sober or, as was more often, not. He couldn't be sure about last night. He'd had a few beers with some friends and was pretty buzzed by the time he came home and then he'd hit the rum and got excited about going over his notes again. Chances are he'd forgotten to lock the door. His head pounded too hard to keep mulling over the same thoughts so he shrugged it off and wobbled back to the bed. Without a way to call his boss, and taking into account he was almost certainly fired anyway, he slowly lay down and hoped he'd be able to sleep. He rolled onto his side, causing his head to spike in pain, and carefully reached up and felt the side of his skull. He'd checked for blood when he first came to and was surprised there was none, but a huge knot was bulging just above his left ear. The thug was either useless with a billy club, or incredibly adept, he couldn't decide. By all accounts, two head shots with a club should have rendered him a vegetable, or more likely in the grave. Jonty had been smacked in the head more than a few times with various items but nothing quite as lethal as a billy club. He leaned towards the man having enough skill with the weapon to render him unconscious without splitting his skull in half. Although it still felt like he had. That would explain the first blow leaving him conscious, if the guy was being careful not to kill him. It also explained when he had a second shot at a prone victim he still didn't send him into the afterlife. Or maybe he was over-thinking the whole damn thing, he figured – the concussion might be playing a part too. He felt sleep approaching and the idea of not being awake was overwhelmingly appealing.

Jonty's head echoed with a loud banging noise. It wasn't the droning throb he'd had, this was more of a series of sharp raps. He slowly cleared the cobwebs enough to look at the clock. 9:15 am. "Bugger me," he groaned, realising he'd only been asleep a few minutes. The thumping wouldn't stop and the rattling of a door handle added to the annoyance, but told him the racket was coming from his front door.

"Alright already," he bellowed and clutched the side of his head, regretting his own volume. He eased himself from the bed and staggered over to the door. Assuming another assailant would not be requesting entry, he unlocked and swung the door open.

"Please, be quiet," he muttered and shielded his eyes against the bright sunlight that poured into the room.

"Are you okay, what's wrong?" Came Jules's American accent. Surprised, he peeked from one eye to verify it was indeed her. It was. In her late thirties, Jules was almost everything. Almost cute, but not quite. She had the peculiar quality of appearing less attractive when she smiled or laughed. She was generally a fun, upbeat person, so she smiled and laughed a lot. She almost had a good figure, but somehow the curves didn't all assemble together in an overly attractive way. Her upbeat personality was fine in a bar when the noise of the people and the music gave everyone an excuse not to hear what was being said, but she wasn't big on silence when they were alone either. That meant he had to respond and engage in what some folks call conversation. He considered it mindless, endless verbal spillage. All this added up to the some-times status of their relationship. What on earth was she doing here now, he thought?

Jules stepped inside and put an arm gently around him. "Your work called me, said they'd been trying everyone you know to find you. I got worried and came straight over. What happened to you?"

Jonty allowed her to shepherd him to the dining table and he dutifully sat on the chair. "I'm fine, just a bump on the head. Why are you banging on the door, don't you have a key?"

"I couldn't find it. I'll take you to the hospital, they should check you out," she said, fussing around him and getting him some water.

"I don't need a hospital," he grumbled, already tiring of all the words being thrown around the room.

"They need to see what's wrong, Jonty. I'll take you," she persisted.

"I know what's wrong," he protested quietly.

"You might have a concussion." Jules handed him the water.

"I know I have a concussion." This was getting on his nerves – he had been happily asleep two minutes ago.

"How do you know? That's for a doctor to tell you."

"Because I've had plenty of concussions and I know what it feels like. Plus, when some shithead smacks you upside the noggin with a billy club, you either get dead, or concussed." See, he thought, now she's given me the verbal trots.

"Someone hit you with a billy club? Oh my god. Who was it? We should call the police." She pulled her mobile from her pocket.

"Jesus Jules, calm down, you're making my head worse. I don't know who it was, but the police won't help. He was after all my research paperwork, the bloke took the lot, even my mobile and laptop."

"Can't the police trace the phone somehow? Find the guy?" She plonked herself down in the other chair and ran her hand through her long brown hair. She looked pretty cute when she was worried, he thought; trick was to keep her unhappy and she'd be far more attractive. Well, if she'd shut up for five minutes.

"You watch too much TV, they don't do fancy phone tracing for peons like me." He lifted himself from the chair, "Can I go back to sleep now? I'd just gone to sleep when you woke me up."

She got up and helped him to the bed. "Should I call your boss and tell him what happened?"

Finally, something useful, he figured. "Yeah, that would be a help, tell him you've seen me and I got mugged. Bloody great big knot on me head, tell him you saw it yourself. Maybe he'll believe you, cos I guarantee he won't believe me. Be handy if I didn't lose that gig. Tell him the doctor says I need a few days, okay?"

"But you haven't seen a doctor."

"Just tell him, alright?" he protested.

"Okay, I'll call him back. You sure you're okay? I can stay with you in case... you know, in case you..."

Jonty wondered what she was thinking he might do. Explode? Die? If he died, her sitting there wouldn't change the fact he'd just died and the idea she might attempt resuscitation could only cause him more grief in the hereafter.

"I'm fine, don't worry about me. Just give us a call this evening and check in."

"You don't have a phone?"

"Correct," he mumbled as he laid his throbbing head carefully back down on the pillow.

10

1821 (5 YEARS LATER)

The midday sun was relentless and dirt-laced sweat covered Solomon's body as he walked from the field towards the huts. At age forty he worked as hard as he had at eighteen, but his body ached and muscles grew sore, to remind him he wasn't a young man anymore. He idly chatted with the other two men as they returned to the slave village for their lunch and a break from ploughing the soil. Before he could reach his hut a five-year-old boy, lean and energetic, ran towards him excitedly.

"Papa, papa, you're back, I'm gonna get you some water!"

Cudjo was growing into a fine boy, and Solomon smiled as his son ran back towards their home as fast as he'd greeted him. Cudjo never seemed to walk: he ran, or danced, or skipped everywhere he went and his father wondered where all his boundless energy came from. Polly stepped outside the door as Solomon arrived.

"Don't think you're coming inside looking like that mister," she said, pointing to the water bucket around the side of the hut. Solomon dutifully splashed the water over his bare chest and arms. The liquid was warm from the heat of the day but still cooler than his hot skin and it felt good. His daughter Phibba, now three years old, hugged her father's leg while he washed himself and he playfully dabbed her nose with his wet finger.

"Come on now, leave Papa alone so he can have some food, he been working hard all mornin'," Polly said and she scooped up her youngest child and walked towards the long table under a stand of trees in the middle of the half circle of huts. The other men gathered, and soon all nine adult slaves and their seven children were sitting on various wooden crates and boxes around the table. Polly's mother began scooping ladles of fish stew upon their plates and a loaf of bread was broken and shared. The old mahogany trees, a few of the last remaining on the plantation, offered welcome shade and the ocean breeze kept the mosquitoes away. The group ate, bantered and enjoyed a break from the toils of the morning. Once the food was eaten, the women cleared the plates as the children played under the trees, chasing each other around and around. Pegg was now eight years old and was expected to help the women with their chores, but Cudjo had a boy his age to play with, and the two were rarely apart. In another few years they would start to follow the men and learn the ways of the plantation trade, but for now they were left to roam, amuse themselves and help the women when they could.

Solomon watched his boy shimmy up one of the trees and fearlessly jump down from twice his own height. He had explained to Cudjo, as he'd explained to Pegg before him, that they worked for Mr. Ferguson and were always to do as he commanded. The truth of being owned by the man was a subject for later years, and he wondered how his son, so full of vitality and life, would process the concept that his existence was the possession of another human. It wouldn't be easy to explain as ownership of anything wasn't part of their world. Even their clothes were shared from child to child as each grew. The pots and pans were for the village, regardless of whose hut they resided in, same as every tool, fishing pole and piece of furniture – everything was part of their community. Except one thing. Solomon had one possession no one knew about, not even Polly.

"It is hot for this early in the year," came the voice of Mr. Ferguson, startling Solomon and the others at the table. They all quickly stood.

"Yes sir, hoping it cools some when we come to seeding," Solomon replied, as Cudjo ran to his side and looked down as he'd been told he should do.

"It's in God's hands – let's hope he favours us with a little rain and a cooler spell," Mr. Ferguson said, the deepening wrinkles showing on his weary face as he squinted against the bright sun. "Cudjo, my lad, you're growing more every time I see you, you'll be as big and strong as your father soon."

The boy glanced up and replied hesitantly, "Thank you, sir."

Solomon looked towards the house where he could see Francis, standing on the veranda, staring at them. Francis never came down to the slave village. He never spoke with anyone but his nanny, Sally the housekeeper, whose responsibility the boy had become. Mr. Ferguson practically ignored him, sitting in silence at mealtimes, and leaving Sally to raise him and begin his education. Sally, a slave with two children of her own, could barely read or write beyond some basic English Mr. Ferguson had taught her. Francis, now seven, learnt quickly and soon surpassed his ill-equipped teacher in his abilities to write the alphabet and perform rudimentary math. Still small for his age, the boy was quiet, stern and preferred playing alone, despite being told he could join the children of the slave village. Sally had grown fearful of the boy: he showed little emotion and often told her 'You're not my mother', glaring challengingly at the poor woman. Over time, her sympathy for his solitary life had slowly evaporated as his detached and dispassionate nature left her uneasy in his presence.

"I interrupted your meal, I'll come back shortly," Mr. Ferguson said.

"No sir, I was just done sir," Solomon politely lied.

"Walk with me, Solomon," Mr. Ferguson said, stepping from the shade of the trees and walking slowly from the group. Solomon quickly followed, and walked alongside the man, careful to stay half a step behind.

"I've been thinking about irrigation, Solomon, ways we could control water to the plants at the right times."

"Yes sir, I fear there's too few of us to bucket the water to the fields in the dry spells – we help the soil some, but not enough," Solomon replied, wondering what he had in mind.

"We need water at the highest point and unfortunately our well is down here at the lower elevation of the plantation," Mr. Ferguson said, pausing and looking over to the shrubs and small trees that surrounded the step well.

"We can try digging a well beyond the fields again, sir, but we dug three man deep and saw not a trickle twice before," Solomon responded, praying they wouldn't chase that fruitless and back-breaking task again.

"No, no, I'm thinking we build an old-fashioned cistern," Mr. Ferguson said, pointing to the ploughed soil to the north.

"A sis-turn, sir?" Solomon asked, nervous he was supposed to know the term.

"Yes, a cistern. It's a tank for gathering rainwater to use later. If we constructed an above-ground cistern at the top of the fields we could pipe water along the higher level and let it feed down towards the south. There's not much elevation drop but perhaps eventually we could pipe the water down the fields too. Even if buckets were needed it would be an easier task than pulled from the well."

Solomon was starting to picture what the man was talking about, although he'd never seen a tank such as this before.

"What do we build a cistern from, sir?"

Mr. Ferguson thought a moment. "There lies our first challenge, I'd say. It can be stone or wood but the problem will be sealing it. It's needs to hold the water for days or often weeks. The next hardship will be procuring pipe, as I know of none available here on the island; it'll have to be ordered and shipped to us."

"What size are you thinking this cistern needs to be, sir?" Solomon asked.

"Well, the bigger the better I'd say, but the larger we make it, the more material it requires. Two men long, by one man wide and a man tall should be adequate," he said, using a simple method of rough measurement he knew Solomon would understand. "Using the local limestone and sand, I believe we can form a cement to seal stone, but the stone itself here is porous, so the whole tank would need to be lined with cement. If we used wood, which could be easier to seal, I believe the sun may warp the timbers over time." Mr. Ferguson tipped his hat up and scratched his forehead. "Do you have a thought on the matter?"

Solomon scuffed at the dirt with his sandal while he considered the problem. He felt blessed and honoured the man would even ask the opinion of his slave, and strove to provide a solution to any problem raised.

"For the time being, sir, would a set of barrels be a way to capture some rain before we could build one of these cisterns you been explaining? We could set a row of them along the top of the fields. Bucket from them or tip them over and let the water run when needed."

Mr. Ferguson pulled his hat back down and smiled at Solomon. "We have a half dozen empty barrels behind the house and two more of seed we'll be using in a few days. Come to the house with the other men later this afternoon and we'll set the few we have out. Maybe some stones in the base so they don't blow over before they fill with water." He turned and started back towards the huts, placing a hand on Solomon's shoulder.

"Thank you," he said quietly, and slipped his hand away.

Solomon glowed inside, a pride washed through him in the knowledge he had Mr. Ferguson's respect and gratitude. He glanced over towards the house, thinking of the best way to get the barrels down the veranda steps. Francis stood in exactly the same place, leaning on the railing, staring in exactly the same way. A shiver ran through Solomon, flushing the warm glow from his heart and replacing it with an odd sense of dread. Why should he fear a seven-year-old boy, he wondered? Knowing the secret he shared with Mr. Ferguson, he couldn't believe the man would allow Francis to come between them in any way, but the old man wouldn't be around forever. Solomon looked at Cudjo running towards them as they walked back. He shivered again. The old man wouldn't be around forever, and Francis wouldn't be a boy forever either. One day this plantation would be his.

11

WEDNESDAY AFTERNOON

It had been a few years since AJ had been inside a flooded cave. Saving Jonty Gladstone in fact. She pulled her side-mount BCD from the small storage shed behind her apartment, and gave it a look over. She'd learnt to dive caverns and caves in Florida when she'd lived and worked there. The labyrinth of natural springs in the northern part of the state was the perfect place, and her boyfriend at the time was a keen cave diver. They both worked in Key Largo, but regularly made the 300-400 mile trek north to explore the underwater, and underground, world. Two years ago, when she'd bailed Jonty out of the extensive cave system he himself had named 'Cavern of the Lost Souls', she hadn't had time to grab her side-mount, and used her regular BCD with its back-mounted tank. Some of the spaces were so tight she'd had to remove her entire rig and push it though. This time, she decided, she'd be more prepared, and use the side-mount with the tank in line with her body, creating a much lower profile.

Rummaging around several totes of gear she found her cave reel, and some extra lights which she added to the pile along with a spare mask. Her plan was to man the boat for this venture, which had been Jonty's indication of her role, but she wanted to be prepared in case. In case of what she wasn't sure, but it was Jonty, so anything was possible.

AJ carried the gear inside her apartment and set it down by the door. She checked her email for the umpteenth time since she'd come home after the morning dives. Still nothing from Jackson. In the middle of the long stretches he was gone she found it easier to fall into her regular life and not dwell on their separation. But the few days after he left were tough, and the anticipation in the lead-up to his return left her uncharacteristically scattered. Early on in their relationship she found herself growing more and more insecure about his return, or more specifically about his interest in returning. They'd often go long stretches without communication, when he was unable to get an Internet connection, and she'd doubt herself into a pessimistic fervour. They'd gone through the cycle enough now she felt confident in his commitment, and just missed being with him.

She looked around her tiny cottage and decided she ought to clean it before he got there, one of her least favourite things to do in life. AJ's nature was a dichotomy between neatness and chaos. She was obsessive about having everything organised and systems in place, but once something was built or established, it lost her interest and maintaining was not her forte. Thomas helped keep her in line when it came to the boat maintenance, but her home was a different story. Usually, she let the mess accumulate until it drove her nuts, at which time she'd clean, tidy and rearrange like the Tasmanian devil. Jackson's imminent arrival was a more rational reason for some basic cleaning. Having not showered from the morning on the boat, she figured there was no excuse. Tying her hair back in a ponytail, she wrapped a bandanna around her forehead and started scrubbing the sink and counter tops. After that she found a duster under the kitchen sink and had just begun wiping down the cabinets when her mobile phone rang. She hoped it was Jackson but no such luck. It was a number neither she nor her mobile recognised.

"Hello," she answered, barely containing her disappointment.

"Hey," Jonty said, sounding quiet and subdued. "We need to go sooner rather than later."

"Jonty? Why the sudden rush?" she asked. This was an extracurricular activity in her mind, something she was fitting in as a favour.

"Someone else may be on to it. When can we go out?" he asked.

"You okay? You sound like your dog died," she enquired with a mixture of mild concern and medium curiosity.

"I'm fine, we just need to get out there, when can we go?" he persisted, a hint of annoyance in his voice.

Bloody hung over, again, AJ figured. "I have customers in the morning but we're not going out in the afternoon. I suppose we could go then." She regretted offering it up the moment the words came out of her mouth. Jackson was supposed to be arriving and the last thing she wanted to give up was time with the rarely seen man she loved. Too late.

"I'll be at your dock at one o'clock tomorrow," he answered and hung up before she could respond.

"Bugger," she said, staring at the mobile in her hand. She jumped when it rang again.

"I can't go out tomorrow afternoon, can't we go Saturday?" she blurted.

"Huh?" Casey answered. "Go where?"

AJ laughed. "Sorry, I thought it was Jonty calling back."

"Jonty Gladstone?" Casey said, "What is that nutjob roping you into now?"

AJ rolled her eyes. "Blimey, you been talking to Reg?"

Now Casey laughed, "No, but I bet he said the same thing."

"Okay, so what were you calling me about?" AJ said, deciding it was best to move the conversation on.

"Nets. That net you pulled off our ninja turtle was a gill net, according to the guys here who are big-time fishermen. The floats had been cut off the top and about half the weights were missing off the bottom, but they reckon it was a gill net."

"They're illegal, aren't they?" AJ asked.

"Oh yeah, most places they are, definitely here in Cayman waters. They think it got snagged on the reef which is probably how some of the weights were torn off – when they couldn't free it up they cut the floats off so it would sink. Must have dislodged itself once they abandoned it. Along comes the turtle and he drags it to the surface trying to get a breath. If half the weights weren't missing no way could he have made the surface with it," Casey said.

"I thought gill nets hung like curtains over flat sandy sea floors? Over the drop-off here it's thousands of feet down, surely they wouldn't work?" AJ queried.

"That's right," Casey agreed. "But we're thinking they're dragging it slowly along the wall trying to snag some of the deep-sea fish that come to the edge of the reef. More like a trawling net but moving slowly or perhaps sitting stationary so it doesn't curl around like a trawling net. Tuna, grouper maybe, even wahoo come closer to the wall sometimes. You saw the mesh size was over a foot square so anything small will swim right through. That net's designed to catch big stuff."

"That's pretty ballsy right off the coast here. Did you check out that boat I sent you the picture of? Odd-looking thing isn't it?" AJ said, wandering around dusting half-heartedly while she talked.

"I went by earlier this afternoon but it had left already. Fuelled up at the Yacht Club. The old Caymanian guy at the pumps didn't know the man's accent, but he said he was a foreigner, sort of sounded English, but not like most of the English ex-pats here, he said. They paid in US dollars, cash, a ton of cash. He said he pumped over six hundred gallons and the tank wasn't empty before he started – he watched the guy dip it. And..." The line went quiet while she thought for a second. "Jamaican, that's right, he said the boat didn't have a name but had Jamaica listed as its registered port on the stern. He started talking to one of the crew, who he said was Jamaican, but the white guy yelled at the crewman and told him to go below."

"Did he notice anything on deck? Did he see any nets or any of their catch?" AJ asked.

"He said it looked like everything on deck was covered over but he noticed the boat had what looked like a hold, a lot bigger than a regular fishbox or livewell on a sport fishing boat. Sounds like there were too many crew for a charter boat as well, he said he saw at least three more Jamaicans aboard."

"I saw them cover over whatever it is on the deck," AJ added. "All sounds pretty odd doesn't it? That amount of fuel they could run back to Jamaica no problem at all."

"Yup, wish we could have inspected them but they were long gone. We'll keep an eye out, but my guess is they're well out to sea by now." Casey said. "Well, just wanted you to know I followed up. Sorry it's not with an arrest, but we'll take a keen interest if that boat comes back."

"Thanks Casey, I'll keep an eye out too."

"Oh, and congrats, your boy's back in town, huh?" Casey added excitedly.

"I'm sorry?" AJ responded.

"Jackson, isn't he back? I saw the Sea Sentry boat pull into the harbour just after lunch."

AJ looked herself over, she was dirty, salty and looked more like Rosie the Riveter than a lovesick girlfriend ready to welcome her lover home.

"Oh shit, I didn't know they were here yet." She looked around the apartment at the pile of laundry yet to be done and the bed stripped of sheets. "I better go, I have a bit to do."

Casey laughed. "When you come up for air, tell him I said hi."

AJ hung up and ran through the to-do list in her mind; she needed to prioritise quickly. Grabbing the laundry, she stuffed a load in the small, stacked washer dryer in a built-in cupboard by the bathroom. She poured in some detergent and hit go when a knock came from the door. She froze. Perfect, she thought, this is how he'll picture me forever now. Her excitement quickly overwhelmed her embarrassment and she rushed to the door and flung it open.

Jackson stood outside. His long dark hair tied back, his beard a little longer than the last time she'd seen him, but trimmed neatly. He smiled, his eyes sparkled and he stepped towards her.

"I'm so sorry, I'm a total mess..." she began to say but he put his arms around her, lifted her off her feet, and kissed her deeply.

"You look perfect," he said quietly as he set her down and backed her into the cottage, kicking the door closed with his foot. She was lost for words so she didn't try to say any. She kissed him again instead.

12

WEDNESDAY EVENING

Jonty lay on his bed with his eyes closed. He had all his curtains and blinds shutting out as much light as possible but whenever he opened his eyes they still felt like they had needles being poked in them. So he tried not to open them. He'd already tripped over his shoes on the floor attempting to make it to the bathroom and back, keeping them closed. He'd crawled the rest of the way to the bed. His head throbbed. A rhythmic beat steadily kept a record of every passing second just to make sure any more sleep eluded him. Jules had come back on her lunch hour and fussed around some more, much to his annoyance. She seemed to be taking this opportunity to assume a role of caregiver and concerned girlfriend. He wanted none of the above and sent her back to work so he could sleep, which he hadn't managed to do yet.

The only benefit was he'd used Jules's mobile to call AJ and coerced her into diving tomorrow afternoon. Right now he could hardly get out of bed, but he was banking on a rapid overnight recovery which would make car and boat travel possible within twenty-four hours. It didn't seem likely if he thought about it, so he didn't think about it. Informing AJ she was doing the dive could also wait until the aforementioned bridges were crossed. Finally, he felt himself drifting off to sleep until three deafening thumps came from the door.

"Sod off," he yelled as loudly as he could in the direction of his front door. It actually came out more as a whimper and the enthusiastic knocking continued. Mumbling obscenities, he rolled out of bed and staggered towards the door, trying to half squint, half close his eyes and keep the needles from his eyeballs. He unlocked the door and opened it a crack. The door thundered open, bowling him backwards across the room, landing hard on his backside. For a second he sat motionless and prayed for the billy club, gun shot, samurai sword or whatever other means of death was coming his way. Anything to take him out of his misery and end this shitty day. When nothing happened curiosity got the best of him, and against his better judgement he opened his eyes. Standing before him, silhouetted by the impossibly bright light of the outside world coming through the open door, was a large man.

"Close the door," he mumbled.

"What?" the man growled back.

"Close the damn door."

To Jonty's surprise the man closed the door and shut out the excruciating sunshine. He squinted and tried to get his eyes to readjust to the dim light. He didn't know the man, or at least couldn't recall knowing him.

"Do I know you?" he asked, as often he didn't remember people he ought to.

"No," was all the man replied.

"Then why are you in my house?" Jonty asked, hoping this bloke didn't require long conversations like Jules seemed to insist upon.

"Because you let me in," the man growled and Jonty noted the American accent. He also confirmed this arsehole was going to make him talk himself to death.

"Okay. Why did you wish to come into my house?"

"I was sent," the man said with a hint of humour in his gravelly tone.

Jonty very gingerly picked himself up off the floor and stood on wobbly legs. He could now see the man wasn't very tall but his shoulders could have barely squeezed through the door. He wore a black tee-shirt that fitted like a layer of skin over his muscles, which clearly knew how to pick things up and put them down. Big, heavy things. Jonty turned, staggered back to his bed and crawled under the covers.

"What are you doing?" the man asked.

"Trying to sleep," Jonty said quietly from under the covers, "I've had a really naff day, so if you want to get to your point, go for it, if not please leave quietly."

He heard the man shuffle across the room towards the bed but before he could do anything he felt a vice-like hand grab his ankle and drag him from the bed, bringing him crashing back to the floor. He groaned and lay still.

"Your investor sent me," the big man said. "She's invested, and you ain't produced, so you get me instead."

Jonty peeked through one eye. "Who are you, again?"

"Falcon," the man said.

"That's not a name, that's a bird," Jonty mumbled.

"What?" the man replied, sounding confused.

"McGinnis sent you?"

"Miss McGinnis," the man corrected him as he kicked him in the ribs with what felt like construction yard boots. "Show some respect. And Falcon is what people call me."

Jonty coiled up in pain and the movement made his head pound even worse. Finally he vomited on the carpet and the man leapt back out of the way.

"Ah no, damn that stinks. I barely tapped you and you puked."

"You're late to the party, I already got my head caved in last night," Jonty muttered as he laid back down.

"Seriously? You owe someone else too?"

"No, they just wanted to steal stuff. Actually all my information to get the thing Brenda..." The man stepped towards him again.

"Miss McGinnis, sorry," he quickly corrected himself and the man stepped back.

"They took all my research. I'm supposed to make the first dive tomorrow on the site I've found, but whoever it was took all my papers."

"You don't look in much shape to go diving anytime soon," the man chuckled.

"Well, if you'd stop kicking me I might have a chance, and then I can work on getting Miss McGinnis what she's after. That way we can conclude our deal and everyone can be happy." Jonty managed to stumble out as he propped himself in a seated position against the bed.

"She said I could break a few things if need be," the man said.

Jonty squinted at him. "Like chair legs, or my legs?"

The man shrugged. "She wasn't specific, so I took it to mean my choice."

Jonty nodded towards the little table and two chairs in the kitchen. "I'm confident she meant furniture. Bust up the one on the left, it's got a wobbly leg anyway. The other one I use."

The man chuckled. "So when does Miss McGinnis see a result?"

Jonty breathed a sigh of relief; he might live another day. Although he wasn't sure he wanted to, he didn't want to leave this world as slowly and painfully as this fellow probably had in mind.

"First dive tomorrow and I'll have a better idea if I'm in the right place. If I'm right about the location, my guess is we'll have to do at least five or six more dives to have a chance at finding it, likely more. Could take weeks, or longer, depending on what we come across."

The man nodded. "Alright, sounds reasonable. So, I'll tell Miss McGinnis you'll get her what you promised by Sunday night then."

"That's not even close to what I said," Jonty replied, dropping his head to his chest, accompanied by another jolt of pain.

"I can break one of your legs and give you an extra week, if that helps?" the man said, clearly amusing himself.

Jonty thought about it a moment. Hell, he wasn't going to be able to dive anyway so a broken leg probably wouldn't make much difference. It would make it really difficult to get about on a boat though. Plus, he figured this guy wasn't likely to make it a nice break.

"Nah, I'll pass, but I appreciate you thinking outside the box, you know, giving me options."

"You're welcome. Of course, come Sunday, it won't be a broken leg, it'll be a bullet in the head." The man held up his fingers like a gun.

"If I don't find the artefact," Jonty added.

"Yeah, yeah, naturally. Bring her the goods and everyone's happy as a two-tongued dog in a room full of assholes."

"Okay," Jonty said disdainfully; sitting next to his own vomit, he really didn't want to add that new visual to the mix.

"Till Sunday then," the man said cheerily and walked to the door. He turned and grinned at Jonty before pulling the door wide open and leaving it that way as he stepped out, whistling as he went.

Jonty contemplated crawling straight back on to the bed and ignoring the door and the mess on the carpet, but the disgusting taste in his mouth urged him to move. He teetered over and closed the door so he could half open his eyes and see what he was doing. Making it to the bathroom, he washed his mouth out with water and brushed his teeth. He didn't want to face cleaning up the carpet but the smell was not going away, and as nauseous as he already felt, it would invite more problems. He gathered a roll of paper towel and the only cleaner spray he had in the kitchen, which happened to be window cleaner. He shrugged and set about the mess on the carpet, holding his breath as long as he could as he scrubbed. Finally, he had that job wrapped up, washed his hands and made it back to the bed.

His four-day timeline to perform the impossible task of recovering the Cross of Potosí was one more burden he had to shove to the back of his mind if he was ever going to get some sleep. This one might be harder to ignore. He'd known Brenda McGinnis was a tough lady, but he hadn't imagined she would go to these lengths. Once again, drinks were involved when he talked her into fronting him twenty grand on the promise of splitting the proceeds, seventy-five, twenty-five, when he recovered the cross. At the time, he was between jobs, again, and needed rent money more than cash to pursue the project. For some reason she believed his story of how close he was, which at the time, three months ago, was mostly fabricated. Regardless, she gave him the money and he was happy to take it. He thought the worst that would happen would be she'd make him sleep with her. He might possibly prefer the bullet over that, as she wasn't the daintiest or most pleasant-looking woman around, and had to be in her seventies. Apparently he'd underestimated her commitment to receiving a return on her investment, and her willingness to use violent means to get it. He probably should have known better: she ran high-end hookers working the Seven Mile Beach resorts, and the islands' biggest sports book. A woman who had survived in that line of business since anyone could remember didn't do so by letting debts slide.

He rolled around trying to get settled and comfortable for more than an hour. Finally, exhaustion took over from the dance club drums in his head, along with the new soreness in his ribs, and he felt himself drifting off to sleep.

"Hey, how's my patient doing?" Jules said enthusiastically, as she let herself in the front door. "I found my key. I'm so silly, it was in my car all the time. Were you sleeping?"

13

1821

Cudjo walked along the edge of the bluffs and watched the sea lap gently at the ironshore, fifteen feet below. The bluffs seemed huge to him – towering, insurmountable cliffs. His father had forbidden him from going down to the water alone. He didn't mind that: the water fascinated the young boy, but it intimidated him a little too. His papa was a giant – Cudjo wasn't afraid of anything, or any place, when he was with his father. The top of the bluffs behind the village were partially covered with low scrub grass, ferns and bay vines, wherever they could find enough soil to grow between the jagged limestone that once upon a time, when the island was below the sea, used to be coral. Farther east, they gave way to shamrock and wild tamarind shrubs, and beyond that, taller trees bordered Ferguson's plantation. Years ago, Mr. Ferguson had put his slaves to task, forming a series of pathways along the bluffs by knocking down the top of the sharp ironshore and using the crushed debris to fill in, forming a walkable surface.

Cudjo usually played along the scrubland where he and his friend could run, chase each other around the pathways, and pretend they were swashbuckling pirates. His sidekick had chores to do, so this evening he was a sole adventurer, discovering new lands and fending off the natives. The sun was getting low in the sky behind him, and he knew he should get back soon, his papa would be in from the fields and supper would be served. The rule for the children was to be around the table before the sun went down. If he was late he'd not get any food, and he was hungry. He was always hungry. He'd eat until he felt full but an hour later, after running around playing or doing chores, he'd be hungry again and begging his mama for a piece of fruit.

Standing before the shrubs, he began to turn when movement behind one of the shamrocks caught his eye. He tiptoed closer and a young agouti bolted through the undergrowth. Cudjo gave chase, nimbly dodging between the ferns and leafy plants keeping the odd-looking rodent in view. His bare feet, toughened by his shoeless existence, danced off the sharp stone as though it were forgiving soil. The agouti veered towards the edge of the bluff before making a sharp left turn around a bushy tamarind. Cudjo tried to turn after him but his foot finally slipped on loose debris and he crashed to the ground, scraping his knee across the rough surface. He skidded to a halt with both feet hanging over the edge of the bluff and his heart thumping in his chest. Slowly, he pulled himself clear and sat up, peering over the drop at the water five times his height below. He took a deep breath and looked behind him, but the agouti was nowhere to be seen. Cudjo stood up and brushed himself off, inspecting the graze on his leg. His mama would fuss over it and his papa would just smile and shake his head. He looked up and realised he was only a short way from the trees. He wasn't supposed to wander off the plantation but some of the trees looked like they'd be fun for climbing. He looked back over his shoulder towards the village and couldn't see anyone looking for him. Maybe he'd just have a quick look around, he decided, stepping around the shrubs, and come back with his friend next time they were out this way.

The logwood trees were thick and thorny but in between them were some mahoganies with their convoluted roots and twisting limbs. He ran up to the first one and began scaling the lower trunk until he could pull himself along a big limb and sit and survey the woods. He couldn't see far, as the dense dogwoods mostly filled the view, but he could pick out daylight along the bluff so he figured the woods didn't last long. Another plantation bordered theirs and he assumed there were fields beyond. Scanning the woods for better trees, he noticed something strange. A big mahogany filled the centre of the woods, its thick limbs and branches shoving the neighbouring dogwoods aside. Around its trunk was a dark mark that couldn't be a natural part of the tree.

Cudjo slid down from his perch and trod silently towards the middle of the woods. He stopped at the thick shrubs before the woods opened up around the old tree and peeked around, mesmerised by the strange stripe. The mark was a darker brown than the tree itself, almost a deep scarlet. It was no more than three feet above the ground and about the width of Cudjo's hand if he turned it upright. As he was about to step from behind the shrub, someone came into view around the mahogany tree and Cudjo froze. Francis held something in his hand and dragged it around the tree, adding to the brown stain with a deep red. His face was painted with black and red markings but Cudjo knew it was Francis – he'd seen the older boy staring at them from the veranda of his home. Francis continued around the broad trunk, and Cudjo instinctively knew he should run as soon as the boy went out of sight, around the back of the tree. But he didn't. The curiosity of the five-year-old may have wanted to know more, but it was fear that glued him to the spot as though his feet were nailed to the earth. He held his breath, staying tucked behind the shrubs, and waited for Francis to reappear around the old tree. He didn't reappear.

A lump grew in Cudjo's throat and he felt his legs shake with fear. What should he do now? No choice seemed like the right choice, so he remained frozen in the middle of the copse. He wished beyond all wishes and prayers that his papa was here right now and could pick him up, throw him over his shoulder and stride out of these woods. But he wasn't here. He may as well be back in the strange country he often told his son about, the place he'd come from across the water. Cudjo was alone. Alone except for the son of the plantation owner that his papa said he always had to obey, who was somewhere out there in the woods. The woods that grew dimmer with every passing moment as the sun dipped into the horizon. He had to run. He summoned every piece of courage a young boy could muster: he would run like the wind, he'd run and not stop until he was home in their thatched roof hut. He turned and looked straight into the eyes of Francis. The boy was slightly shorter than Cudjo despite being two years his senior, but he stood firm, arms spread, the severed body of a blue iguana in one hand, and a blood-stained knife in the other.

Cudjo was paralysed in place. His instinct was to scream, but he could make no sound. He could outrun every kid in the village, but his legs wouldn't move. Francis glared at him with steel blue eyes and didn't move a muscle. Blood dripped from the mutilated mid-section of the iguana where it had been cut in half and dragged around the rough bark of the tree. The paint on his face was a mixture of blood and what appeared to be charcoal, forming vertical alternating stripes. His lips curled slowly into a grin.

"What are you going to do, boy?" he hissed.

Cudjo was powerless to respond. All he could think about was how far it was to his hut, and the arms of his mama and papa. The arms he'd never feel wrapped around him again. This boy may only be two years older, but it seemed like there was no boy left inside him. He didn't have size, but he had confidence and intimidation in spades. Cudjo was sure he was about to die by the long, gleaming blade in Francis's hand.

"Nothing to say, boy? Huh?" Francis took a quick step towards Cudjo, who closed his eyes and waited for the blade to plunge into his flesh. He felt the strike like a thump in his chest that knocked the wind from his lungs. Forced backwards, he staggered, whimpered and dropped to his knees, anticipating the searing pain that would come before his impending death. But the pain didn't come. He slowly opened his eyes and touched his chest. His fingers came away with blood but he couldn't feel a wound. He realised Francis had prodded him with the bloody remains of the iguana. Cudjo swung around and looked for the older boy, but he'd vanished as hastily as he'd appeared, and was nowhere to be seen. He took a few deep breaths and felt life return to his legs. He staggered to his feet with his head on a swivel, looking for Francis, but it seemed he was alone in the woods.

Cudjo ran. He ran faster than he'd ever run before, plunging though the low branches of the dogwoods, feeling the thorns and tiny branches scratching his arms and legs, but he couldn't stop. The sun had disappeared below the horizon and the remaining low, dim light cast long shadows from every tree and shrub. He dodged, swerved and jumped until his feet felt the softer vines and scrub grass, but he didn't slow. Bursting through the half circle of huts he saw his mother, under the trees, setting out plates at the table. He threw himself around her and clung on as tightly as he could, gasping for breath. If he could stay right there and never let go he'd be happy. He jolted when he felt two big hands grip his sides, but quickly realised it was his father's powerful grasp that lifted him up into an embrace.

"What's troubling you, son?" his papa asked.

But Cudjo couldn't speak, he clung to his giant's neck and buried his face in his chest. He was finally safe.

14

THURSDAY LUNCHTIME

AJ made a right on Boggy Sand Road, turned sharp left along the waterfront and parked by the low wall overlooking the ocean. She glanced at her Rolex watch, a birthday gift from her family and friends the year before, grabbed her wallet and stepped from her fifteen-passenger van. Jackson came around from the passenger side and they walked across the narrow road to Heritage Kitchen, a local owned and operated food shack.

"It's 12:25 so we better get this to go. I still have to switch the boats out before one," she said as they reached the counter.

"Hi there, AJ," a smiling Caymanian woman said in a thick local accent. "And who's this fine fella you have with you?"

"Miss Grece, this is my boyfriend Jackson," AJ replied. "Jackson, meet the wonderful Miss Grece."

Jackson lifted his sunglasses to his forehead. "Very nice to meet you."

"Jackson is a vegan Miss Grece, can you put something together for him with just veggies?" AJ asked.

"Really now? You eat fish but no meat, right?" Miss Grece directed at AJ.

"That's right, I'll only eat what I'm willing to kill myself," AJ said.

Miss Grece nodded. "But handsome here, not even fish you say?"

"No ma'am, nothing with a face I'm afraid," Jackson replied.

Miss Grece laughed. "Alright then, nothing with a face, he say. We can make you a wrap filled with good veggies, no problem."

"That sounds really good actually, I'll just have the same please," AJ decided. "And one of whatever your fish special is for Thomas, please."

They sat down at the colourful wooden tables and chairs next to the little hut while they waited for their food, and watched the lunch crowd steadily arrive. The sun was beating down from overhead with occasional relief from the billowy clouds that would continue building over the island as the day wore on. The large umbrella offered welcome shade and the ocean breeze helped offset the tropical humidity.

"Oh, I meant to tell you about what happened a few days back," AJ blurted. "We got busy yesterday evening and I forgot," she added quietly with a smile. "We pulled a gill net out of the water, right out here off the west side," she said, pointing north-west.

"A gill net? You sure?" Jackson asked. "This isn't really the environment for gill nets."

"I can ask my friend Casey at the DOE if you can take a look at it and see what you think, but the guys at the DOE think that's what it is. A turtle was caught up in it and dragged it closer in, but they think someone might be using it off the wall, trying to catch grouper, tuna and other big stuff."

"Everything about that is illegal here, right?" he asked.

"Oh yes. I saw an odd boat too, looked half like a sport fisherman and half like a small trawler. Casey tried tracking it but they left the island before she caught up with them."

Jackson scratched his beard thoughtfully. "They must be doing this at night, surely? Everyone would see them during the day."

"That's our guess, but if they run blacked out in the middle of the night I don't know how we'd find them."

"Radar," Jackson replied. "Watch radar and rule out anything with lights. Can't be too much boat traffic out by the wall in the middle of the night. If there's a boat on radar, and you can't see any running lights, you've found your trawler."

"Duh, of course. See, that's why I wanted to tell you about it," she said with a smile.

He laughed. "It's kinda what we do every day, chase these bastards down."

"Yah veggie food wrap specials are up here, AJ," came Miss Grece's voice from the hut.

They grabbed their food, added three fresh fruit smoothies, paid and drove back to Reg's dock. AJ wasn't completely surprised to find Thomas had already switched the Newton out for her smaller RIB, which sat tied to the dock. He was carrying tanks down to load on the boat as they pulled in.

"Thomas, you should have waited, I could have helped."

Thomas beamed back at her. "No problem, I got Hazel's Odyssey all set so I went ahead and switched them."

AJ and Jackson walked down the dock loaded with food. "Well stop now and eat your lunch while it's hot."

Thomas set the tanks in the RIB and joined them sitting on the side of the dock, out the way of Reg's crew loading their boats.

"Thank you, I'm starving," Thomas said.

AJ laughed. "You're always starving."

"True enough, gotta put fuel in the tank to keep this motor running," he said with a big grin.

"Want to come out with us this afternoon? Not sure what we'll be diving, but it might be interesting," AJ offered.

"Thanks, but I promised my sister I'd help her paint their apartment this afternoon," he replied.

Thomas's sister had recently graduated from university in Miami and was back on the island. She and her Cuban fiancé,

Carlos, who worked for Reg (and occasionally AJ), had just got their own place.

They sat and enjoyed their lunch and chatted about the morning dives until a quiet voice grumbled behind them.

"You ready then?"

AJ turned to see Jonty standing there. He did not look good. He wore a wide-brimmed sun hat, dark glasses, shorts and a tee-shirt that didn't appear to be from the clean drawer. His complexion was pasty white.

"Hey Jonty, where's your gear?"

"Let's get going and I'll explain," he muttered and stepped around them and onto the boat.

"I put six tanks on board, that enough?" Thomas asked as he finished his sandwich and stood up.

"Yup, looks like that'll be more than enough by the state of happy pants there," she replied, nodding towards Jonty.

AJ went back to the van and brought her side-mount BCD and other gear to the boat. As she stowed it aboard she took another look at Jonty, who she presumed was severely hung over or still drunk.

"We don't have to do this today if you're not feeling well," she offered.

He looked at her blankly. "What? Let's bloody go, time's wasting." He looked at Jackson stepping aboard the boat, "Wait up, who's this? It's just me and you going, nobody else."

AJ put her hands on her hips and turned to Jonty. Jackson grinned and waited for the man to get 5'4" of straightening out from her.

"That's Jackson, he's with me, and who goes on my boat is my decision, not yours. If you want to charter the boat we can discuss the crew, that clear?"

Jonty looked back and forth between them and shook his head. "Whatever, let's go."

AJ and Jackson cleared the lines to the dock and she started the twin outboard motors. In short order they were idling away and she turned to wave to Thomas. Thomas stood at the end of the dock, and next to him was the hulking figure of Reg, who looked even less happy than he usually did. She stuck her tongue out at him.

They pulled clear of the boat moorings in the shallow water and AJ eased the throttles forward. The RIB responded instantly picking up out of the water and getting on plane. They had a long ride ahead, about fifteen miles in total, around the south-west corner of the island and along the southern coast. The RIB could cruise comfortably at 20 knots and AJ expected the first half to be smooth waters, but wasn't sure what to expect along the south coast. She was about to push the throttles up to cruising speed when she remembered Jonty hadn't brought gear. She eased the motors down so she could be heard.

"Hey, so what's the plan here, seeing as you didn't bring any gear?"

Jonty turned in the seat he'd chosen forward of the helm. "You've got gear don't you?"

"Of course, but I thought I was providing the transport – you said you knew the dive?"

"I never said I knew the dive, I said I knew where it was," he retorted, looking annoyed.

"So you want me to go in an unexplored cave as well as provide you with a boat? Bloody hell, Jonty, it's a bit much to ask isn't it?" she said, and Jackson stepped to her side, interested to hear where this was going.

Jonty sighed and his shoulders slumped further down than they already were in his wilted state. He struggled to his feet and faced them as AJ knocked the throttles back to idle. Jonty started to take his sunglasses off but winced and put them back on.

"Look, someone came by and gave me a smackin' the other night, knocked me out and stole all my paperwork on the project. No idea who, but if they're smart enough they'll figure things out from my notes, which is why we needed to go now," he explained.

AJ was taken aback. It was one thing helping Jonty on a fun dive to see if his theory was right, but another when people were breaking in and assaulting over it.

"Are you okay, did you go to the hospital? You might have a concussion."

Jonty shook his head, but only a little bit, as it appeared to hurt. "Of course I have a concussion. Why does everyone think I need a doctor to tell me I have a concussion? You know what he'll tell me? Mr. Gladstone you have a concussion. Too bloody right I do, that's what happens when some plonker smacks you upside the head with a billy club."

AJ considered turning around. She tolerated Jonty, and actually found his abruptness amusing, but sometimes it wasn't worth the aggravation, or in this case, the risk.

"Look," he said in a more pleasant tone, "I know I'm asking a lot, but believe me there's a lot at stake here. It really would be doing me a huge favour if we could go out there and just check it out. Nothing crazy, just have a look around and we'll see if what I'm thinking is plausible. We'll know pretty quick if it is or isn't."

To Jackson's credit he stayed quiet, which AJ appreciated. She could sense he was concerned and was sure he would prefer them to go back rather than her take a risk for a guy she didn't even refer to as a friend.

"Why can't we come back when you've recovered? You think these other people will get there first? Who the hell could it be, anyway?" she asked.

"I don't know who they are. It was an islander with his hair in those cornrow things, that's all I saw before he cold-cocked me. But I can't risk whoever it is beating us to it. I could spend the afternoon explaining it all, but the short version is I have to do this, with or without you. But I'd really appreciate doing it with your help. You know I'll look after you if this all works out."

AJ looked at Jackson, who shrugged. "It's your call, I don't know enough about what's going on here, but I will say something if things get too crazy."

Jonty grinned for the first time. "If the dive's over yer head, I get it, I'll just borrow your gear and go in, concussion an' all."

"Sit down, you bloody moron, before you bang your head again." AJ shook her head and pushed the throttles forward.

15

THURSDAY AFTERNOON

Jackson stood next to AJ at the helm so they could chat over the wind and engine noise, but Jonty stayed up front for the rest of the ride out, which was fine with everyone. She couldn't imagine the headache he must have, and the pounding of the boat as they headed into the waves rolling in from the south-east couldn't be helping. They passed Pedro St. James, the historic plantation house now restored by the government for visitors to tour, and AJ slowed, knowing they were getting close. Jonty just waved her on from the front so she sped back up. A few minutes later he waved again, this time indicating she should slow down. She eased the throttles back and Jonty shakily stood up and scanned the coastline. This section of the southern coast between Spotts and Bodden Town was the only part of the island with any kind of bluff or cliff; the rest of the shoreline was sandy beaches or ironshore only a few feet above the high tide mark.

Jonty beckoned AJ to the bow and Jackson took the helm to keep the RIB pointed into the three-foot waves while she went forward.

"See those two small inlets?" he said, and pointed to the bluffs. "The one to the right is where we're going. The entry to the cave is outside the inlet. We'll have to anchor about a hundred feet out, it's sandy there and fifteen feet deep. If we play out the line we can let the waves swing us around in close."

AJ nodded and went back to the helm, taking a good look at the direction the waves were meeting the shore. The tide was coming in: she could clearly see the stains on the rocks where the ocean usually rose to at high tide, and she knew low tide had been earlier that day. She turned to Jackson.

"Can you go up front and get the anchor ready? There's twenty feet of chain, so figure on letting over another ten foot of rope. I'll signal when to drop it, if it catches, lock it in the cleat. Once we're sure it's firm we'll play out more line and back ourselves in towards the bluffs. These waves are gonna make it a bit exciting getting in and out of the water."

"Probably be pretty exciting underwater too in these shallows. They'll be a ton of surge, make sure you don't get pounded against the ironshore," he replied, and she could see the concern in his eyes. She smiled, hoping it was reassuringly.

He headed to the bow and AJ piloted the RIB in close to the shore, before turning back out into the incoming waves to find the sandy sea floor. Jonty was right, it was about a hundred feet out when AJ signalled for Jackson to release the anchor. The heavy chain chased the steel prongs over the side and Jackson wrapped the rope through a cleat after ten feet had followed. The swells quickly moved the boat towards the rugged shoreline and AJ was relieved when the line jolted them to a stop, indicating the anchor had bitten into the soft sandy floor. With the motors idling and the drive in neutral she waved to Jackson to start playing out line and they slid backwards with each wave that came in. AJ carefully watched behind, ready to slap the motors in forward drive if they came close to a shallow rock, or the anchor gave. She could see a large outcrop of dead coral forming a plateau about six or eight feet down and they edged back over it.

"That's good," Jonty grunted, and Jackson locked the rope in the cleat.

"We can probably get closer to the bluff, we're still in at least six feet of water here," AJ shouted towards the bow, now pointing south, out to open water.

"Nah, this is good, the cave is in the side of this shelf we're sitting over," Jonty replied, peering over the side of the boat into the clear water. "Gear up, I'll give you the skinny on the cave as you get ready."

AJ started suiting up; she'd brought her 3mm full wetsuit to have some protection against the sharp ironshore and hoped the wave action had smoothed the worst of it inside the cave. As she put her rig together, they all hung on as the waves rolled under them, and Jonty gave her what information he knew about the dive.

"So I stumbled across this spot years ago when I was working my way along the shoreline here looking for anything interesting. I'd come out on a day off and scour along a section, mark it off on a map, then start where I'd ended the next day I came out. There's a bunch of caverns, caves and tunnels along the shore here." He glanced over at Jackson, who was staying respectfully back, but could obviously hear what was being said. AJ was about to tell him to get over it, when he must have come up with the same conclusion and carried on.

"Entrance is on the east side of this shelf, you can't miss it, but it actually slants slightly back towards the shore. That's how it hasn't got filled up and blocked over the years. The entry is snug but it quickly opens up into a decent-sized room. I found a turtle skull in there; see if it's still there, I left it alone."

AJ had one tank hooked up and ready on her BCD. She paused. "I don't need twin tanks for this do I? It's not deep?"

"Nah, you'll be fine on one," Jonty affirmed. "So, at the back of the room towards the shore there's a tunnel. It'll be to your right as you go in. It's only three feet high, but it's pretty wide. Set your reel outside the tunnel before you go in. The tunnel goes back a ways," he looked off the back of the boat to the bluffs, "I'm guessing halfway up the little inlet there. You'll be under the bluff for sure.

The tunnel opens into another room that's not very big, but enough to manoeuvre yourself around in. It's also quite high, and when I went in there I found fresh air in the top of the chamber, but no light source. That's as far as I got. There were a few skinny tunnels off that chamber and I always intended to go back and explore some more, but never got around to it."

"Wait, so how does this lead to the well?" AJ asked.

"I don't know," Jonty replied and shrugged his shoulders. "That's what you're going in to find out."

"I thought you'd figured out how they were connected? This is a total shot in the dark then," AJ said.

Jonty pointed to the top of the bluffs behind the inlet. "Look, the well is up there, about 150 feet back off the edge. It's right in line with this cave system. If you go farther inland there's a second well; it must have been the one they dug afterwards as it's still in use. It's also in line. We know the well went brackish, and the new well is beyond the hidden one. So if salt water got to the well water it must have come from this direction, not from inland. I think this cave and tunnels brought the sea water that finally made it upstream enough to ruin the well. Could have been the floor fell out into this system even. I don't know that, and I don't know if this system is passable that far back either. That's why we're going in."

"That's why I'm going in," AJ corrected him, as she slipped into her BCD.

"Fair enough. Anyway, get to the inner room and see if you can figure out the best way from there. North is good, anything that keeps going north." Jonty slapped her on the shoulder.

Jackson stepped forward and looked at AJ. They rocked back and forth together as the swells swept under the RIB, and she could see the worry on his face.

"I'm just going in for a look around, be back before you know it," she said, hoping to make him feel better.

"I know you're good at this, but I just ask you to be careful, okay? Anything doesn't seem right, then abort and come out," he asked softly.

"I promise I will."

She checked her gear over one more time and moved to the rubber pontoon side of the RIB that rose and fell with the waves. She made sure it was clear behind her, pulled her mask in place, and put her regulator in her mouth. She winked at Jackson, before back-rolling over the side into the crystal-clear water.

16

1821

Cudjo sat on the edge of his parents' cot while his mama wiped the blood from his chest with a cloth and kept one arm around him. He didn't want her to stop holding him. His papa stood silently in the doorway, his brow furrowed and his powerful arms crossed. His mama had asked him what happened and listened while Cudjo retold his story between sniffles and trembling legs. He was gripped by fear all over again as he pictured himself back in the woods. His mama kept glancing up at his papa but the man just stood there, listening to his tale, his expression hard to see in the dim candle light. None of them had eaten but Cudjo couldn't think about food. Finally, his father spoke, his voice a low rumble.

"You absolutely sure it was Mr. Ferguson's boy? Couldn'ta been another boy about the same age? Maybe from the next plantation over. You said he were painted up, his face and all, maybe you mistook him, son?"

Cudjo looked up at his father. "No sir, it were him."

His papa took a step towards the bed and leaned over, hands on his knees. "You never actually met Francis before, am I right? You only seen him way over yonder at the house."

Cudjo swallowed. He wasn't sure if he was about to be in

trouble but he was sure of who he had seen. "It was him, sir. I know I only seen him far off but he stares across at us all the time, I swear Papa it was him."

His father stood up straight. "Mama, go get yourself some supper, save some aside for me and the boy."

Polly nodded and stood, stroking her son's head gently before she walked out of the hut. The moment her touch left him, Cudjo felt open to the evils of the world once again and longed for her to stay. He was relieved when his papa, his giant, sat down in her place, and rested a strong, reassuring hand on his shoulder.

"Hoping we'd have more time before we'd be having this talk, son, but I believe there's things you need to know and understand."

Cudjo had no idea what his papa was saying, but figured he must have done something wrong and was now in trouble. His papa's hand on his shoulder didn't feel like trouble; he'd felt that hand across his backside a couple of times and that stung like a bunch of trouble.

"This is gonna take some explaining, so sit back here and listen good, son," his father said and slid across the bed to lean against the wooden footboard. He motioned Cudjo to sit back against the woven lattice wall.

"I told you before, I ain't from this island, I was brought here when I was a boy, about twice your age I reckon. What I never said is how that came to be."

His papa was struggling to find the words but Cudjo did his best to follow along, listening intently as he'd been asked.

"My people were the Akan, we lived near the ocean in a place the English call the Gold Coast. The villages near to us were other Akan people, but sometimes people from villages farther away come and fight with us. These fights were very bad, many people hurt and killed. My father was a strong man, he was a great fighter. One day the other people attack our village but they have muskets now, and a white man with them. There was no fighting that day, they would have killed us all. They held us until big ships full of white men came, bigger ships than we'd ever seen. They put us in the belly of the boat, with no room to move, and sailed away across the water. We were all in shackles, which were like heavy metal bracelets, tied to the ship, and each other. We never see the ocean, but we sailed for what seemed like forever, so I knew we were a long way from our village. I was small, so I was lucky, I could find some room to sit up but many, they were not so lucky. Some of the men and women died and they dragged their bodies out. I think they threw them overboard because we never saw them again. Children died too, anyone that got sick just got worse and died. They gave us a little water and some food occasionally but we were always hungry and thirsty, they gave us just enough to keep most of us alive. We were on that ship for seven weeks."

Cudjo, for now, had forgotten about Francis Ferguson and was fascinated by his father's incredible story. He sat transfixed as the man recounted the tale, his face shadowed in the light of the flickering candle.

"Why, Papa? Why did they take you from the village?"

Solomon held up a hand. "I'll get to that, I'll explain, but it's important you hear the whole story."

Cudjo had a hundred more questions but he stayed quiet.

"After seven weeks, they let us out of the ship and we could barely walk. Most that lived hadn't been able to stand up that whole time and now they made us walk for miles. We was in Jamaica, this big island closer to here than it was to my home. They put us inside these fences with people from villages all over the place. There was some people that spoke Akan, but mostly people we couldn't understand. Some wanted to fight, and crazy as it was, dark-skinned men were killing each other while we were all imprisoned by the white men. Those other men were all white skinned, some spoke different tongues, but they was all white. I didn't know any of their language back then. They had some black men working for them to speak to us all, but the men in charge, they were just white men. They talked to us in English a lot and expected us to learn the words, which I did some. A man I didn't know, who spoke Akan, explained we were now slaves and would be sold to work for someone. We were to do what they say or they shoot us. I see them shoot many men, and some women too, so I know they mean what they say. Things were bad, son, we were treated no better than livestock, worse in fact. They'd take a whip to a man just for looking up from the ground. I saw things no boy should have to see.

My papa and mama had been on the same ship but after we'd been behind the fences for some weeks they took them both and I was alone. I ain't never seen them again. I stuck with some people from my village but one by one they all got taken. One day they come grab me and I was taken too. They put me on another ship, this one was smaller and had some more room as there was maybe twenty of us in the belly, but not much. This time we sailed for two or three days and when they took us out we were here, on this island. They walked us into the town, to a marketplace, and that's where Mr. Ferguson came and took us."

"And he took you out of the metal bracelets and asked you to help him?" Cudjo asked, with the innocent logic of a five-year-old.

"That's not how things are, son. Mr. Ferguson took off our shackles, but me and the four others, he bought us with his own money. He paid the men for us, and he owns us. We belong to Mr. Ferguson, so when I says to you, we must do everything he says, I mean that. If we don't, he can whip us, beat us, shoot us, do as he please, and ain't no one gonna care. That man own our lives, Cudjo. I helps the man, but it ain't because he asked, or I chose to, it's just the way it is. Don't ask me why God made things this way, but he did and I figure we blessed that Mr. Ferguson has treated us just fine."

Cudjo looked at his father, his giant. He couldn't comprehend how the powerful man before him would be a servant to the weak old man that depended so heavily on his father, and the other men and women of the village. Surely he could strike him down in one blow.

"Papa, you are much stronger than that man. I've seen him, he walks slowly, he's old, and he's alone. You and our village could beat him at any time." Cudjo exclaimed.

Solomon reached out and firmly grasped his son's shoulder. "Listen to me, son, and listen good. It's not Mr. Ferguson, he's just the man that owns us, it's all of them. You haven't seen the men with their muskets and blades. They cut our people down like a scythe through a field of spring grass. We rise up against Mr. Ferguson and they start coming, believe me. They come from everywhere, and besides, where we gonna go? This island ain't but so big. There's nowhere to hide, there's nowhere to go. We can't go home, I don't even know which way to row. Can't see no land from here and wherever I been there's white men with their muskets, son."

He squeezed the boy's shoulder. "You get all them thoughts about rising up outta your head, you hear me? Mr. Ferguson been good to us, I hear of far worse around other plantations, and I see a lot worse back on Jamaica. You gonna grow up big and strong like your Papa, and you gonna work the cotton fields like I done. Be proud of that, this place don't grow nothing 'less we plough the ground and harvest the crops, you hear? It's important you understand me, son, you don't want no trouble with Mr. Ferguson. We work hard for him and he treat us right."

Cudjo nodded. "I understand, Papa."

He thought about his father's words. Mr. Ferguson seemed different now in his mind. He'd always seen the man as someone important, like the village elder, a respected man, but now, it was different. Was he respected or just feared? What about his own father, the man he looked up to beyond all else, the man who feared nothing and nobody. But he did. He wasn't a giant. Cudjo's mind raced back to the blood-painted face that had stood before him earlier this evening, and the fear returned.

"What about Francis, Papa? Do we have to do what he says too?"

Solomon looked down and hesitated before replying. "You need to stay clear of that boy, understand me? Don't ever go back to those woods again. He stays up at the house and never comes down here, and that's just fine."

"But Papa, if he does come down here does he own us too? We his slaves? We have to do what he says?" Cudjo persisted.

His father reluctantly nodded. "We do, son. But he ain't coming anywhere near us for a long time yet. We worry about that when the time comes, for now you stay out of those woods. If you ever run across him you call him Mr. Ferguson and you use all your please sirs, and thank you sirs, understand? Sometimes you have to choose your times to fight, son. My village tell stories of wars with other villages from before my father's father was even born. But that day, when they came with their muskets and blades, and all those men, my father knew that was not a day they could win. You have to know those days, and those people, son. We can't win against the white man, Cudjo. Not Mr. Ferguson, or that boy of his, not any of them."

"Yes sir," Cudjo replied, but the knot in his stomach didn't ease. He could stay away from Francis best he could, but that didn't mean Francis would stay away from him.

That night, Cudjo lay on his straw-stuffed mat, where sleep eluded him. His mind filled with visions of a red and black painted face, peering through the open windows. Every rustle and scratch sounded like the mutilated body of a blue iguana being dragged around the outside of their hut. Marking them for life. He edged over closer to Phibba's mat and took his sister's tiny hand in his. He would protect her as long as he could, if the knife came for them. He would have to fight like a man, now they didn't have a giant to protect them.

17

———

THURSDAY AFTERNOON

The surge immediately swept AJ towards the bluff and then pulled her back the other way. She kicked hard to make sure she didn't get carried back into the hull of the RIB. It was about thirty feet to the east edge of the shelf, where she dropped down to fifteen feet and got clear of some of the surge. She quickly looked around for the opening to the cave but couldn't see anything. She let the pull of the waves carry her towards the inlet for a while and then turned to look back at the outcrop of old, dead coral. Sure enough, sheltered from the incoming seas was an opening in the ironshore. Wedged up against one side of the entrance was a large piece of limestone that must have broken free from somewhere else and become lodged. It narrowed down the opening, but she figured there was still enough room to fit through. The problem was the surge. She would have to time it right with flawless aim as the movement of the water could throw her into the opening, or the side of the shelf if she got it wrong.

She really wanted to shine a light inside the cave to see who might be hanging out, but it wasn't an option while she was being thrown back and forth. She put the safety strap for her torch around her wrist and cinched it tight; she couldn't afford to lose a light, financially or tactically. Kicking beyond the opening she waited for the surge to draw her a few feet farther out and, as soon as it swung back, she kicked hard towards the shelf. It wasn't pretty, and her side tank slapped against the wedged piece of iron-shore, but she pinballed her way inside the cave where the water was isolated from the wave action.

AJ swung her torch around the cave and silver flashes reflected back at her from everywhere. The cave was full of large silver tarpon, which were almost as shocked as she was to have company. A few bolted for the opening, but most stayed back against the sides and circled the room. AJ sucked down a few deep breaths and tried not to startle the big fish more than she had to. The base of the cave was covered with sand and the room was about six feet high in the centre, sloping down to walls that formed an irregular circle. She spotted the tunnel between the tarpon cruising the room and finned gently that way. She paused at the wide opening and shone her light into the pitch black. The tunnel looked more like a wide crack over three feet high in the middle, tapering quickly down each side, then extending three or four feet farther but only inches high. A few lobster antennae probed the water from crevices along the side, otherwise she saw no signs of life. The first part had scattered sand on the floor but it quickly thinned and revealed the smooth and polished surface of ancient ironshore, worn down by centuries of water flow.

AJ wrapped the end of her reel line around a protrusion of rock, tied it in place and looped it a few more times so it wouldn't slip. The tarpon had slowed their laps and hung over the far side of the cave, blocking more of the entrance light. She thought about shooing them out but didn't have the heart, and wasn't sure what panicked tarpon might do. They didn't have teeth, but some of them were over five feet long and probably weighed eighty pounds. She decided to ignore them – she'd be in complete darkness soon anyway. She was about to pull herself into the tunnel when she noticed something wedged under the low side of the crack. It was Jonty's turtle skull peering back at her. That old fellow had probably guarded this cave for centuries. She briefly wondered whether he came in here to die, or was dragged in here to be eaten. She quickly pushed that thought aside with a shiver, and started down the tunnel. She could still feel some effect from the surge and made a note that it would be harder coming back against it. The crack stayed straight for a while and then widened, turned and narrowed to quite a bit tighter in height. It was still heading a few degrees off north and there hadn't been any options to turn, so she kept going. Her torch beam cast dancing shadows from pillars of rock that ran from floor to ceiling at either side of her. It was a little like swimming down a hole bored through a giant honeycomb of dead coral. In the early part of the tunnel AJ had been confident she could turn herself around, but now she wasn't sure she'd be able to. All she could do was hope the second room was where Jonty remembered, and wasn't blocked or collapsed. She didn't fancy shuffling backwards out of this mess. Her light showed a wall ahead, and the ceiling of the tunnel steadily raised until it opened into the second room as promised. It was almost a vertical tube in the old coral, about six feet in diameter. She shone her light up and watched the beam dance off the underside of surface water. She wondered nervously what was above. The water in the room looked hazy in her light beam and she realised there was a layer, called a halocline, where the lighter fresh water was sitting above the heavier, salinised sea water. Maybe Jonty's theory wasn't so crazy after all.

AJ eased into the room and noticed the floor dropped away about a foot, indicating water may have poured into the base and shaped it at some time. Loose rocks scattered around the base made it hard to kneel so she rose up slowly inside the room, inspecting the walls for any openings or tunnels. There were only a few cracks and indents that led nowhere. Her fin tips were barely touching the floor of the room when her head broke the surface. She hesitated a moment and gathered her wits; it was creepier than the narrow tunnels, poking her head blindly through the surface to an open cavity. She had no idea if she'd bump into tree roots, more rock or some critter's waterfront home. Her mask cleared the surface and she quickly shone her torch around. After the silence of being submerged with only the rhythm of her breaths through the regulator, every little sound echoed loudly around the chamber. Each drip sounded like a cymbal crash.

The ceiling was low and claustrophobic above her, her hair rubbing the rock before her shoulders broke the surface. The edges of the room seemed to splinter into a series of cracks, fissures and openings, making it hard to tell what was passable, but several directions appeared to have promise. She checked her compass to see what options lay north and had to turn almost ninety degrees from the direction she instinctively thought was correct. A good reminder of how disorientating caves could be. She also took a look at her dive computer. She had plenty of air, the diving had been shallow, but she'd already been down for twenty minutes. She thought about Jackson, sitting on the boat in the rolling surf, worrying about her. She considered going back and calling this a good first reconnaissance, but her curiosity wouldn't let her. Jonty had been this far before; they'd learn nothing new unless she pushed on farther.

A wide crack with enough height in the centre headed twelve degrees off north, slightly east, and seemed like the best option. The biggest problem now was her scuba gear. The crack had a few inches of water trickling down it so she'd be crawling with her heavy tank and BCD, not to mention how hard it would be dragging herself and her gear out of the pool into the crevice. Or, she could ditch the gear and crawl in her wetsuit, which would be much easier. If the air was breathable. She tentatively eased the regulator from her mouth. She'd tasted stale, rank air before inside wrecks, and it took ages to get the foul taste from her mouth and it made her nauseous. She took a shallow cautionary inhalation and to her surprise and relief the air was damp and musty but perfectly breathable. Somewhere this system vented to the outside world. Another promising sign, she thought.

Removing the leash from her wrist, she set the torch in the rocks and began slipping from her BCD. She put some air in the bladder so it would float and make it easier to push up into a space to the left of the tunnel she intended to explore. It was still incredibly awkward and banging her head on the ceiling repeatedly reminded her how cramped she was. After a fair amount of effort and a lot of swearing she had her gear stowed, what she thought was securely, with her fins hooked to her BCD. She kept her mask with her in case she encountered another room or pool to navigate. She also unhooked her reel and carried that to track her path. As she hauled herself into the confined crack in the worn ironshore she remembered to grab her dive knife from her BCD. She'd want to tie off the reel line at her furthest point which would require cutting the line. Holding her torch and knife in one hand, and the reel in the other, she shuffled herself along the confined tunnel. She was glad she'd kept her mask on as each movement splashed the water running along the floor into her face, and condensation dripped constantly from the ceiling. It tasted a little salty but not like pure sea water. There was definitely some amount of fresh water in the mix.

The crack was sloping gently up, hence the water running back down, but it also zigzagged back and forth with the ceiling dropping and raising indiscriminately, making it tricky to choose a path. The hole through the honeycomb was much less defined, so she looped the reel line around anything she could find at each redirection, and kept a close eye on her compass. She was averaging a northerly direction but it certainly wasn't a straight path.

She checked her watch in the beam of her light. Thirty-five minutes since she'd back-rolled into the water, and she wondered how far inland she was by now. It would take two minutes to reach the well, walking on the surface, but belly-crawling through this tiny, rocky hole was much slower going. She really had no idea how much ground she'd covered. She was about to call it good and start back when her light beam played on an opening ahead. She shuffled along, cursing some more as she felt her body grinding against the polished ironshore, steadily wearing holes in her expensive wetsuit. Another room appeared but it was much smaller and she realised it was more of a junction than a cave. To her right, aiming, at least initially, back towards the water, was one passage, and to her left, staying north, was another. She swore she could hear the ocean from the tunnel to her right. An echoing rumble of waves above the constant, tinny dripping of water droplets everywhere.

She crawled into the opening to the north and realised quickly it was narrowing and getting lower. Her light beam shone on rocks not far ahead: the path was blocked. It was tight enough already that she'd have to shuffle backwards to retreat, there was no way to turn herself around. The restricted, blind end gave her a shiver and she fought back a surge of claustrophobia. She closed her eyes and took some deep breaths. Settled, she started to drag herself awkwardly backwards but then stopped. Something caught her eye in the rocks. She shuffled forward again until her back wedged into the ceiling and she could barely tip her head up. She shone her torch over the rock wedged in the right side and could see a lighter stone beyond it. Grazing her cheek on the ironshore, she wriggled herself around to be able to peek with one eye past the blockage. The lighter stone was uniform in its shape and had a similar stone staggered back and above it, disappearing into the rubble above. She was looking at the bottom steps of the well.

18

———

THURSDAY AFTERNOON

AJ could see the concern on Jackson's face as he helped her back aboard the RIB in the rolling seas. It was over an hour she'd been gone. Jonty, on the other hand, showed little concern for anything other than information.

"What did you find?" he asked, flinching at the sound of his own raised voice over the noise of the ocean.

AJ slipped out of her BCD and caught her breath while Jackson helped stow her gear.

"I found the steps," she said with a grin as she towelled herself off.

"Bugger me, seriously? Are you sure?"

"Cut slabs, leading up, yeah, I'm sure. But they must have thrown rocks and dirt down there when they filled it in. The base is blocked pretty good. Guess a lot depends on whether the cross was thrown down before the well was blocked up or after, right?" she said, trying to think it through.

"Why would someone throw anything down a blocked hole?" Jackson offered.

"No, no," Jonty said impatiently. "He would have filled it in after he threw, well, more likely placed, the cross down the well.

You'd cover it over afterwards. Remember, it's a step well so anyone could walk down and put their hands, or a bucket, in the water, hardly a great hiding place unless you filled it in."

AJ peeled off her wetsuit and examined the scuffs and tears in the knees. "There's another way in I think. From the room you made it to, there's a tunnel that heads north for a ways, which meets a junction. There are two main leads off that junction, one goes farther north, which I took, the other comes back to the water I think. Pretty sure I could hear the waves."

"You could hear them underwater?" Jackson asked.

"I wasn't underwater," she replied with a smile. "I ditched the gear at the top of the second room. It reaches above the water line; I crawled to the base of the well." She wiggled a finger through the threadbare knee of her wetsuit to accentuate her point.

"Shit," Jackson mumbled, clearly impressed.

"Knee pads," Jonty said, waving a hand at her wetsuit.

"You owe me a wetsuit," AJ waggled a finger back at him.

He scoffed. "Not likely. I ain't buying you new gear 'cos you don't know to wear knee pads, love."

AJ threw her long-sleeved tee-shirt on and stepped to the helm.

"Jackson, do me a favour, dear, and throw this wanker off the boat, I'm pretty sure he just asked to swim home."

Jackson grinned at AJ then scowled at Jonty, tensing his tall, lean, muscular frame.

"Piss off Yank," Jonty blurted. "Don't listen to her, she's just touchy when it comes to her diving shortcomings." He sat himself back in the bow seat and pulled his hat down to shade his face.

AJ started the motors. "On second thoughts, grab the anchor, let's drop him in deeper water."

The ride back was a little more comfortable and a bit faster rolling with the swells on the south side, but it was still late afternoon by the time they pulled into the dock in West Bay. Reg stood at the end of the jetty as though he'd been staring at the ocean since they left. Coop sat patiently by his side. That was, until the RIB nudged against the dock and then he went nuts, his tail wagging so hard it threatened to launch his rubbery puppy body into the water. Reg stood by stoically trying not to smile at his dog's antics. Jackson tied the lines to the dock cleats and scratched Coop's ears, as the puppy helped by running around and sticking his nose in the way. Coop took the fuss from Jackson, but had his eyes on AJ. Once she'd shut the motors down she looked up at the dog who quickly sat and stared at her intently, waiting.

"Permission to board," she finally said, and Coop leapt over the rubber side of the RIB and half fell, half scrambled to AJ's feet, rolling over and wriggling around for the belly scratches she was happy to provide.

"Damn, never seen a dog wait for permission before," Jonty mumbled as he shakily hauled himself up to the dock.

"Discipline and training ain't something you're around much, I suspect," Reg jabbed without looking at him.

"Beat him too, do yer?" Jonty barbed back. AJ leapt to the dock and shuffled Jonty away before Reg could say anything more.

"You trying to get another concussion? Or a worse concussion, or whatever it is when you get smacked in the head when you already have one," she said as they walked away.

"He never liked me," Jonty mumbled.

"Perceptive of you," AJ replied as she halted them once they were out of harm's way. "So what's next?"

"I'll get some gear to move the rocks. How big are they, you think? Can you drag them back down the tunnel or shove them to the side?"

AJ pictured the constricted end of the passageway; it was like crawling towards the narrow end of a funnel. "It's really tight, I had to reverse out for maybe thirty feet before I could turn, and that was without dive gear on. The two I could really see are about twice the size of a football, probably weigh a hundred pounds each. The other problem is when you pull the bottom rocks away, if you can under the weight of the rubble above, the rest will start falling down. It'll be like playing Jenga, but in a tiny cave, underground, miles from help," she said, chuckling.

Jonty frowned. "What the bloody hell's Jenga?"

"Forget it." AJ rolled her eyes. "It'd be a bugger to shift the rocks, so see what you can come up with. If we get lucky, we'll pluck a rock or two from the bottom and get a decent look before everything collapses. Hopefully we'll see if it's there or not. This thing's pretty big, right?"

"Oh yeah, it's over a foot long, it'll weigh a shit ton."

"Well, that won't matter so much," she said, looking at him carefully. "If we find it we'll leave it in place and register the find so it can be excavated properly, right?"

Jonty nodded. "Yeah, exactly." But she couldn't see his eyes behind his sunglasses and wasn't convinced. Still, she thought, he won't be the one in there, she would be. Wouldn't be his call to make.

"Tomorrow afternoon, can we get back out there tomorrow?" he asked.

"I can't tomorrow, we're on the boat in the morning with customers and then I have a Dive Against Debris trip in the afternoon, it'll have to be Saturday."

Jonty scoffed. "Dive Against Debris, what's that rubbish? Can't you blow that off or have someone else do it? I'm telling yer, we don't have time to bugger about on this deal, someone's got all my bloody notes and they'll be at it before us if we're not careful."

AJ really wondered why she helped the man at all. "No, I'm not bailing on the debris dive, it's important, and people are relying on me to go out. Saturday, we can go in the morning, gives you a bit more time to figure out how the hell I can move those rocks."

Jonty grunted and stomped off up the dock towards his car. AJ walked back down to join Reg and Jackson who were sitting on the end, chatting. Coop did another round of twirls and rollovers as though he hadn't just seen her five minutes ago.

"Jonty said he's still sorry for the Pearl thing and wishes you'd give him another chance," AJ said as she sat down next to them.

Reg laughed. "Bullshit, and no."

AJ shrugged. "Worth a try."

"So, he didn't get you killed this time, that's good," Reg bantered.

"No," she said, "but we'll try again Saturday."

Reg shook his head. "This better be worth it, whatever wild goose chase he's got you on. Don't suppose you can tell me what it is?"

"It's a cave system on the south side past Pedro St. James. It's pretty cool actually, I made it a ways in there today. There's a piece of treasure he's figured out might be in the cave somewhere. Who knows, but the diving is fun. The crawling was less fun."

"Why is it he's not diving? I thought you were providing the boat?" Reg asked.

"He's got a concussion," AJ said, and waited for the flak she was about to hear.

"Another one? Didn't he miss a dive on the U-boat because he had a concussion, just last year? He didn't have any bloody sense to start with, keeps getting his bell rung and he'll be getting fed baby food from a spoon."

AJ chuckled, but couldn't think of anything to say that would help her cause.

"What do you think of all this?" Reg asked Jackson, who'd been sitting quietly.

"I trust AJ's judgement. She's promised not to get herself into a bad situation and I need to believe that," he said in his soft, laid-back Californian accent.

Reg looked at him with a scowl. "What kind of lovey-dovey boyfriend crap is that? She put herself in harm's way just associating with that buffoon."

Jackson grinned. "I reckon she can give better than she can get, Reg, don't you?"

Reg smiled. "Ah, you may be right."

AJ nudged Jackson, and felt all warm and fuzzy inside.

Reg looked over at her. "You're still daft as a brush."

Jackson turned to her as well, but with a look of confusion.

"It's an old English term of affection," she lied with a grin.

"Oh, almost forgot," she said, as she took her mobile phone from her pocket and dialled a number.

"Casey? You have radar on your DOE boat right?"

"Hey, yeah, we do," Casey replied.

"What are you doing tonight?" AJ tempted.

"No plans, what do you have in mind?" Casey asked.

"How about we go hunting some gill netters?"

"Have to go out late to stand a chance – it's a long shot if they're even still around," Casey said sceptically.

"Jackson says the Sea Sentry guys use their radar to track the fishing boats when they run blacked out at night," AJ said.

"He coming?" Casey asked.

"Hell yeah," AJ replied, grinning at him.

"Can I stare dreamily at him without you getting mad at me?" Casey asked.

AJ laughed. "I don't mind in the least, but your husband might."

"I can handle him," Casey chuckled. "I'll get it cleared with my boss, so unless you hear otherwise, I'll pick you up at your dock at midnight."

19

1821

Solomon checked the last of the barrels set up to collect water at the top of the fields. Mr. Ferguson had managed to buy, or borrow, half a dozen more from the Eden plantation to the west, making their total fourteen. Solomon had placed them twenty-five paces apart to set them evenly across the north side of the fields. They'd had some rain over the past week and each barrel had filled up to about mid-calf when he stood beside the wooden vessels and took a rough measurement. He estimated each to hold at least eight to ten buckets' worth already and was satisfied he'd saved them that many trips from the well for each barrel. The sun was getting low as he started across the field towards the slave village, where he'd already told the other men to go ahead of him. It was a pleasant evening and the breeze was a touch cooler than usual, which he thought might bring them some more rain. Looking up, he saw Mr. Ferguson waiting for him at the south edge of the fields and he quickened his pace. The plantation owner was pacing back and forth, which Solomon found unusual for the patient man. As he neared he noted a worried look on his face.

"Sir?" he said, as he approached, and Mr. Ferguson stopped pacing.

"Solomon, tomorrow morning I need you to go into the port. Can you leave at first light?"

"Of course, sir," Solomon replied. "What am I collecting, sir? Should I take the hand cart?" He wondered what had been delivered; the walk to the port took about two and a half hours and usually four back, pulling a laden cart. Cudjo was old enough to make the trek now, and had gone with his father the last time he'd picked up seed. The boy had been filled with awe at the sight of a sailing ship and Solomon was excited to take him again.

"Delivering, not collecting. No cart needed, just you. Be at the house at daybreak and I'll give you instructions then." Mr. Ferguson nodded, and turned towards the house.

Solomon waited a few moments to see if the man had anything more to his cryptic request, but he kept walking. He knew he should leave it be, but Cudjo, who'd known nothing but the plantation for his first five years, hadn't stopped talking about it for a week after his first trip. He loved seeing the joy in his young son.

"Sir, if I may ask, just me, but can I take my boy?"

Mr. Ferguson stopped and turned. "No," he said, and Solomon was taken aback by the man's tone, immediately wishing he hadn't asked. Mr. Ferguson paused and looked at the dirt beneath his feet.

"Not this time, Solomon," he said quietly. "Not this time." He looked like he wanted to say something more but turned again and walked towards the house.

"Yes, sir," Solomon said. "Sun up, sir."

Solomon made his way slowly towards the little village of huts, thinking about the next morning, but couldn't come up with a reason he'd be going to the port. As he joined his family at the large table under the tree for their supper, he pushed the concern to the back of his mind. If Mr. Ferguson needed him to go, then there would be good reason for it, and he'd find out in the morning. He looked at Cudjo, beaming back at his father, waiting for prayer so he could start his supper. He sure wished he could take the boy.

Next morning, with the sun not yet breaking the horizon but a soft glow of light spreading across the fields, Solomon was glad his son wasn't with him. He stood at the base of the veranda steps and waited for Mr. Ferguson. After a while he heard feet shuffling inside the house and the door opened. Mr. Ferguson came on to the veranda, already dressed for the day and carrying a small leather suitcase in his hand. He held the door and Francis trudged through and stared blankly at Solomon. Mr. Ferguson closed the door behind them and set the case at the top of the veranda steps, nodding to Solomon.

"Francis is going to America – he'll be staying with his mother's family while he gets his education."

Solomon took the suitcase from the veranda and didn't know what to say, so he stayed quiet. The boy just stood and continued to stare at him.

"There's a ship in port, most likely the only one. Please deliver Francis to the quartermaster and hand him this letter." Mr. Ferguson reached down and handed an envelope to Solomon. "That should be all he needs."

Solomon took the envelope and waited. Mr. Ferguson looked down at the boy.

"Go with Solomon, Francis, he'll take you to the ship. Your kin will meet you at the port in Savannah. Go on now," he urged, without touching the child. Francis briefly glanced up at the man and then trudged down the steps and kept walking towards the trail that led towards George Town. Mr. Ferguson shook his head.

"Put the boy aboard that vessel, Solomon, no matter what he says. Make sure he goes aboard."

"Yes, sir," Solomon replied and walked after Francis, suitcase in one hand, envelope in the other.

The two walked in silence for the best part of an hour, Solomon maintaining a step behind the seven-year-old boy. The sun rose, the heat built, and the mosquitoes fed keenly upon their flesh. Solomon was lost in thought about irrigation piping when Francis surprised him by speaking.

"What if I refuse?"

"Sir? What's that Mr. Ferguson, sir?" Solomon asked.

"What if I refuse to go aboard the ship?" he said without breaking stride. "He told you to be sure I went aboard."

"That he did, sir," Solomon said, unsure what the boy was meaning.

"So, if I refuse, what will you do?"

Solomon thought a moment. The idea hadn't occurred to him that the boy wouldn't do what his father had instructed.

"Well, sir," he replied tentatively, "I'm sure you'll do as Mr. Ferguson asked, that's what your father's expecting."

The boy stayed quiet for a few minutes and Solomon hoped he'd stay that way.

"You're supposed to do as I say," Francis finally said.

"That's true, sir," was all Solomon could think to reply.

"So if I refuse to board the ship, what will you do?"

Solomon could not think of a response. He was in an impossible position. He'd been given a clear instruction by his owner to deliver the boy, yet the boy, who also owned his life, might refuse. His loyalty lay with Mr. Ferguson, the senior, but once in town if Francis, the white son of a plantation owner, claimed a slave was refusing to do his bidding, he knew who would prevail. He'd heard the stories of slaves being whipped, beaten and even hanged for disobedience. The boy truly held his life in his hands. For the first time he wondered why Mr. Ferguson had sent him into port alone with the boy.

"I figure I'm hoping you'll do as your father expects, sir, and we won't need to make no trouble for either of us," he replied, settling on the truth being his only hope.

"My father?" The boy said quietly. Solomon stayed silent.

They arrived at the edge of the small town formerly known as Hog Sty Bay, and now called George Town. It was smaller than Bodden Town to the east, but had the only naturally sheltered bay, which formed the port. For the sleepy island, with less than a thousand inhabitants, two thirds of them slaves, the waterfront was a busy place while a ship was in port. Solomon looked about at the strange mixture of people going about their business. Several well-dressed white men talked amongst themselves, or ordered others to do their bidding. Some had fancy-looking women at their sides, dressed in elegant dresses, but Solomon dare not look their way. Crew from the ship were less well dressed, in dirty, threadbare clothes from hard months at sea. But the majority of men in the port were slaves. Dark-skinned men from many villages and nations across the horizon. Solomon wondered how many of these fellow slaves would have been his village's enemies in his youth. Didn't matter, that was a life they'd never see again, and they were all in this as one now, no reason for them to fight each other. There were plenty of other ways for them all to suffer and die.

They walked closer to the dockside and came across a well-dressed man who appeared to be directing the loading of goods.

"Pardon me sir," Solomon said, looking at the ground. "I'm supposed to deliver young Mr. Ferguson here to the man they call quartermaster."

The white man paused briefly before turning and yelling something up to the ship. He turned back.

"Stand over there, out the way."

Solomon stepped to the side, set the suitcase down and tried to watch the comings and goings without making eye contact with anyone. His only experience with ships had not been a pleasant one, but the incredible sailing vessels still fascinated him. After a few minutes a man descended the gangway and approached them.

"Are you Ferguson?" the man asked Francis in an English accent. Francis nodded in reply.

Solomon offered the man the envelope he'd been charged with carrying. "Here, sir, from the master, Mr. Ferguson, said for me to give this to Mister Quartermaster."

The man snatched the envelope and looked at Solomon with disdain. He opened it and read the contents.

"The slave going with you?" he addressed Francis.

The boy turned and looked at Solomon who kept his focus on the crushed coral pathway.

"This one? No, sir." A slight smile crept upon the boy's face.

"He's to return to the plantation right away. Although I'm not sure he can be trusted to do so."

Solomon looked up, confused by why Francis would say such a thing. In a flash he realised why. The quartermaster turned to the man they'd first spoken to.

"Make sure this slave understands he's to return straight home."

"Certainly, sir," the man replied as he grabbed Solomon by his loose cotton shirt and hauled him along the dockside away from the ship.

"Don't know your place, is that your problem, boy?" he said through gritted teeth.

Solomon had the strength to fight and overpower the man in an instant, but he knew it would be the last thing he'd ever do. The man tried to push him to the ground but Solomon resisted; he might need to run and he couldn't do that from the dirt. The man shouted for help from two of the ship's crew and they gladly restrained an arm each. Solomon couldn't believe what was happening, and looked back towards the ship. Francis was being guided aboard by the quartermaster, but he stopped at the top of the gangplank and stared back at the melee. Solomon thought it might be the happiest he'd ever seen the boy appear, and then he was punched violently in the face.

20

THURSDAY NIGHT

The shoreline was sprinkled with lights from hotels, luxury homes and condominiums, but the ocean was dark under a moonless sky. The perfect cover they needed to stay unseen. The same cover they hoped would entice the gill net boat out into the night. Casey pulled the DOE boat, Sea Keeper, up to the dock at a few minutes before midnight. It was a forty-six-foot diesel-engined former dive boat, used for mooring maintenance, patrols and whatever else needed attention in the waters around Grand Cayman. AJ and Jackson hopped aboard with travel coffee mugs brimming full, and a soft cooler containing snacks and sandwiches. They greeted Casey, stowed their stuff, and then the three gathered around a map to plan their night.

"My boss was a little sceptical about this, I had to talk him into it, so I'm under strict orders not to engage. We'll call it in to the Joint Marine Police Unit for back-up if we find anyone, and wait for them before we approach a boat," Casey explained.

"I understand that's your boss's rule, but they'll be long gone by the time back-up gets here," Jackson said, politely, "Same way we'll use radar to see them, they'll use radar to see another boat approaching. We'll have the element of surprise if we position and time it right. A new boat approaching, from wherever the Marine Unit is coming from, will spook them for sure."

Casey shrugged. "Unfortunately them's the rules. He didn't like the idea of civilians on the boat at all, but I told him AJ had witnessed the boat, and you had done this kind of thing before and would be an asset, so he finally agreed."

"Fair enough, let's get out there and see what we can find, and go from there," AJ said. "It's a long shot they're even still around; we're presuming it's them who already lost one net. They may have packed up and moved on – we know they have a full tank of diesel."

"Worst case, we miss a night's sleep, right?" Casey said with a grin. "It's worth it to give it a try. You think the boat you saw had radar?"

"I didn't notice to be honest, I was trying to see what the guy was busy not letting me see on the deck," AJ replied.

"If they're from Jamaica they're pretty ballsy to travel this far without radar," Jackson added. "The boats we chase, sometimes they're the biggest pieces of crap you've ever seen. Old wooden boats with fifty-year-old diesel motors, but one thing they all have is modern electronics. Depth finders, radar, and sat phones. That's what helps them find the fish, and keeps them from being caught."

"Dang. Well, let's go see what we see. Where should we start?" Casey asked.

They looked at the map of the island and AJ pointed to the north-west area.

"Here's where we found the net and we presume it came from further around the corner where the currents run. How about we pull around by Lighthouse Point and cruise along there?" AJ suggested.

"Should we patrol an area or pick a spot and wait?" Casey asked, looking at Jackson.

"Stay still. Remember they're watching for us as much as we're looking for them. They see a boat moving at one in the morning they'll assume it's trouble. We sit still, lights out, far enough off the coast so we're not lit by the shore lights and hope we're where they choose to go."

Casey looked at AJ. "He's good to look at, and he's useful, huh?"

Jackson blushed and AJ gave him a hug. "Yeah, I think so."

They left the dock and idled along the west coast with their running lights on. The radar showed clear in the open water and they didn't want to black their own lights out until they got in position in case they came across a local fisherman in a small skiff. They rarely had lights on their boats, and while they shouldn't be fishing over the reef, they could be coming back in late to the handful of docks and launch areas along the coast. They cruised past Bonnie's Arch and curved around the corner to Lighthouse Point. Picking one of the mooring buoys on a shallow site in front of an empty lot on the shore, they avoided being illuminated by the landscape lights around the homes and condos. Once tied in, Casey shut the motor down and killed all the lights. The radar showed them alone on the water.

They bobbed quietly in the gentle swell, the water slapping against the hull and the breeze through the open windows of the cabin the only sounds. They'd turned down the brightness on the radar screen to its minimum and their eyes slowly adapted to the darkness and more details towards the shore became clear. The open water was still indiscernible between ocean and sky. Clouds were light and the stars provided a dim glow but with no land for three hundred and fifty miles between them and Cozumel, Mexico, the horizon was ink black. Time ticked away slowly as they lazed comfortably in the wheelhouse seats, enjoying the tranquillity and sipping coffee.

"Seems awfully risky on their part to fish so close to the island," AJ thought aloud.

"Gotta go where the fish are, right?" Casey replied. "Little fish on reef brings bigger fish to hunt them."

"It's a big ocean out there, so unless you know of a specific spawning or feeding area, it's a needle in a haystack to catch any volume of fish in the open seas," Jackson added. "Cayman is pretty unique with abrupt drop-offs all around the coast where deep water instantly meets shallow reefs."

"I suppose so," AJ agreed. "If they can haul in enough of whatever they're trying to catch in a short visit, they're here and gone before we know it."

"We wouldn't have known a thing unless you'd found that net. Probably wouldn't have thought twice about the boat you saw either if we weren't already thinking about poachers," Casey said, sleepily.

"Of course, the two may still be unrelated," AJ mused. "But there again, you know what they say, looks like a duck, quacks like a duck, usually means..."

"It's a duck," Casey and Jackson said together, and they all chuckled. At one in the morning simple humour seemed funnier than it should.

"What are they trying to catch along the wall, do you think? Not exactly fresh grouper by the time they get it back to Jamaica, huh?" Casey wondered.

"Yeah, I think I may know," Jackson said tentatively, "But let's just see what we see."

AJ was about to quiz him further when the radar chirped and they all jumped up. Something was approaching from deep water and headed for the north-west corner of the island. The radar was set to three nautical miles and as the object drew slowly closer, Casey zoomed the range in to get better definition. They all looked out the window in the direction of the blip but could see no lights. Casey handed Jackson a pair of binoculars and he scanned the water.

"He's definitely running blacked out, I can't see a thing. I reckon that's our guy."

"Is that for sure a boat?" AJ asked.

"It's either a boat, or a flock of pelicans that fly low, tight and straight." She laughed.

"Want me to pull the line?" AJ asked, getting excited.

"Only thing they've done wrong so far is run without lights," Casey said. "Let's see what they do. Question is, whether to call the Joint Marine Police Unit. If Jackson's right, and I'm sure he is, they'll see them coming and take off."

"We need their nets in the water," Jackson said quietly, still hunting the darkness for any discernible movement. "Means they can't just take off: they either have to pull the net in or cut it loose, and both take time. That's our chance to grab them."

They watched the blip on the radar as it slowed about a quarter of a mile from where they sat at the mooring buoy, and came to a stop. They were lined up in deep water just beyond the drop-off. AJ scoured the darkness to the west but couldn't make out anything, despite knowing there was a boat so close to them.

"Let me call it in and have the Marine Unit hug the coast and start slowly this way – hopefully they'll be lost against the land mass of the island," Casey said, picking up the VHF handset.

"Got a cell number for them?" Jackson asked quickly.

"Uh, yeah, I think I have the guy's number they said was on duty tonight. You think they're scanning VHF traffic?" Casey asked as she thumbed through her phone contacts until she found what she was looking for and dialled.

"I would be," Jackson replied. "Which way's the cavalry coming from?"

"It would be George Town unless they were already out here for some reason," Casey replied before her call was picked up.

Jackson nodded. "Perfect, yeah, the island will hide them if they're careful."

"Hey Ben, it's Casey with DOE. I think we may have our poacher out here off north-west point. Can you head this way? But you'll need to hug the shoreline or he'll see you on radar."

"Sure thing," came the reply in a thick Caymanian accent, "We'll run hard along the beach and ease up before West Bay. I take it you want to stay off VHF?"

"Figured it's better, in case they're listening," she replied. "Call me when you're close."

"No problem," the man said, and hung up.

They stared at the radar again, where the blip seemed ominously stationary.

"What do you think they're doing? Putting their gear in the water?" AJ asked.

"Probably," Jackson replied. "If it's a gill net they'll face into the current and either keep the boat in one place or slowly trawl into the current, depending how strong it is."

All three were alternating between staring at the radar blip and out the window into the blackness, picturing the fishing boat setting up a few hundred yards away in the night. The blip began to move, almost imperceptibly, but they all agreed it had shifted from a few minutes before. AJ glanced at her watch; it was almost 2am.

"We need to grab them now, the net must be in the water. If we wait too long those arseholes will have another turtle – surely we can stop them before then?" AJ urged.

Casey put a hand on her shoulder. "We gotta wait, Ben will be here soon. We've got no way to stop them on our own."

AJ nodded and looked at Jackson. "What would Sea Sentry do?"

Jackson laughed. "We'd probably ram them or foul their props."

Casey rolled her eyes. "Guys, I work for the government here, cut me some slack. Believe me I'd love to shove this bow right up their butts."

To her relief her mobile rang and she quickly answered it. "Ben, you close?"

"Coming round the corner, lights out, steaming slow and in close. What do we have?"

Casey pointed to the mooring line and AJ ran outside.

"You should see them on your radar, they're less than a quarter of a mile offshore from us, moving slow. We think they have their net in the water," Casey replied.

"Okay, once we come past you on your starboard side we're gonna make a run for them – we'll go to their bow and block them.

You go around their stern and block them running offshore. That sound good?" Ben said calmly.

"Perfect," Casey replied.

"Oh, and don't get between us and them, or in line with us and them, okay? Just in case there's any shooting," Ben said with amusement and hung up.

Casey looked at Jackson. "Damn, I'm hoping they see flashing lights and just put their hands in the air."

Jackson smiled. "You know when they do that?"

Casey shook her head.

"Never," Jackson replied.

AJ came back into the wheelhouse. "Line's clear."

Casey pointed towards the shore. "Watch out there and tell me when you see Ben, he's gonna come around front of us and sprint for them. As soon as he goes we're to head around their stern and stop them turning out to deeper water. I just need to stay wide enough not to catch their net if they're pulling it in or have cut it loose."

"Here he comes," AJ said sharply. "Another minute and he'll be alongside, he's going slow."

"They've stopped," Jackson said, looking at the radar.

"You think they've spotted the Marine Unit boat?" Casey asked.

"Yup, they've seen it silhouetted by the shore lights," Jackson replied.

"Shit." Casey dialled her mobile. "They've seen you, just go now Ben."

The Marine Unit boat leapt out of the water, it's bow riding high as the pilot gunned the powerful motors and it soon tore around the front of the Sea Keeper towards the open ocean. Casey tossed her mobile aside and fired up her motors as she whipped the wheel hard to port. She opened up the throttles and gave chase. They hung on to whatever they could as the wake from the police boat rocked them just as the Sea Keeper came up on plane and accelerated hard. The Marine Unit, several hundred yards ahead already, lit up like a Christmas tree with flashing red and blue lights on their roof, and two powerful spotlights glaring off their bow. Casey turned all her lights on and looked up from the radar screen she was navigating from as the fishing boat came into view in the police spotlight beam. All hell was breaking loose on their deck with men thrashing about, pulling, waving and frantically handling equipment. Casey veered a wide arc around the stern where they could now see the men on the fishing boat were trying to winch in the net. She pulled the DOE boat around their port side and shut down the throttles once she was sure they weren't in the line of potential fire. The Marine Unit boat was bow to bow with the fishing vessel and two officers in full bulletproof tactical gear stood braced against the railings with automatic weapons aimed. The raucous noise of straining diesel engines, wind rushing and water churning subsided as the boats sat idling.

"This is the Royal Cayman Islands Police Service Joint Marine Unit, cut your engines and put your hands on your heads. Stop all activity now."

The fishing boat motors kept idling in neutral and a man appeared from the wheelhouse and descended the ladder.

"Cut the damn lines!" he barked in an Irish accent as he put his hands on his head and walked around the cabin to the bow.

A Jamaican back on aft deck pulled a large knife and began sawing at the lines.

"Alright, alright, what's yer problem?" shouted the Irishman towards the police boat.

Casey ran out of the wheelhouse but Jackson had beaten her to it.

"Freeze, do not move or I will shoot! Put the knife down on the deck, step back with your hands on your head," he yelled forcefully.

AJ had never heard her boyfriend even talk loudly before, he was the softest spoken man she'd ever known. She noticed he was standing in the shadow of the cabin where they couldn't see him. The man with the knife complied and joined his friends with their hands up. The two armed police boarded the fishing boat and just like that the stand-off was over. AJ's heart was thumping in her chest and adrenaline was causing her hands to shake.

"Jeez Casey, this is dramatic stuff, I don't know how you do this every day."

Casey laughed. "I couldn't do this every day. This was a first for me."

Jackson stepped alongside the two ladies. "That worked out," he said nonchalantly, grinning.

Casey nudged AJ. "You better hang on to this one."

They tied the police boat alongside the fishing vessel and hand-cuffed all the men aboard, sitting them on the bow under guard. Ben, a large, imposing man, took one look at the mess of netting off the back of the boat and had Casey tie Sea Keeper alongside them.

"Can you help us sort out this mess?" he asked her once she had stepped over to the long aft deck of the fishing boat.

"I'll see what I can do," she replied, looking at the outriggers swung as wide as they could go trailing lines back into the water. "Can those two come help me?" she nodded back towards AJ and Jackson.

Ben looked them over. "That Miss AJ?" he said in a booming voice.

AJ waved back sheepishly.

Ben laughed. "Sure, come on over, I'm getting used to seeing Miss AJ in the middle of all sorts of goings-on around here."

AJ and Jackson stepped across and shook Ben's hand.

"Hello again," AJ said. "I think the last time we met we were plucking girls from the water outside the North Sound."

"I think that's true," Ben replied.

"Mind if we take a look in their hold, sir?" Jackson asked.

"This is Jackson Floyd, he's with Sea Sentry, they're stopping over for a few days," AJ said.

"I saw your boat in town, welcome to the Cayman Islands," Ben said with a grin. "Sure, let's see."

They stepped back and examined the large, hinged doors in the floor of the deck, towards the cabin. Jackson lifted one side of the heavy metal closure and shook his head.

"Yeah, figured," he said quietly.

The others peeked into the cavity and stared in disbelief at the shark fins packed in ice. Hundreds of them. Jackson dropped the door closed.

"Let's get this net in, we may be able to save anything caught up in it."

They set to work trying to figure out how to work the winch to pull the lines in and, after a little trial and error, soon had the motor whirring. The top of the net was lined with small flotation buoys and the bottom hung down in the water under the weight of the ballasts. Once the top of the net was to the stern, reeled in by the outrigger lines, they grabbed it and began hauling it aboard.

"I'm pretty sure this isn't how you're supposed to do this but it seems to be working," Casey grunted as she dragged the heavy net onto the deck.

With most of it hauled aboard they began to think they'd stopped the poachers in time, but the last part of the net was proving hard to pull up. Harder than just the resistance of the ballast weights. With all three tugging with all their might, the last of the net and weights slid onto the deck, along with a young Caribbean reef shark which writhed and bucked on the deck.

"Where's that knife the guy had?" AJ shouted and one of the policemen slid it across the deck to her from where they'd gathered anything that could be construed as a weapon. Jackson and Casey pinned the three-foot shark down against the deck while AJ started cutting the netting away. The young shark was surprisingly strong and fought them frantically as they tried to free it from the nylon. Ben stood back and watched in amazement as they freed the snare and Jackson picked the fish up by its tail, cradling its jerking body with his other hand, and guided it off the open aft deck into the water. The shark convulsed a few times as it pumped water back through its gills, then flicked its powerful tail, and disappeared into the darkness.

"That's not something you see every day, right there," Ben said, chuckling.

"What part of this night is?" Casey answered, wiping her hands on her pants and grinning.

"Good point." Ben replied. "Fortunately."

21

1821

It was nearing sunset when Solomon staggered back to the plantation. When the men had finished beating him, adrenaline fuelled his retreat out of town, but once clear of homes and people, he'd collapsed by the side of the trail. Lying in the scrub and ferns, under the shade of an old mahogany tree, he believed he was in his final resting place. How long he'd been out, he didn't know, but the sun had moved across its zenith and he was surprised to see the sky once more. He'd struggled to his feet and began the long, seven-mile walk home. He couldn't see out of his left eye, and was certain his nose was broken, but the worst pain came from his gut. After bloodying his own fists, punching Solomon's face and stomach, the man had found a wooden club to continue his beating. Every breath felt like knives drawn across his ribs and with each inhalation came a strange wheezing sound.

Solomon stumbled past the plantation house and, halfway to the huts, Cudjo spotted his father. Instead of running to him as he'd usually do, the boy stood still, terrified, and called for his mama. Solomon was helped to his hut and lain down on his simple bed, where Polly began to clean his wounds, with tears running down her cheeks. She told Pegg to take her brother and sister to their grandmother's hut and keep them there. The children reluctantly left, confused and scared. Polly kept asking him why. Why had this happened. Solomon could hardly speak and he didn't know what to tell her anyway.

"Bad luck," is all he managed to utter.

Although Solomon tried to protest, Polly's mother ran to the house to tell Mr. Ferguson. Ten minutes later she returned with the plantation owner, who leaned over the bed and examined his slave. When he heard the wheezing from his chest and saw his ribs heave and collapse on one side, he called for one of the other men, and told him to get the doctor.

"Tell him to hasten," he said. "And tell him it's me that's not well – don't mention Solomon, he'll not hurry if he knows he's summoned for a Negro."

The doctor resided in Bodden Town, almost three miles to the east, but he was not a man given to be rushed on anyone's account.

"Run man, as fast as you can, for the fool doctor will dawdle back, I know of it."

Solomon tried to sit up, but Polly stopped him and Mr. Ferguson laid a hand carefully on his chest.

"Don't move, not on my account. Lay still until the doctor arrives."

"I'm sorry, sir," Solomon whispered through clenched teeth. "I don't mean to cause no trouble."

"I should have gone into town with you, I doubt you brought this upon yourself," he said, leaning in closer. "The boy? Is the boy aboard the ship?"

"Yes sir, I watched him board myself, sir," Solomon managed before a bout of coughs caused unimaginable pain through his chest. Polly held a cloth to his mouth and when he finally stopped coughing, she removed it and saw traces of spittle and blood.

"We must sit him up, he can't be laid flat, Polly. Here, I'll help you," Mr. Ferguson said, and they heaved him up and propped more straw-stuffed pillows behind him. When he lay back, Solomon felt his head go light from the searing pain, and he thought he would pass out, but after a few agonising minutes it subsided and he remained conscious.

"Can you tell me who did this, Solomon? Who beat you?" Mr. Ferguson asked.

Solomon didn't know what to say. Your boy made them do it? What good could come of that? Francis was on a ship bound for America and his mother's family, where, he hoped he would stay and not be seen again. Not for his own sake, but for Cudjo and the girls. He'd witnessed first hand the evil that lived inside that child, and he feared more than anything what Francis would be capable of if he ever returned.

"Was it someone from the island?" Mr. Ferguson asked.

Solomon meekly shook his head. "No, sir. Man from the ship did it, sir."

"Why, in God's name, did he see fit to do this to another man's slave?"

Solomon wanted to tell the man the truth, and indeed let it rest in God's hands. The Bible scriptures read to him told him to be truthful, and never tell a lie. But this wasn't a lie. It was an incomplete story that he hoped would save the slave village from more problems. If Mr. Ferguson marched into town and demanded answers nothing would change. He'd still be lying on this cot with a broken body and Francis would still be leaving. Best to leave it be, he kept reminding himself.

"I must have looked his way wrong, sir," he wheezed. "I'm sorry for causing this trouble."

He broke into another coughing fit and his broken ribs stabbed and jerked in his chest where they'd punctured his lung. Mr. Ferguson rose and looked at Polly.

"My presence is causing him more anxiety, I believe. I'll bring the doctor down as soon as he arrives." He stepped back and shook his head. "Please send for me if there's anything I can do before then." He looked as though he had something more to say but he mumbled to himself, turned and left.

Once he was gone, Solomon took hold of Polly's arm.

"Get Cudjo," he struggled to say between shallow breaths. "Have him bring a shovel."

"I'm not leaving you for a moment, whatever nonsense you have in your mind. You best forget it until this doctor has you fixed up." Polly replied, wiping the tears away from her cheeks.

Solomon leaned towards her and squeezed her arm as firmly as he could. "I ain't never raised my voice to you, so don't make me now when my words may be my last. Get our boy, Polly, and a shovel."

"Don't say that, don't you dare. I'll get you our boy, but I don't want to hear no more about last words, you hear." She leaned over and kissed his beaten and bloody forehead. Then she stood and quietly left the hut.

Solomon could feel his breathing becoming more laboured, with every inhalation came intense pain, but not enough air, and he felt the need to quickly breathe in again. Fear was taking hold of him, not a fear of dying, for he believed he belonged in heaven, but a fear of leaving his family to the clutches of a future unknown. Perhaps the doctor would arrive, and perhaps he could fix his injuries but if there was nothing to be done, then he may never have another chance.

The wood-framed wattle door opened and Polly ushered Cudjo into the room before her. In her other hand she carried a shovel. His son looked scared as he looked at his father's battered face. Solomon tried to smile and beckoned the boy towards him. Solomon took a few quick breaths before he could speak.

"Be strong for me son," he said and caught his breath again. "Take that shovel and dig me a hole, son, right under your mat, there," he said, pointing to the straw-filled mat in the corner where Cudjo slept.

Polly handed the boy the shovel and pulled the mat aside, looking as confused as her son. Cudjo poked the shovel at the packed dirt and looked back at his father. "Here, Papa?"

Solomon nodded and waved his hand for him to start. "Slow and steady, son, it'll take some time."

Polly moved over and sat on the floor next to her husband, touching a wet cloth to his brow. "What is this all about?"

"Anyone comes, pull that mat back real quick, you hear? This is just for you two to see," he struggled to whisper.

For twenty minutes, Solomon sat still on the bed fighting for every breath, and Cudjo wielded the shovel that stood a foot taller than him. Finally the shovel hit something solid and Solomon held up his hand.

"Easy now, son, careful with that shovel and use your hands." He wheezed and waved a hand for Polly to help.

Mother and son sat on their knees, and pulled handfuls of dirt from the floor of their hut, until they'd uncovered the object wrapped in an old dirty cloth. Cudjo tried lifting it free but it was too heavy and Polly had to help him. Solomon looked over from the bed as they peeled back the dirty cotton to reveal the gleaming silver cross hidden beneath.

"What in God's great name is this?" Polly said, turning to her husband.

Cudjo ran his hand down the ornately sculpted, bright metal and circled each, vibrant green emerald, sparkling in the candlelight.

"Alright now, wrap it back up," Solomon said as loud as he could manage. "Bury it, same as it was."

Polly and Cudjo carefully swathed the cross in its filthy cloth and laid it back in its hole. They shovelled and packed and tamped down the earth before sliding Cudjo's mat back over. When they were finally done they sat next to the bed, sweat glistening from their faces, and let Solomon take his time to speak.

"One day son, things will be different, different from how they are today," he said weakly, resting a hand on his son's shoulder. "When that time comes, that cross will pave the way to your freedom. Until that day, you best forget about it, for all it can bring is pain and suffering, you hear me, son?"

Cudjo nodded.

"If that day don't come along in your lifetime, you do same as I done with your son. Tell him same I told you." Solomon wheezed, and struggled to speak, but continued, "Mr. Ferguson be a good man, be proud to work for that man, and work hard like I done. I pray that how things be, and how they stay, but one day most likely they won't be, and you'll have to make your own decisions. But don't ever let greed take hold of that cross, not by you, not by nobody."

"Where did it come from Solomon?" Polly whispered.

He looked at her and tried to smile. "It was a gift from God," he said. "I can think of no other reason it came to be in my hands. I've had it hidden since I was a young man."

He squeezed his son's shoulder and looked at his wife. "Promise me now, you'll tell no one, show no one, and not touch it until the day?"

"How will we know the day, Papa?" Cudjo asked.

Solomon nodded. "You'll know, son, it'll be the day you can walk into town and not have to look at the ground. The day a white boy can't have you beaten for his own pleasure of seeing it. You'll know the day."

He waved a hand towards the door. "Take that shovel and put it back, son, then get back to your sisters."

Cudjo stood and retrieved the shovel leaning against the thin wall.

"Sleep at your grandmother's tonight, son, okay? Look after your sisters," Solomon said.

"I'll come see you in the morning, Papa," the boy replied.

"That you will, son," Solomon mumbled as Cudjo closed the door behind him.

The next morning Cudjo did see his father. He saw him lowered into a hole in the ground and covered with dirt. The same way he himself had buried the cross the night before, he watched his giant laid to rest, and the world he knew change forever.

22

FRIDAY MORNING

Metallica made it all the way to the first chorus before AJ startled awake and turned her mobile phone alarm off. It was 6:30am, and they'd been in bed for just over three hours. She groaned and nudged Jackson under the covers.

"You coming diving?" she asked.

"Have a lovely time," he mumbled back.

"Thought you wanted to spend every minute you could with me?" she grumbled, as she swung her legs out of bed.

"I'll be dreaming about you the whole time you're gone," he replied and pulled the covers over his head.

"Fair-weather boyfriend," she ribbed, as she plodded to the bathroom.

Even the sun seemed reluctant to come up, a bank of low clouds stifling the morning light on the eastern horizon. AJ gathered ice, snacks and fruit and topped off her travel mug with coffee as she'd already downed half she'd made at her apartment. She doubted there was enough coffee in the world to compensate for the lack of sleep, but she'd give it a try. The same Caymanian lady manned the checkout.

"Well, good morning sunshine, you look less enthused than normal this morning," she said with a laugh.

AJ sat her purchases on the belt and groaned. "Long night working, short night sleeping."

She wasn't sure if her part in the night's events constituted work in anyone's eyes, but it sure felt like it was at that moment. Of course, she thought somewhat guiltily, to save one more shark from being brutally killed by its fins being severed and the helpless fish being tossed back in the water to slowly die, she'd go out every night.

"Have a good day, dear," the lady said, handing AJ her change.

"Thanks, you too."

As she walked to the van, she was overwhelmed with sadness and frustration as she thought more about the poachers. It was the tip of the iceberg; millions of sharks were slaughtered throughout the world every year for their fins because some cultures consider it a delicacy with healing properties. Scientists can find none of these values in the soup. Sea Sentry were known for aggressively challenging the poachers, as well as whalers and many other illegal and unethical fishing practises. She sat in the van and thought about Jackson, and how every day that's exactly what they did. Hunt down these poachers, often in international waters where no nation will commit the expense to patrol and enforce the laws that exist. As much as she wanted to be with Jackson every day, and wished he would join her on the island, she couldn't ask him to stop doing the work he was doing. It was too important. Maybe they'd have to go on indefinitely as they were, seeing each other sporadically whenever he could drop by, or fly in on short breaks from living at sea. It would be instinctive to push for more permanency in their relationship, but a lot harder to do the opposite, and allow their lives to continue as they were, in a difficult and lonely existence filled with love. She started the van and vowed to be stronger. They were too good for each other to undermine what they had in desperation for more. It would go against her nature to let things be, but she was determined to do her best.

Thomas had Hazel's Odyssey at the dock and he'd already brought the Campbells' gear up from below and was busy setting it up on tanks.

"Good morning, boss," he beamed. "This cloud's gonna burn off I reckon, be another fine day."

AJ slid her sunglasses down her nose and peered over them at Thomas as she stepped aboard.

"Oh looka here now, that man of yours not letting you get enough sleep I see by those eyes."

With her arms full of groceries she couldn't punch him so she went for a kick up the arse, but he quickly dodged her sluggish attempt.

"We were out half the night with Casey – busted the poachers too, mister smarty pants."

She walked under the covered section and set the bags down on the bench, slipping off her rucksack and depositing that as well. Thomas followed her.

"Really? That's great, how did you catch them?"

AJ gave him the rundown on the night's events between a barrage of questions, until they spotted the Campbells coming down the dock.

"Want me to take both dives this morning, boss? Let you relax and maybe nap a bit?" Thomas asked as they stepped to the gunwale to help their clients aboard.

"You're a life saver, Thomas, thank you," she replied quietly.

Thirty minutes later the Newton bobbed gently on the water, tied to the dive site named Easy Street. It was a wall dive in a row of great sites between their dock and the north-west point. Thomas and the Campbells had just descended and once AJ was sure everyone went down okay, she propped herself on the padded bench and leaned against the cabin. Pretty soon she found herself nodding off, and dropping her coffee mug was the only thing that woke her. She was supposed to be on watch and ready in case of a problem, so although she desperately needed sleep, she sat herself back up and looked about. Rummaging in her rucksack she pulled out a notepad and a pencil. On her mobile she went to maps, switched it to satellite view and zoomed in on the south coast until she found the spot she'd dived yesterday. Using the map on the mobile as reference, she sketched the inlet and the coastline on her notepad. She added the shelf from memory, as best she could recall, and the location of the entry into the first cave. From there it was pure guesswork on distances and exact direction, but she knew she'd headed north, and for the first section she must have paralleled the side of the inlet. She hadn't seen anything Jonty may have marked with the location of the well, which had all been stolen now anyway, but he'd told her it was straight north from the shelf. About 150 feet from the bluffs she recalled he'd said. Estimating the inlet to be a roughly half that, she marked the well on her sketch. From there she worked backwards, adding the junction, the vertical room and finally the first cave next to where she'd noted the entrance in the shelf.

She sat back and studied the map she'd produced. She could easily see how a relatively short tunnel or crack from the back of the inlet could meet the junction where she'd heard the sound of the water. Maybe it was that channel that had broken through and turned the well brackish, she thought. A large amount of water had to have passed through the tunnels she'd traversed to have smoothed the old dead coral that way and turn it from sharp, jagged ironshore into the traversable passage. It must have taken centuries, or more likely thousands of years. Sea levels had been rising for 20,000 years and the last time the oceans were higher than they were now was 130,000 years ago. She wondered if the caves and tunnels she searched through were shaped that long ago, when this island was completely submerged and the ironshore was living coral. Probably some of both, she decided.

She looked at her map again. Next to the entry cave she wrote 'Turtle Skull Cave'. Next, she named the vertical room the 'Tank' as it reminded her of a barrel, or a large vat. The junction she named 'The Junction' because she couldn't think of anything better, and then she paused and tapped her pencil on the pad next to the well.

She thought about the story Jonty had told her of the Spanish agent who leapt from the ship along the southern coast. The young slave who wrote the poem with the clue that led them to that spot. Jonty had said he'd traced the father's name to be Solomon. According to his son's poem it was he who'd dug the well. Next to her mark on the roughly sketched map she'd made she wrote the words 'Solomon's Well'.

23

———————

FRIDAY LUNCHTIME

The dock was a busy place when they pulled back in after the morning dives. Two of Reg's boats were going out again in the afternoon, as well as AJ's. They tied alongside the jetty at their usual spot on the south side and helped the Campbells disembark. AJ reminded them she'd be off the next day, but would see them Sunday for their last dives this trip. After hugs and waves she stepped back aboard Hazel's Odyssey and helped Thomas wash the dive gear from a fresh water hose running down from the dock.

"I think we have enough tanks for this afternoon, Thomas," she said, counting the scuba tanks with the protective caps still on their valves. Cap on meant the tank was full, cap hanging by its tether meant the tank had been used, a universal system adopted around the world.

"We have six divers, plus us, oh and Jackson, if he's woken up by now. So we need sixteen tanks to do two dives."

Thomas backed up her count and they both came up with twelve full tanks.

"Well bugger, guess I'll have to run and get some filled," AJ cursed.

"How many you need?" came Reg's gruff voice from the dock.

"Need four – I'd take six to be safe and have a couple of spares," she said, squinting up at him.

"I'll pull six off the boat that ain't going out," he replied, and shouted to one of his crew.

"Thanks Reg, saves me a mad run into town and back," she said as she and Thomas lifted six empty tanks to the dock and traded for the fresh ones brought over.

"Compressor comes next week," Reg said. "Got them pouring a base by the hut on Monday, then we'll frame a room around it off the side of the hut."

AJ finished switching the tanks and stepped up next to the big man. "That is going to make our lives so much easier, you have to let me chip in something towards it, Reg, it must be costing a fortune."

Reg grunted. "I'd be putting it in whether you're here or not. Just keep a tally of your fills and we'll come up with something."

AJ knew he'd probably never charge her a cent but she'd conspire with Pearl, who did all the books, and pay for a maintenance service when it was time.

"We gonna run a hard line down the dock?" she asked.

"Was thinking we would, put two outlets both sides so four boats can fill at the same time." He looked up towards the hut. "Just gotta figure out how to run it across from there without digging up the car park."

Thomas had been listening from the boat and stepped up alongside them. "Run it down the edge of the tarmac over there, and then across the front here," he said, pointing to the edge of the car park. "Dig a trench and have the concrete guy fill it over the hard line when he does the base for you."

Reg and AJ looked at each other and Reg shrugged. "That'll work."

AJ grinned at Thomas, who beamed a toothy smile back.

Reg started back up the dock. "Lads will be excited to dig up some ironshore this afternoon, they thought they were getting off early today."

Thomas quickly called after Reg. "Don't tell them it was my idea, they'll be mad at me for days."

Reg waved a hand in the air. "No problem, I'll tell them the 'Thomas line' was my idea."

AJ laughed and Thomas shook his head.

"Alright, you need lunch?" AJ asked.

"Nah, I got something my mama gave me," Thomas replied.

"I'm gonna pick Jackson up then, be back in a bit, we're going back out at one," she said, looking at her watch. "Almost noon now."

"I'll be here," Thomas replied. "Take a nap, boss," he said, as she walked sleepily up the dock with her rucksack slung over her shoulder.

AJ started the van and took a deep breath; she felt desperately tired, but hungry as well. She pulled her mobile from her rucksack to call Jackson, figuring she'd ask him to fix them a sandwich while she was driving there, but she noticed her notepad instead. She dialled Jonty's number. It went straight to voicemail and she hung up. She put the mobile down and drove out of the car park, turning right to the junction with West Bay Road. She paused, waiting for a car to go by, and when she looked back to the left she remembered Jonty's little apartment was not far. She switched her indicator to turn left and drove up Town Hall Road.

When she pulled up to the detached garage over which Jonty lived, she noticed a car she didn't recognise alongside Jonty's well used pick-up truck. The main house was a hundred feet away and the garage was an extra storage building with the flat the family rented out above. She tore the map from her notebook and trotted up the wooden stairs at the side of the garage. She knocked on the door and was surprised when a woman opened it.

"Oh, hi, is Jonty here?" AJ asked.

The woman frowned and looked her up and down. "Who are you?"

"I'm AJ, I'm a friend of his. If this is a bad time..."

"Damn it Jules, let her in," came Jonty's voice from inside the room, "and close the bloody door."

Jules stepped back, somewhat reluctantly, and AJ stepped inside. The room went dim when the door was closed, with only the light from a bedside table, and Jonty stood in the kitchen looking just as bedraggled as he had the day before.

"Feeling any better?" AJ asked.

"Yeah, a bit," he said unconvincingly.

"Here," she said, handing him the sketch she'd made. "I made this while it was still fresh in my mind."

Jonty sat in one of the chairs at the small dining table, nodded towards the other chair, and studied the map. AJ sat down and noticed several sheets of paper already on the table that appeared to be copies of old documents and maps. Jules moved next to Jonty to look over his shoulder. AJ wondered who she was as she still hadn't been introduced.

"This is good," Jonty mumbled and ruffled through the papers on the table until he found one he was looking for. He held the paper next to AJ's map and compared the two.

"You're close on the location of the well," he said, spinning them around and sliding the two papers in front of AJ. "I marked where I found the well on that map," he said as AJ examined both.

Jonty's paper was a print from a satellite map on which he'd marked the well.

"Jules brought me more copies of some of the paperwork that got nicked the other night. I marked the map from memory but it's accurate," he said.

AJ looked up at the woman, "Where did you get the other papers?"

The woman glared back but then seemed to decide to be friendly, and extended a hand.

"I'm Jules, sorry I didn't introduce myself, I've been helping Jonty with this for a while. I work part time at the museum," she said, squeezing Jonty's shoulder as though claiming him. He's all yours, AJ thought, no need to get all jealous, you're welcome to that one.

"So, you think this other tunnel leads to the inlet from the junction you marked?" Jonty asked.

"Yeah, I'm pretty sure it does. That's where I could hear the waves."

"Might be easier access from there," he wondered.

"I don't know," she replied. "Be tough with the waves pounding you into the inlet. I think we're better off through the way we already went. If there's time I could take a look down that tunnel on the way out though."

"I bet that's what broke through a few hundred years ago and sent the well bad," Jonty said.

Jules leaned over and tapped on AJ's map where she'd marked the well. "But you say it's blocked right here? At the base of the well?"

AJ looked at Jonty, wondering how much he'd shared with this woman, and how much she should say. He didn't look up so she assumed Jules must be part of the team.

"Yeah, there are rocks piled there from when they filled the well. I could just see the steps but we need to clear some of the blockage to get a better look."

"I'll put together some tackle this afternoon. Do you think there's somewhere back in the tunnel we can wedge a bar across? We'll need an anchoring point to set up a winch or a lever to pull the rocks."

"Put something cross ways in the tunnel you mean?" AJ asked, picturing the funnel-like tunnel leading to the well.

"Yeah, like a piece of steel bar," he said. "I have a four-foot bar with a lever on a hinge I've used before. The hinge is in line with the bar so it folds flat to carry it in. Then you swing the lever up and pull it towards you, the rope clips on lower down the lever so you get some mechanical advantage."

Jules looked puzzled and seemed like she wanted to ask a question, but didn't say anything.

"I think that'll work," AJ replied. "Just give me plenty of rope as I may have to set it back down the tunnel pretty far. I was wedged solid in the end by the rocks, I'm not even sure I can move my arms enough to tie anything in that space. To work a fulcrum lever I'll need some room so it'll have to be farther back."

Jonty nodded and AJ looked at her watch: it was 12:44pm. "Bugger I'm late, I gotta run," she said, jumping up. "Keep the map, just bring it tomorrow, although I think I have it memorised."

"What time in the morning?" Jonty asked.

"Seven-thirty at the dock?" AJ replied, and immediately wished she'd said later.

"Seven-thirty it is," he said.

"Nice to meet you Jules," AJ said, as she opened the door.

"Great to meet you too," Jules replied, with a smile. Guess we're friends now, AJ thought, as she hurried down the stairs to her van. Her tummy grumbled as a reminder how hungry she was, and still dead tired.

24

1831 (10 YEARS LATER)

It had been a week since the storm off to the south had thrown high seas against the bluffs. It had rained for three days straight, turning the fields into a muddy mess and threatening the crop. Cudjo stood above the well and looked down the stone steps. The well made him think of his father: even after ten years, he thought of the man every day. His mama told him he looked just like him, now he was grown. Once Cudjo had turned thirteen he'd begun filling out and his muscles grew from the hard toil on the plantation. At fifteen he was already becoming a leader like his father had been.

Phibba, herself a young woman at thirteen, climbed the steps with a pail half filled with water and put it at her brother's feet. She shook her head.

"Ain't no better," she said, standing next to him as they both stared at the pail of brackish water.

He looked at the water level of the well and then out towards the ocean that had calmed since the storm, the gentle, harmless waters glistening in the early morning light.

"Dip a bucket and check it each day for some time yet, but seems we've lost the well, something's changed." He looked back towards the fields of cotton, a sea of white amongst the green of the tropical trees and shrubs beyond. At the top of the 50 acres was a cistern they'd finally built to replace the barrels his father had set out so many years ago. A series of pipes ran from the tank to the rows of cotton plants where they could drip-feed water to them in the dry spells. The plants didn't need any water right now – they'd had more than their fill the past week.

"Tell the other women, everyone's to take water from the cistern, and make sure they boils it first, you hear me? Don't need nobody getting sick off that water, it's been sitting."

He grinned at his little sister, who was turning into a pretty young woman before his eyes. She'd recently started the things that made her a woman, according to their mother, and the only eligible young man on the plantation was already trying to gain her attention. He didn't much care to think about such things for his baby sister, but it would fall on him to decide what's best for her.

"Go on now, you best hurry. Mr. Ferguson will be ready for his water soon," he said, giving Phibba a playful shove.

She tipped the tainted water back down the well, gave her brother a quick shove back and ran towards the huts giggling. He turned and chased after her, his long powerful legs quickly catching up, and he swept her up in his arms and threw her over his broad shoulder. She writhed and laughed and pounded on his back to put her down.

"You acting like a little girl, I'm carrying you back home like a little girl," he said, laughing himself.

"Put me down," she squealed and kicked her legs in the air.

"That boy been getting all friendly with you gonna see you just a little baby still, thrown over a shoulder and might even get a spanking when we get there," he teased.

"Cudjo, put me down. You the meanest brother anyone ever had." She giggled as he put her down on the table under the trees in the middle of the half circle of huts.

"You two stop playing around like fools." Their mother, Polly, called out with a big smile.

"Yes ma'am," Cudjo said, leaving Phibba standing on the table with the pail in her hand. "Just teaching that girl of yours some manners, ma'am."

"She be needing a lesson if she don't get up the house soon, Miss Sally about ready to go," Polly added.

Phibba jumped down from the table and started up the fields towards the cistern. "I gotta go get water from the tank again. Tell Miss Sally I'll be back soon as I do."

"Still no good, huh?" Polly asked Cudjo.

He shook his head. "No, something happen in that storm, since then it's been bad. Keep hoping now it's settled, water would go back normal, but ain't yet. Reckon I need to start digging a new one."

"Well, Mr. Ferguson's up early, he's coming down," Polly said, looking towards the plantation house. "Hope he ain't mad they ain't been up there yet."

Cudjo walked towards the man and met him halfway.

"Morning, sir."

"Good morning," Mr. Ferguson replied. "Well still bad?"

"Afraid so, sir. Women will be up shortly once they boiled some water, sir, sorry it's a little late."

"They're not late, I'm just up early." He looked past Cudjo, over the fields towards the well. "Best start a new well I suppose."

"I was thinking same, sir, whatever happen in that storm seems to be staying. Do you have a spot in mind we should try, sir?" Cudjo asked.

Mr. Ferguson started towards the old well and Cudjo fell in step with him. At sixty-one, the old man still got around better than most at his age, but he was slower than he used to be. Cudjo still stayed a respectful half step behind him.

"Your papa tried up the top a few times, but we could never find the seam," Mr. Ferguson said as they approached the well. "My guess is the heavy seas broke through downstream of the well, which has tainted it." He continued, "It may clear eventually, but every storm we have it'll do the same again."

"Maybe we try a little farther up the edge of the field, sir?" Cudjo suggested, pointing to a spot a hundred yards away.

"That's my thinking," Mr. Ferguson replied. "Gives us some distance from the sea water and slightly more elevation. Have to dig this one deeper, I'm afraid."

"That ain't no bother, sir, just hope we hit the water down there."

Mr. Ferguson turned to Cudjo and thought a moment. Cudjo knew to pay attention – he was about to learn something from the plantation owner. Soon after Solomon had passed, Mr. Ferguson had taken an interest in Cudjo and began teaching him to read and write. At first, no one in the slave village knew what to make of the arrangement, but soon it became accepted that Cudjo would spend two hours a day at the house taking lessons. After a few years, when the boy became proficient with his alphabet and basic math, Mr. Ferguson urged Cudjo to start passing on that knowledge to the other children. Mr. Ferguson had many books in his collection, and would often let Cudjo take one at a time to read to the group in the evening after supper. He'd even taken to joining them on occasion to listen to the reading, and would help Cudjo when he stumbled over a difficult word. The first time he sat with them, everyone nervously wondered why he was there, and the group sat in silence. After a few more times, everyone relaxed in his presence, as he seemed to enjoy the company.

"The rock this island is formed from is mainly the porous limestone as you know," Mr. Ferguson started. "How deep it goes I don't know, we've never dug past it. The fresh water drains through that porous stone, from the inside of the island to the sea."

"Porous, sir?" Cudjo asked.

"Means it's not solid, has holes that allow air or fluid to pass though," Mr. Ferguson explained.

Cudjo nodded, "I believe you've told me that before, sir, I'm sorry."

Mr. Ferguson waved a hand. "No matter. Anyway, the fresh water runs through this porous rock and in places it runs more freely than others. Where the water runs, it wears the stone away over time, and makes the holes bigger so we have a seam. It's like a small stream underground where the fresh water congregates and is more prevalent. There's more water there is what I'm saying. The old well," he nodded towards Solomon's well in front of them, "hit a decent seam of water. So we want to hit that same seam but farther away from the sea."

"How do we know where that river runs under the ground, sir?" Cudjo asked.

"Good question," the old man replied. "We don't. We have to make our best guess, and dig a hole to see if we were right. Your father and I hoped it ran all the way down from the top of the fields but we couldn't find it up there."

He walked next to the well and looked to the sea. "See the inlet in the coastline?"

Cudjo stood by him and looked where the man was pointing. "Yes sir, where we have the steps down."

"Exactly. My guess would be the fresh water finds the swiftest way to the sea and that would be that inlet. If we turn and face inland, trace a line from the inlet through the current well and up the field, that'll give us a place to start."

Cudjo looked back and forth, drawing an imaginary line up the field. "Runs off the edge of your land, sir, maybe two hundred paces away."

Mr. Ferguson placed a hand on Cudjo's shoulder and pointed at the fields. "See how the land slopes just a little down towards the edge of the property, and of course towards us?"

"Yes sir, I see that."

"The water on the surface will drain down that slope, and that water is what filters down and feeds the seam underground. Our best chance will be in this line, at the base of the slope, before the property line. That make sense?"

"Yes sir, it does. Let me walk that way and place a mark, sir. If you could direct me from here, sir?" Cudjo asked.

Mr. Ferguson nodded and by hand signals and some pacing

about, they settled on a spot to try. They both stood near their mark and looked back towards the slave village.

"Longer walk for the water I'm afraid." Mr. Ferguson said, wiping his brow as the heat of the day built with the rising sun.

"It's no bother, sir, the women be fine." Cudjo said. "Most important we have fresh water, sir, better than walking to the top of the fields and boiling every day."

"Let's hope we hit that seam then," Mr. Ferguson said quietly and the two men stood in silence for a few minutes, each with their own thoughts. Finally Mr. Ferguson took a few steps towards the cotton fields, stopped and stared over the crop.

"We're one of the last, you know?"

"Sir?" Cudjo asked.

"Cotton growers. Here on the island, we're one of the last still able to grow cotton. Most others have given up. A few tried sugar cane and failed. Most have simply given up, harvested all the hardwoods from the land and retired, moved into another trade, or left. This soil is not ideal for growing these crops."

"You've made it work, sir, maybe they weren't as clever as you are with the cotton, sir."

Mr. Ferguson laughed. "I don't know that I'm clever, lucky perhaps. Your father had something to do with it too."

They fell silent again, and after a moment Mr. Ferguson started walking back towards the house.

"He was a good man," he said softly as he left.

25

FRIDAY AFTERNOON

Jonty couldn't stop looking at the map AJ had sketched. It had been a few years since he'd been inside the cave so he couldn't remember it well, but the map helped him picture what it must be like. He desperately wanted to dive it with her, but he knew in his condition he'd be more of a burden than an asset. If only he had more time. He'd been racking his brain trying to think who the cornrow guy could be working for, but he'd come up dry; the man didn't seem like the treasure hunting type himself. There was no shortage of people who wouldn't mind seeing him done over, mainly former female acquaintances, but none who could have known about his research into the cross, and how close he was. He looked over at Jules who was making the bed and tidying up the apartment for him, against his wishes.

"You haven't told anyone about this project, right Jules?" he asked.

"Of course not," she replied, putting her hands on her hips and looking indignant.

"No one saw you copying any of the stuff? Maybe asked what you were doing it for?"

"No," she insisted, "I told you, I always do it when there's no one around. I'd be in big trouble if they knew I was helping someone hunt for any historical item or treasure, you know how they are. They want it all by the book and proper procedure, with an archaeological dig and all. What's bothering you?"

He shook his head slowly, as it still hurt to move quickly. "I can't figure out who the hell the bloke was that broke in here."

"Maybe it was just a random break-in, he wanted the computer and phone. He took the papers just because they looked important," Jules suggested, as she carried on moving his stuff around and dusting.

"Nah, he didn't even take my wallet." Jonty mumbled.

"He was smart then, there's nothing in your wallet," she retorted.

"He didn't know that," he growled back. "At least, he shouldn't have known that. It was still on my bedside table."

"Was there any cash in it?" she asked, looking around, running out of things to clean in the tiny place.

"No," he admitted, "But there's a credit card and a debit card in there."

"Card's maxed, right? And he wouldn't have your PIN for the debit card," she said, as she threw clothes in a laundry basket.

"What was he? Clair-bloody-voyant or something? He couldn't know any of that."

She scoffed, "Apparently he did know you then, didn't he? Anyone who's spent two minutes around you knows you're always broke."

"Cheers, love," he retorted. "Thought you said you were coming round to make me feel better? Maybe you want to smack me about a bit too, while you're here? Everyone else has."

Jules pouted and walked over to him. "I'm sorry, I didn't realise you were Mr. Sensitive all of a sudden," she said, and kissed his cheek.

He waved her away from him. "Sod off, I've been called a lot worse, by a lot worse. I'm just trying to figure out who this bloke was – he was here for the research paperwork, I'm sure of it. He had to be working for someone else, 'cos he definitely wasn't a treasure hunter, he was just a thug."

Jules put the laundry basket on the floor by the bathroom and looked at Jonty. "What do you mean everyone?"

"Huh?" he said.

"You said smack you about like everyone has. Who else did?" She walked over to him.

"Ah, it was nothing, just some other bloke came round, he didn't do nothing. It's not important," Jonty said, playing it down. See, he thought, this is the crap that happens when you have conversations.

"Jeez Jonty, who else is after you? What did he want? Was he with the first guy?" she barraged him.

"No, no, no. Different guy, different problem, just some people I have some business with. Came round to see how I was doing," he said, trying to dig himself out of the hole he seemed to be in.

"If he came to see how you were doing, why did he smack you about? Doesn't seem like a business partner sort of thing," she said, brushing his hair gently with her hand.

Why does she always want to touch me, he thought? My head is killing me so she thinks stroking my noggin will help. He tried to stay calm.

"Look, I was exaggerating, one guy knocks me out and steals my stuff, the other one came round to talk about business, alright?"

"Okay dear, I just worry about you. You seem to have a lot of people angry at you, that's all," she said and went back to shoving laundry into the stacked washer in the bathroom.

"I'm fine," he mumbled. He picked up AJ's map again. I'm fine, he thought, providing the cross is at the bottom of that well, and we can pull it out tomorrow. Some pretty heavy 'ifs'. He also knew AJ would want to handle it properly and leave the cross where she found it, so they can report the artefact, officially. The bureaucratic red tape would take forever, and Brenda wasn't interested in donating the cross to any museum in exchange for her name on a plaque. She'd have her weightlifter friend snap his spine in two if he didn't have an emerald-encrusted silver cross in his hands come Sunday.

"I gotta go," Jules announced, after starting the washer and coming back to the kitchen.

Jonty managed a smile. "Okay, cheers then."

"What are you doing tomorrow?" Jules asked. "Going back out with your fancy tattooed girlfriend again are you?"

Jonty looked at her blankly. "She's not a girlfriend, and never been a girlfriend. What she has is a boat. Well, and she can dive caves, which is handy right now."

"Whatever," Jules said, kissing his cheek again. "So you'll be down south doing that all morning I suppose? Going early she said, right?"

"Yeah," he replied, still looking at the map and not paying her much attention.

"I'd like to see it, if you get it," Jules said as she walked to the door.

"What's that?" he asked.

"The cross. The thing you're looking for. I feel like I've helped a little bit, I'd like to at least see what all this fuss was about," she said, and smiled.

"Oh, right. Of course. If we bring it up I'll text you a picture."

"You don't have a phone," Jules quickly replied, as she stood in the doorway.

Jonty rolled his eyes. "I know, I'm gonna get one of those cheap ones from the store this afternoon." He waved a dismissive hand in her direction. "Don't worry, I'll text you."

"Cool, thanks. Don't forget to switch your laundry," she said, and slipped out the door.

Once she'd left and the talking stopped he realised the washing machine was the latest thumping he heard in his head. Perfect, he thought, she's even loud when she's not here.

26

FRIDAY AFTERNOON

Once a month, on a Friday, Mermaid Divers took a group of divers out for the sole purpose of cleaning debris and rubbish from the reefs. AJ was a big proponent of the Professional Association of Diving Instructors program they called Dive Against Debris, but she wished it could be a different day than today. By the time she'd picked Jackson up from her apartment, she'd had no time for lunch, so a dry bagel and an energy bar grabbed from the kitchen cupboard would have to do. She desperately wanted more coffee but didn't have time to stop on the way for that either. They pulled into the car park with a minute to spare to find most of the afternoon's divers already on the boat.

The DAD dive was made up of local residents who cared about protecting the coral and enjoyed getting to dive a spot they normally wouldn't visit. The main dive sites were kept pretty clear of any rubbish that showed up, but some of the areas between the buoyed sites, where the divers didn't go, could accumulate harmful debris. Most of the rubbish inadvertently blew off passing boats, things like plastic bags, cups, cans, bottles and assorted other human litter that went overboard. Fortunately, fishing line wasn't the big problem it was in other places around the world as the reefs off Cayman were a marine sanctuary, with no fishing allowed. Still, they always found some of the nylon line and wondered how it got there.

The last of the group arrived, so Thomas cleared the lines and AJ eased the Newton away from the dock with half a bagel between her teeth. As she idled away, she ate the rest of it and chased it with some water. Jackson leaned against the hard-top frame beside her.

"You need an early night tonight. I can cook us up some pasta, just relax a bit," he said.

"Sounds perfect," she replied, giving him a sleepy smile. "Oh, we can't," she remembered, "it's Pearl's night at the pub."

"Can't we skip one? They'd understand if they knew what your night had been," he said.

She laughed. "I could, probably, but you can't. They've been dying to take us out one night you're here. I reckon they might have to settle for having us there tonight."

"Yeah," he said quietly. "I'd like you to myself Saturday night. I'm afraid we pull out Sunday."

She took a deep breath, then leaned over and gave him a kiss. "I'll share you tonight then, but tomorrow you're all mine."

She reminded herself of her decision she'd made that morning: whatever it took, she'd make this work. With only a few hours' sleep, it was a test she didn't feel up to facing and a tear crept down her cheek, carried away on the wind, to her relief.

The wreck of the former USS Kittiwake was the most popular dive on the island, which meant many dive boats, but also many snorkelling tours moored up there. Divers in general were incredibly conscious of their impact on the ocean, but some of the tourists, ferried out en masse in boats to bob around and peer down from the surface, weren't always as careful. As the swell usually came from the north-west, anything going in the water around the Kittiwake tended to drift south-east towards the shore. AJ piloted the boat to the south of the Kittiwake's bow buoy and pulled the throttle back to idle and disengaged the drive. Standing at the back of the fly-bridge she shouted down to the divers on the aft deck below.

"Okay guys, here's the plan. We'll splash here, just south of the wreck, and make our way at an angle towards the shore." She pointed south-east. "Over there, the buoy you can just see is Mitch Miller's reef. Thomas will moor up there once we're all in the water. The goal will be to regroup there. There's ten of us in the water, so let's split into two groups of five. Just after we get in we'll come across a large coral patch that's oval shaped – we'll take a group each side and focus on that area. It's big so it'll take most of the dive. Hopefully we'll all meet up on the other side in the sand flats before Mitch Miller's. Make sure each group has a couple of lift bags, at least one SMB and everyone has a mesh bag for debris. Sound good?"

Everyone gave her an okay sign and began sorting their groups and gear in preparation. AJ started down the ladder. "I have a lift bag and an SMB, so I can take three of you along with Jackson, so my group needs one more lift bag, in the hands of someone trained to use it, I should add."

After a few minutes of organising they were ready to go, and one by one they took a giant stride into the water from the swim step. Once below, the visibility was superb and current was non-existent. AJ took a quick compass reading and headed south-east, with the group following. Almost immediately the coral patch she'd talked about came into view as they angled down to the sea floor at sixty feet. Splitting into two groups, then fanning out, the divers began to search the reef for anything that shouldn't be there. Jackson stayed close to AJ, and she soon forgot how tired she was, enjoying being in her happy place, with him alongside. Sunday would be tough, she knew, but there was no point ruining the little time they had together by moping about it. She soon found a plastic shopping bag caught around a sea fan and carefully removed it, stuffing it in her mesh bag. The ringing sound of a tank tap caught her attention, and she kicked across to where one of the group had found something. When she reached the woman she was pointing at a crevice in the coral. AJ saw what appeared to be an old piece of metal, wedged in the reef. It had been there for a long time and was covered with growth. The rule was take what does no harm, and in this case they'd be harming fresh coral growth by removing the object. She waved a hand, indicating to leave it in place, and they moved on. She saw Jackson had found something and finned over to him. He'd come across an anchor wedged in the reef. It was a smaller, modern Danforth anchor from a pleasure or fishing boat, and hadn't been there long. Its chain lay across the coral and AJ estimated there was twenty-five feet of it, but they'd measure it when they got it aboard. The boating rule of thumb was a foot of chain rode for every foot of craft, so if the person knew the rule it would indicate a twenty-five-foot vessel that had lost its anchor. Not that they'd ever find the boat, unless they'd marked their anchor with their name, which was unlikely for someone illegally anchoring on the reef. From the chain stretched a further length of rope which also draped and wrapped around and over the delicate coral, fans and sponges.

Jackson was able to wriggle the anchor free and AJ clipped her lift bag securely to it. Using her regulator, she blew some air into the lift bag until the anchor hung freely with neutral buoyancy. They coiled up the chain and wrapped it around the anchor, using a spare carabiner to clip it in place. It took a lot more air in the bag to float the additional weight of the chain. They cut away the rope from the chain and stuffed that into a mesh bag. Once they began their ascent, and the surrounding pressure decreased, AJ would have to bleed some of the air from the lift bag to stop it accelerating towards the surface, but for now she could tow it along like an overgrown balloon. By the time they reached the end of the coral patch, they'd added several plastic soda bottles, one length of fishing line, and more rope, which appeared to be attached to nothing. They'd been down over forty minutes so when the other group caught up, they crossed the sand flats to Mitch Miller's reef and AJ guided them to the mooring line. She carefully began to ascend, bleeding air from the lift bag as she went. At fifteen feet from the surface she levelled off and the divers hung there for three minutes allowing some of the excess nitrogen in their systems to dissipate. When everyone had completed their safety stop, they surfaced and began the chore of hauling their bounty aboard Hazel's Odyssey.

Thomas reached in and helped pull the anchor onto the swim step.

"Oh, that's worth some money right there, boss, I can sell that no problem."

AJ climbed the ladder and rolled her deflated lift bag up. "Perfect, we'll throw the money in the fund for next month's trip, discount the cost for everyone a bit," she said, turning to help drag mesh bags of rubbish aboard. "Just don't sell it back to the wanker who snagged the reef and lost that anchor in the first place."

For the second dive they stayed moored to Mitch Miller's reef and made a wide arc to the west. They didn't come across anything large or heavy enough to require a lift bag, but filled their mesh bags with more plastic bottles, bags and a miscellany of discarded items. AJ took her sling spear and shot four good-sized lionfish, removing the invasive predators from the reef and bringing them up in a lionfish container she made Jackson carry.

As they motored back to the dock, the boat was abuzz with the satisfaction of clearing a large amount of trash from the reef, and saving some of the delicate coral from being smothered. By the time they had pulled up to the dock and AJ had shut down the diesel engine, her exhaustion caught up with her and she sat in the pilot chair for a few minutes while everyone unloaded gear and piles of rubbish. One of the divers loaded all they'd gathered, apart from the anchor, into the bed of his pick-up truck and volunteered to run it by the dump in the morning. AJ wearily made her way down the ladder and bade farewell to the group, politely bowing out of the impromptu celebration they headed for at Calico Jack's bar on the beach.

Jackson wrapped his arms around AJ and she buried her face into his neck. All she wanted in that moment was to curl up with her man and sleep in the warm sanctuary of his embrace. He kissed the top of her head and her calves ached from standing on tiptoe to snuggle in his neck.

"I gotta sort out the fish, and I have to take the tanks to be filled," she moaned. "I just want to sleep."

"Tell you what, how about Thomas and I take care of the tanks and you trim the spines off your lionfish. If you're done before we're back lay down on the bench and take a nap; we'll take the boat out once we get the tanks back."

AJ would never normally let them do all that work, but she was too tired to even protest.

"Okay," she said, "I love you."

He kissed her again and nodded to Thomas who'd started to pull the empty tanks from the boat.

"Alright if you and I do the tank turnaround, Thomas?"

The Caymanian grinned. "Sure thing, man, boss should get herself a nap, been telling her all day."

27

1835 (4 YEARS LATER)

Sweat ran down Cudjo's shirtless body as he walked between the rows of cotton plants. His loose-fitting cotton pants were stained the colour of the earth, evidence of working with it every day. It had been a long, hot day and he and the two other young men laughed and joked as they headed home for the evening. Much had changed on the plantation as times grew harder. Polly's mother had died several years back, and the older man who fished for the village had passed on as well. One of the younger families was sold to another man on the island when cotton production was low one year, after an autumn of exceptionally heavy rains. The only son of Sally, the house cleaner, who worked the fields with Cudjo, had married the cook's daughter, and they'd moved into Polly's mother's hut. The cook's husband had taken over the fishing duties. They were down to ten slaves, the least there'd been in forty years. It meant each man, woman and child had to work a little harder, and work a little longer every day. If it meant they could keep the plantation going, food on the table and shelter over their heads, they all considered it their only choice. They knew nothing else.

Phibba greeted her brother with a pail of water to wash the dirt away and a coconut opened up to drink. Cudjo knew the real reason she was standing there was not him, but the other young man working with him, who she'd be marrying in a few weeks. He'd made her wait longer than he should have, but at nearly seventeen he figured he should let them be together, or else there'd be a baby anyway. Nature would be what nature would be. He and Pegg had lost out in the eligible partners numbers on the plantation, there simply weren't enough of them. Mr. Ferguson had talked with the neighbouring Eden plantation a few years back about allowing their slaves to socialise occasionally, but both had run across hard times and had to reduce their numbers. Babies were a burden in such times, so there wasn't any incentive to have their slaves married, and nothing came of it.

"Mr. Ferguson has a visitor at the house," Phibba announced. "Man came this afternoon, had someone carry his bags for him, so must be important."

"That's good for Mr. Ferguson to have some company," Cudjo said. "Did they say where he was from?"

"Nope, he seemed surprised to see him and then told Sally and me to head on out," Phibba said. "Cook's only one been back up there, she's still there. I been helping mama around here."

Cudjo wondered who it might be and looked towards the house as he washed his hands. Standing at the railing, staring back towards him and the slave village was a well-dressed man, not much older than Cudjo. Even at a distance, he immediately recognised that stare. He had been five years old the last time he saw Francis Ferguson. The morning his father left with the boy for the port. Cudjo had stood outside their hut in the early light, and watched the two walk away down the trail. By the following morning his father was dead. Fifteen years ago Cudjo had felt nothing but fear for Francis Ferguson, but now, as a grown man, he felt nothing but hatred and contempt. He looked at his little sister, chatting and flirting with her future husband, oblivious to the danger that had walked back into their lives. He wanted to warn her, to warn them all, but he calmed himself into waiting. Fifteen years was a long time. He had no way to know what kind of man

Francis Ferguson had grown to be. Maybe he'd taken after his father after all.

The following morning Cudjo rose before the sun, as he always did. Letting his mother and sisters sleep, he quietly left the hut and walked over to the new well they'd dug four years before. They'd hit the seam of water first try, where Mr. Ferguson had directed, and it had flowed plenty of cool, fresh water since. Cudjo walked down the dozen steps to the narrow base of the well and dipped the pail in the stream. Walking out he placed the pail beside him and sat on the top step. The sun cracked the horizon behind him to the east, and bathed the countryside in a pale, yellow glow. This was his favourite time of day, when he was alone with a few birds in song, the occasional cock crowing, and his thoughts. But this morning, those thoughts were interrupted by a voice behind him.

"You probably don't remember me, do you?" The man's voice startled Cudjo.

He turned to see Francis silhouetted by the rising sun. He stood and faced him.

"I remember you, sir," he said.

"Last time we met, you were a scared little boy in the woods," Francis said in an even tone.

Cudjo had no response. Everything he wanted to say he knew would bring trouble upon him, so he urged himself to stay quiet. He hoped the boy had grown into a reasonable man but the stare he'd seen last night reminded him too well of the look that dark, lonely boy had always had. He couldn't see his expression now, with the early morning light silhouetting his face.

"I hear your father is no longer with us. My father thought a lot of him, I know. Unfortunate what happened," he said, his voice still flat. He had a strange accent, tinted from the English he was raised with.

"I'm told my father favours you now," he continued, and Cudjo listened carefully, staying quiet. "Even taught you to read and write, I hear." He laughed and took a step closer.

"Quite unacceptable in America, I assure you, wasting time on educating Negroes. You should expect things to change around here now I'm back. We're going to run this place like a proper plantation should be run, how my family in Georgia showed me. No more wasting money," he said, his voice slightly raised. Cudjo remained silent.

"No 'Yes, sir'?" Francis hissed and before Cudjo knew it a whip whistled through the air and slapped across his bare arm and shoulder, stinging ferociously. He staggered to one side and kicked the pail over, clutching his arm and feeling the welt from the whip raising up.

"Still nothing?" Francis said, and cracked the whip again, wrapping around Cudjo's arm and slapping his back.

Cudjo groaned at the pain. "Yes, sir," he managed to say.

"Yes, sir, what?" Francis replied, laughing. "Yes, sir, whip me again?"

He cracked the whip again and Cudjo cowered, turning his back to the blow from the sharp leather.

"Certainly, I can whip you every time you ask," Francis said, putting more strength into the lash.

"No, sir." Cudjo winced in pain.

"No, sir? You're telling me no, boy? You don't get to tell me no. Damn you, boy," Francis growled and snapped the whip again.

Cudjo dropped to his knees and looked at the dirt. Confused, and reeling in pain, he was at a loss what he could say or do to make Francis stop. He thought of his father's words all those years before. Do as they say, whatever happens, do as they say. He wanted to lunge at the young man, he knew he had the strength to win a fair fight and he could stand one whip lash to get in close. But then what? He kept his head down and heard Francis begin to laugh again.

"Good, we have an understanding already, I see. That's more like it." He stopped laughing. "There'll be no more lessons at the house, boy, no more lessons down here with your other Negros either. When the sun comes up you'd better be in the fields already. If I see you back from the fields with any daylight to work, you'll all be whipped. The food my father has been wasting on you people, that's to be cut in half. Grow your own food, in your own time, hear me?"

Cudjo stayed looking down but quickly responded this time, "Yes, sir."

"Should I take my whip to the others, or do you think you can pass along the new rules, boy?"

"I'll tell them, sir, I swear, I'll tell them, no need to be whippin' anyone," Cudjo said through gritted teeth.

He heard Francis take another step towards him but fought the urge to look up. He felt the end of the whip handle under his chin, lifting his head. He kept his eyes looking down as his head was tilted up.

"That cock crowing means more to me than you do. You need to understand that. I've sent better than you to an early grave for looking at me wrong, boy. One step out of line and you'll regret the day you were born."

He released his chin and Cudjo let his head drop, never looking up.

"Get to work," Francis muttered and Cudjo watched the man's boots walk away.

He slowly stood, and started back to the village where everyone was emerging from their huts to begin the day. He saw Francis pause and take a long look at Phibba. If he took one step towards her, he knew he wouldn't be able to control himself, but thankfully the man moved on towards the house. As Cudjo limped into the half circle of huts he wondered what Mr. Ferguson's part in all this could be. The man had been so fair for so many years, and they'd all worked hard because of it. How could he stand by and let his son change everything in a day? Phibba looked over and saw he was moving slowly.

"Cudjo, what's wrong with you?" She ran to him. "My goodness, what happened to you? What did this?"

"Weren't no what, it was him," he said quietly, nodding towards the man walking up the steps to the plantation house. "Get everyone gathered Phibba, and hurry about it."

"But you need tending to," she started to protest, but he took her arm firmly.

"Be a lot worse I don't get to tell everyone right now, so do as I say girl, get them gathered."

"Alright," she said and ran to each hut in turn.

Cudjo sat at the long table under the trees and winced as he touched the welts, some of which had broken through and were bleeding. He felt a cool, wet cloth touch his back and turned to see his mother, Polly, dabbing his wounds.

"Damn whipped me, Mama," he said under his breath.

"I know, it's been since I was just a little girl, but I seen plenty of these marks before, when we was being brought here all those years ago. Ain't never seen them since we been here, though. Not under Mr. Ferguson."

"It weren't him, Mama, I don't believe he ever would. It's his boy, Francis is back, and he's all grown up and means to run things it seems."

Polly shook her head. "That boy never been right, evil from the day he could walk. Ain't never said nothing, 'cos never thought it meant nothing, after he'd gone and all." She leaned in close to his ear, "But your Papa tell me the night he died, he say that boy ain't Mr. Ferguson's. It was his wife's alright, she paid for her sins day she gave birth to him, but Mr. Ferguson ain't his papa."

"Mr. Ferguson know that?" Cudjo asked, stunned by his mother's words.

"Him that told your Papa, best I know," she said. "But you listen to me now son, that Francis already took one man from me, I swear he had something to do with your Papa's beatin'. You don't let him take another one from me, you hear? Let him boss you around and say what he wants, take it all with a 'yes sir'. Don't give him no reason to take you too."

"I'll do my best, Mama, I promise," he told her, but he knew he couldn't keep that promise if Francis laid a hand on her or the girls. He wished he could talk to his Papa, ask him what to do. It had been fifteen years, but he still missed his father every day. He looked up, and saw nine faces turned to him for wisdom, and he felt the weight of responsibility on his shoulders with more pain than the whip had delivered. Their lives might depend on his words and his actions. He took a deep breath and hoped his father would guide his words.

"Everything we know has gone changed today, and it's important you all understand and hear me now," he began.

28

FRIDAY AFTERNOON

Jonty rummaged through the paperwork on the dining table, although he knew he'd looked at it all several times already. Jules had only been able to get a few of the articles, newspaper clippings and maps she'd accumulated for him over the past few months, and had focused on the maps as he'd asked. History of the Ferguson plantation was thin, but information on the neighbouring and much larger estate of William Eden was relatively plentiful. There were details of the stone house, which had been taken over by the government and restored in modern times, along with extensive research into its past. None of the paperwork he currently had covered any of that, but he recalled reading that the Eden estate had acquired Ferguson's property in 1835.

Jonty didn't usually spend much time thinking about the people involved. His focus was treasure and where it may lie, but for a few minutes he wondered what happened that drove the slave to write that poem. He hadn't looked very hard, but to his recollection he hadn't seen any records of what fate befell anyone past the sale of the plantation. It puzzled him slightly why the slave would hide the cross and write the cryptic poem, seemingly for someone to figure out at some point, just when he would have been granted his freedom. In May of 1835, a representative of the governor in Jamaica, who at the time presided over the Cayman Islands, held court at Pedro St. James to issue the proclamation ending slavery in the British Empire. The sale of the Ferguson plantation happening at that same time couldn't be a coincidence, he pondered. Why didn't the slave take the cross and start a new life on the wealth it would have brought?

The front door bursting open put an end to his wandering thoughts, and he jumped as the large American from Wednesday night stood in the doorway.

"Hello Gladstone," the man grunted, with a smile.

"Oh, Bird-man, I see you've let yourself in." Jonty's heart stopped for a moment when he thought he'd got his days mixed up in his concussed state and perhaps it was Sunday already. No, he assured himself, it's still Friday.

"It's Friday," he blurted.

"It is," Falcon said, and stepped farther into the apartment.

Jonty's eyes were steadily becoming less sensitive to the light, or perhaps anything following the afternoon on the boat just felt better, but he still had to squint to look towards the open door. He was surprised when a short but wide figure blocked much of the sunshine from the doorway.

"Brenda?" he muttered, and Falcon took a step towards him.

"Miss McGinnis," he quickly corrected himself, and the man checked up.

"Jonty Gladstone," she said in a thick Scottish accent. "How are you today? Falcon tells me you've been under the weather lately, I hate to hear that, you poor wee lad."

"It's only Friday," Jonty repeated.

Brenda laughed, and things jiggled that shouldn't really jiggle. "Ay lad, it is, I just thought I'd drop by and check on you myself, you being poorly and all. And us being in business together, of course."

She pulled out the chair on the opposite side of the table and plonked herself down. The chair wobbled slightly, as did Brenda.

"I have to say, you caught me in a weaker moment when I agreed to your proposal a few months back. I confess to being a bit of a romantic when it comes to the old Errol Flynn swashbucklers." She chuckled, and Jonty couldn't help being transfixed by her dancing jowls as she spoke. "But business is business, and since I did agree to get involved in your flight of fantasy, I now need to make sure I make back my investment, one way or another." She put her hands on the table, "Preferably with a suitable profit, or at least a gain of some description."

Jonty nodded, and took the plunge to see if he could buy more time. "You'll make it back, and then some. Now we've found where the artefact is located, all I need is the time to retrieve it. Which I explained to Birdy over there, but he seems to be stuck on this Sunday deadline. Quite honestly, Miss McGinnis, you and I both know that's unrealistic."

Brenda smiled but her eyes, peering out from under her droopy eyelids, didn't change their expression at all. "You give me far too much credit, Jonty, I have no idea what's realistic or not, when it comes to finding hidden treasure. Though what I do know a lot about is making commitments, and keeping those commitments. Call me crazy, but over the years I've learnt to insist upon that sort of thing, you see. I believe it has a lot to do with why I've managed to stay afloat, and in business, for all these years. Plenty of men, with balls much bigger than your wee little excuses for manhood, have tried to test me on this."

"That's a bit uncalled for..." Jonty mumbled.

"How do you think they've fared, eh?" she asked.

Jonty shrugged his shoulders. "Not well is my guess, otherwise you wouldn't be making much of a point right now."

"That's right, not well is exactly how they've fared," she said, sitting back to a groaning from the chair legs. "No exceptions."

"But, not contradicting you in any way here, but Eddie the Eagle over there tells me I have a bullet in the head coming Sunday if I don't produce. Surely you don't run around shooting everybody that's five minutes late on a payment or delivery, do you? The island has a couple of murders a year, you'd go double digits alone if that were the case."

"Say the word, Miss." Falcon growled from where he stood behind Brenda. She held up a hand.

"You're right of course, we don't go around topping people every time they're a wee bit late on a payment. That would be..." She thought a moment, "Well, quite American really." She laughed and glanced over at the Falcon. "But also bad for business. Dead men can't pay back debts." She leaned forward again. "Most of the time a simple roughing-up of the offender, or someone close to them, is effective enough. But every once in a while I find it's important to make a statement, you know, let everyone know we're still serious."

She turned and looked at Falcon. "When was the last time? Do you recall?"

"Been a while, Miss, maybe as long as five years," he replied with a grin.

"I believe you're right," she turned back. "And I've been thinking lately, we're due. We can't have anyone thinking we've gone soft now, can we?"

"Nah, no one thinks you're going soft. Well, not in business, anyway," Jonty said, hopefully. "As you can imagine, I may be coming from a biased perspective, but I for one take you very seriously and am fully aware of the gravity of the situation."

"Ay, I'm not surprised you'd see it that way, but considering my error in judgement getting involved in the first place, along with a general need to make a show of strength to keep the punters in line, I'm afraid it might just be your unlucky day."

"You say that like it's a foregone conclusion," Jonty pointed out.

"Well, surely it is really," she replied with a smile. "You've come up with jack shit in months, and now you're claiming to be so close you'll have it by Sunday. Hardly likely now, is it?"

"I didn't say Sunday, I said I need a few more weeks. Your pet budgie came up with Sunday, which as I mentioned, is unrealistic,"

Jonty protested, sensing the situation cascading out of control, at least for him.

"Besides, you're in no condition to go treasure-hunting with that bash on the head you have," she said with a sympathetic tone as she heaved herself up from the chair. "Or your poor wee hand."

Jonty frowned, and by the time he'd wondered what his hand had to do with anything, the Falcon had taken a step forward and brought his fist down on the back of Jonty's fingers, crushing them against the table. The sound of crunching bone was almost worse than the searing pain that shot through his hand. He picked his hand up but three of his fingers dangled helplessly and he could feel broken bones grating against other shards of broken bone. He screamed more in terror at the mess than the intense pain. Damn, he moved quick for a big thug, he thought.

Brenda laughed as she waddled to the door. "Take care of yourself, love," she said. "We'll see you Sunday, one way or another. I'd like this fancy cross and all, but if not I'll write my investment off as an incentive for others to be timely on their debts."

Falcon followed her to the door. He paused and looked back at Jonty. "I gave it a little extra there, because of the birdie cracks, no one likes a smartass," he said. "I'll be thinking up something fun for Sunday too, you know, maybe something more drawn out, and enjoyable for me. Till then." He finished with a grin and left.

Jonty stared at his mangled fingers. He thought he was going to be sick again, but managed to keep the nausea at bay. He knew this latest affliction required a hospital visit, he couldn't shake this off with some sleep and a few paracetamols. His truck was a manual transmission and he didn't think he could drive himself one handed.

"Damn it," he said out loud, and begrudgingly dialled Jules's number on the cheapest mobile he'd found at the store a few hours earlier.

29

FRIDAY EVENING

AJ slowly woke and for a second had no idea when or where she was. The room was dimly lit, with only a sprinkle of light filtering around the curtains covering the window over her dining table. Jackson was sitting on the edge of the bed and she smiled up at him.

"I hated to wake you, but you made me promise," he said.

"What time is it?" she asked and rubbed her eyes.

"Quarter to seven," he replied and stroked a gentle hand through her hair. "Sure you're feeling up to it?"

She pushed the covers away and sat up next to him on the bed. He looked at her naked body and smiled. "Maybe we should stay in."

She turned; taking his face in her hand she kissed him, then pushed his face playfully away.

"Later, if I can stay awake by then," she said as she stood and walked to the bathroom.

She turned on the light and stood in front of the sink, staring at herself in the mirror. Her hair was a mess – as usual she wore no make-up when she worked, and her eyes still looked weary. She made a face at herself in the reflection, and groaned.

"I'm getting old," she grumbled.

"Nonsense," Jackson commented from the room. "You're maturing with grace and beauty."

"You're only saying that 'cos you want to get lucky later," she retorted and splashed water over her face. She could hear him laughing.

She put on a light touch of eyeliner, mascara and a subtle shade of lipstick and went searching for clean clothes to wear. She found a pair of tan shorts and a Ducati motorcycle tank top which she slipped on over a sports bra that she was pretty sure she hadn't worn since it had been washed. The tank top was a gift from a friend who'd been over to Florida recently. AJ had told them she was craving a motorcycle and had been looking at Ducati Monsters on the Internet. She'd have to settle for the shirt for now. Her Rainbow sandals completed the outfit, and in nine minutes from consciousness, she was walking out the door.

"Fish?" Jackson said before she locked the door.

"Oh, bugger, thank you. I almost forgot," she said, and ran to the refrigerator to retrieve one reusable Ziploc bag of lionfish fillets, and a smaller bag of spines.

Usually she rode her bicycle to the pub but she only had one bike and they were going to be tight to making it by seven, so she thought it best to take the van. She was surprised by how refreshed she felt, after only a few hours' nap, but doubted it would last long. Tomorrow should be her day off and she didn't want to think about getting up before dawn to meet Jonty. She wished she'd told him a later time but she'd been thinking about spending the rest of the day with Jackson so it seemed like a good plan at the time. Not so much now. After a few minutes' driving, she pulled the van into the car park of the Fox and Hare pub off North-West Point road. She realised Jackson had been quiet while she'd been lost in her own thoughts.

"You okay?" she asked as she shut the engine off.

"Yeah, I'm good," he said but didn't move to get out of the van. She took her hand off the door handle and turned to him.

"What's on your mind," she persisted, convinced he had something bothering him. A flash of panic sped through her sleep-deprived mind. Is he about to tell me we're over, she wondered, and a knot instantly formed in her stomach. Her face must have shown her concern as he reached out and touched her.

"Hey, it's nothing bad. Well, I don't think it is anyway," he said, and smiled.

Her stomach unclenched a little but still wouldn't relax all the way until she knew what was up.

"I've been thinking," he continued, "about all this time apart we keep having."

Her stomach didn't release its knot and all she could do was stare at him and forget to breathe.

"I think I've done my part for Sea Sentry. I'm going to tell them this next tour will be my last."

AJ let out a sound somewhere between a groan and a gasp when she finally took a breath.

"Are you sure?" she heard herself say instead of 'that's wonderful', which is what she felt inside.

He laughed, but it was his turn to look concerned. "Well, yes, I thought I was, but that was based on figuring you'd be pleased about it."

She lurched over and threw her arms around him. "I am pleased, I'm more than pleased, I'm extra super crunchy pleased," she blurted and let him go. "But I feel incredibly guilty taking you away from what you love, and all the good you do aboard that boat."

He pulled her back close. "You haven't pressured me at all, in fact the opposite, which is why I've wondered if you wanted me around more or not."

She kissed him. "Oh, I want you around more, don't worry about that. You sure I won't drive you nuts?"

He laughed. "I'll happily go nuts if that's the case."

"But, seriously, this is a big step for you, you've invested so much into a life with Sea Sentry," she said.

He nodded. "I have, and as you know it's all voluntary, so I've done pretty well to make my savings last this long. I really thought I'd do a couple of tours with them and then I'd move on. I'm surprised how long I was able to stretch my money. My only real expense was health insurance, which as you know from when you lived in America, is incredibly expensive. But after nearly four years with them, I feel I've done my part, and my savings are finally running low. It's time I moved on."

She beamed at him, but her smile quickly melted again. "Moved on where? I guess I've been assuming a bit much."

"Well, I have to do the next tour, which will be six to ten weeks, and then I need to go home to California – my family have seen me less than you have. But then I was hoping to come here."

She leapt at him again and kissed him passionately. "Correct answer, Mr. Floyd, you may advance to the next round."

The door to the pub opened as a couple walked in and loud music could be heard from inside, fading again as the door closed behind them.

"We're late!" AJ exclaimed and quickly kissed him again, before opening the van door and leaping out. Closing the door she waited for Jackson to come around and they started towards the pub.

He stopped suddenly. "Fish?" he asked.

"Bugger it," she said, and ran back to the van.

30

1835

It had been four days since Francis had returned to the plantation, yet it felt like a month. He'd made good on his promise to reduce their food, the yams, sweet potatoes and vegetables they either grew or bartered from other growers. Their eldest man caught fish or turtle, which was plentiful if the seas were calm, but now a larger share went to the house. Mr. Ferguson had not been seen. Sally and Phibba reported he had taken ill, and had been confined to his bed since his son arrived. Cudjo desperately wanted to see the man – he couldn't believe the new way of things was as he wished. Mr. Ferguson had been so fair and reasonable through good times and bad. He'd sheltered the slaves inside his house during the worst storms, concerned himself with their welfare and health. In Cudjo's lifetime he'd never know the man to raise his voice, let alone a hand.

Francis seemed like he was everywhere, watching them at all times. When Phibba's boyfriend was sent back to the village for a shovel, Francis was there and whipped him for not being in the fields. When the sun went down he could be seen on the veranda under the lanterns of the house making sure they didn't stop working until the last light had faded. The invigorated feeling of having put in a good day's work was replaced with acute fatigue and weariness, compounded by their fear of what was to come. No one was sleeping well, and Cudjo even dreamed of the painted face at the window one night, a vision he hadn't thought about since he was a child. Chatter around the table at supper time was subdued and Cudjo dare not read a story to the group.

As the women finished clearing the table, Sally, the house-keeper, pulled Cudjo to one side, under the trees by the half circle of huts.

"I didn't want to say nothing, but it don't feel right not speakin' up either," she whispered.

"Say what's troubling you," Cudjo urged. "Can't fix nothin' if I don't know what it is."

"That's my trouble," she said tentatively. "You can't be fixin' it and I'm scared you'll try."

Cudjo had no idea what Sally was mumbling about but he was tired, his whip wounds were still sore and all he could think about was laying his head down.

"Out with it now, Miss Sally, our days are too long for drawn-out talk."

Sally looked down at the dirt. "You notice your sister getting awful quiet around the table?"

Cudjo sighed. "Everybody quiet, Miss Sally, times like these everybody feel it some."

Sally looked up at him and he could see the fear and dread in her shadowed face. "No, she being more quiet than most."

"Phibba?" he asked.

"Yes, sir," Sally replied.

Cudjo felt a wave of dread consume him. "Francis? He been touching her?"

Sally put a hand on Cudjo's arm. "It ain't gone all bad yet, settle yourself before you turn all crazy. He been mostly looking, but today he watched her for a long time when she was cleaning the floors, and then he said something I didn't hear."

"What she say about it?" Cudjo asked.

"She wouldn't say nothing about it. I asked her and she said it were nothing to bother over, but I saw the look on her face even if I can't hear what he says. Believe me, it weren't nothing."

Cudjo turned to go and find his little sister but Sally grabbed his arm.

"Go careful now. I don't know what can be done, but I do know it can be made worse for everyone – that man ain't like his father, he take after that mother of his for sure. Phibba be mad I told you I don't doubt, but I had to say something. Lord, I hope I did right."

Cudjo paused. "You did right, Miss Sally. Better she mad at you for a day than something worse."

"What you gonna do?" Sally asked, taking her hand away.

"I need to speak to Mr. Ferguson, that's what I'm gonna do. Tomorrow, after sun's up, I'm gonna talk to Mr. Ferguson, even if I have to break my way in there."

Sally shook her head slowly. "I don't know what ails him, but it don't seem to be getting any better. I thought he was just down with a little stomach trouble, but it ain't passed yet. That son of his ain't sent for the doctor neither. This afternoon he had a fever starting, too. If you go to the house, you be careful Cudjo, Francis got eyes everywhere. That man shows up and I don't hear nothing, he scared the life outta me more than once, I tell you."

Cudjo, and the two other young men, began work in the fields before dawn the following morning. He hadn't slept much, and sensed Phibba hadn't either. She'd been angry at Sally for saying something, but knew it was from love, and told Cudjo she didn't want him to know for fear of what he might do. He'd assured her all he planned to do was talk to Mr. Ferguson, the senior. As the sun finally began to climb above the eastern horizon, he kept glancing at the plantation house, trying to figure out how to get to his owner without Francis intercepting him. He hadn't seen Francis on the veranda so far that morning, and somehow not seeing him was worse than knowing where he was. Finally, when he saw Sally and Phibba walking to the single-storey house from the huts, he decided he could wait no longer.

Telling the other two men to keep working, he dusted himself off, and started towards the house, crouching low along the rows of cotton to remain hidden. At the edge of the field he faced more than a hundred feet of open space to the corner of the house. The two women had already gone inside and there was still no sign of Francis. The shutters were all closed from the night and he could see a faint glow of lantern light at the edges of a couple of them. He'd spent plenty of time inside the house, taking lessons from Mr. Ferguson, but he'd never set foot in several of the rooms, Mr. Ferguson's bedroom being one of them. Cudjo jogged swiftly across the open space and stepped quietly up the steps of the veranda. He followed it around to the side entrance, used by the slaves to go in and out of the house. He could hear Sally's voice speaking quietly inside and the sound of water being poured. He eased the door open and carefully looked inside. Both women looked up in surprise and he slid into the room and held a finger to his lips. Phibba glared at him, clearly afraid of what his intentions were. He stepped over to her and whispered in her ear.

"Have you seen Francis?"

She shook her head. "We just got here and starting our chores now, ain't seen nobody."

"I'm gonna talk to Mr. Ferguson, stay in here," he said, and moved quietly across the open living room towards the hallway which led to the bedrooms and Mr. Ferguson's study. It was dim inside the house, the only light from the single lantern the girls had lit, but Cudjo could see Mr. Ferguson's bedroom door haloed by a light inside the room. He must be awake, he thought with relief and was pleased to see no light from any other room. Every rough-hewn floorboard seemed to creak and complain as he placed his weight upon each foot, but he kept moving slowly towards the door. Reaching for the handle, he deliberately turned the primitive wooden lever and pushed the door open. He wasn't sure exactly what he was going to say, although he'd been over it a thousand times throughout the night, but his first concern was not startling the poor man at this early hour. He entered the room and looked over at the bed, which was raised above the ground and covered with a quilted blanket. Mr. Ferguson lay with his head propped on two luxurious-looking cotton-covered pillows and Cudjo paused, waiting to be beckoned over, or asked to wait outside while he prepared for the day. Mr. Ferguson didn't move, and Cudjo, squinting in the low light to see better, took another step into the room. The plantation owner's eyes were open, but stared blankly at the ceiling, and the man's skin was pallid.

"Come to pay your respects, boy?" came Francis's voice from the shadowed corner of the room.

Cudjo startled, and for a moment thought about running. But how would that leave Phibba? He stood motionless and looked at Francis. The man leaned on a wooden dresser and appeared to have been standing there, waiting.

"Seems I made it back just in time, it would have been tragic if I'd not been able to say goodbye to my dear father," Francis said coldly. "But the question is why are you inside this house? Tell me, boy, why do you see fit to enter my home?"

Before Cudjo could respond, Francis lashed his whip and the slave felt the sting across his arm and chest before he heard the snap of the leather. He turned and ran. Sprinting down the hall, he turned across the main room, passed the stunned women, and burst out of the door into the soft morning light.

31

FRIDAY EVENING

AJ and Jackson entered the Fox and Hare to the sound of applause as Pearl finished up a song. The place was busy as usual on Friday nights when Pearl played – she had a loyal following on the island. The pub was a simple two-storey stucco building from the exterior, but once inside the place was a slice of the old country. Union Jacks, bulldogs and Premier League football dominated the decoration, and the bar itself was a hefty oak wood structure with a floated resin top over maps of England and the Cayman Islands. A picture of the Queen took pride of place behind the bar nestled between rows of glass shelves containing an impressive array of international spirits. In the back corner, several dartboards hosted a keen tournament, not a single barstool was unoccupied and every wooden table was taken, leaving many standing and focused on the tiny stage in the front of the pub.

Between the crowd, all taller than her, AJ waved to Pearl, who winked back as she strummed the intro to Ellen Foley's 'We Belong to the Night'. Reg had two tables pushed together near the middle of the pub and they made their way through the crowd to join him, AJ having to pause and say hi to regulars every few steps. With Reg at the table was Thomas's sister Sydney and her Cuban boyfriend

Carlos who worked for Reg, Thomas himself and, to AJ's surprise, a young woman with him. Thomas's love life was a subject of constant conjecture as he seemed to always have several ladies on the go at the same time, but never brought any of them around, or apparently stuck with them very long. Each new possibility was of great excitement to him and a week later he'd report on a newer, more exciting prospect. She grinned at Thomas and enjoyed the worried look on his face.

"Hey guys, sorry we're a few minutes late," AJ said loudly to be heard, and extended her hand over the table to Thomas's date. "Hi, I'm AJ, Thomas and I work together, and this is my boyfriend Jackson."

The young woman rose from her seat and shook AJ's hand firmly, "Hello, I'm Jacqueline," she replied with a soft Caymanian accent, and shook Jackson's hand as well. The girl was stunningly pretty, with a tall, slim figure and curly black hair that cascaded down her shoulders.

"I think we've met somewhere, haven't we?" AJ asked, recognising her but unable to place where their paths had crossed.

"I work in the bank at Governor's Square, I've seen you in there," she replied with a smile.

"That's it," AJ said, sitting down next to Reg. "Well, it's very nice to meet you."

Thomas looked a little more relaxed as the introductions seemed to go smoothly. Meanwhile, after Jackson had said hi to Sydney and Carlos he turned to AJ.

"What would you like to drink?"

AJ realised she was still carrying two bags of fish parts and jumped back up again. "I'll get them, I need to do something with these." She held up the bags.

"Will you stop bouncing around like bloody Zebedee," Reg grunted. "You're worse than a five-year-old."

AJ leaned over and kissed him on the cheek then laid the bag of lionfish spines in front of him. "Here, these are for your wife."

Reg ignored her, still watching the stage, but held up his empty glass.

"Alright, alright, I'm going," AJ said. "Anyone else need a drink?"

The others declined and Jackson sat back down as AJ made her way towards the bar. AJ waited patiently, listening to Pearl, until the busy bartender worked his way over.

"Hey Frank, mind having the chef throw these in some tacos?" she shouted over the music.

"No problem. Drinks?" he replied, taking the bag of fish fillets from her.

"Bourbon over ice for Reg, and a couple of Strongbows, please. Oh, and three veggie tacos please," she remembered just in time.

He nodded and took the fish to the kitchen before serving the drinks.

By the time AJ made it back to the table, Pearl had just wrapped up her first set and came to join them. AJ gave Pearl a hug and offered her the seat next to Reg.

"Brilliant, as always," AJ said as they all sat.

"Thank you dear," Pearl replied, "and hello, Jackson, nice to see you. She's had you squirrelled away since you came into town."

AJ blushed but Jackson didn't miss a beat. "Have to make up for the months apart," he said in his laid-back tone, and AJ blushed even more.

"Besides, she's had me diving or on the boat every day."

"You two still taking that idiot Gladstone back out tomorrow?" Reg asked.

AJ rolled her eyes. "Yes, I wish I'd told him later though, I really need some sleep."

Reg held up his glass to Jackson. "Good work, lad."

AJ glowed like a beacon in the night. "Shut up you dirty-minded old goat, we were out all last night catching poachers."

Pearl looked at Jacqueline who, by her expression, was slightly bemused by all the banter.

"You poor dear, I'd like to tell you it's not always like this, but I'm afraid it is."

"Don't worry," Thomas replied, "Jacqui can take care of herself, she keeps me in line no problem."

"So how did you two meet?" Pearl asked.

"We went to school together," Jacqui replied. "We dated back then."

Everyone at the table wanted to ask the next question but no one wanted to be the one, so they sat and looked awkwardly at each other. Jacqui helped them out.

"Took him a little time running around to figure out he'd started in the best place and went downhill from there," she said with a grin, looking at Thomas. "Then he came back begging, and I finally took sympathy on him."

Everybody laughed, and it was Thomas's turn to look embarrassed.

"Oh, you're gonna fit in just fine with this group of misfits, my dear," Pearl said.

"You're the only one he's brought to meet us, so that's saying something," AJ added.

"Yeah, probably more about us than Thomas's dates," Reg chuckled and Pearl nudged him with an elbow.

"Don't listen to him. So how long have you been back together?" Pearl asked.

"About a month now," Jacqui replied.

"Which is a record for Thomas," Sydney chimed in, and they laughed some more.

AJ looked at Jackson. "Mind if I tell them?" she asked quietly.

"Tell us what?" Thomas jumped in, glad of any conversation away from his love life.

Jackson shrugged his shoulders. "Sure, don't see why it should be a secret."

AJ beamed. "Jackson is doing one more tour with Sea Sentry, and then coming here."

"To stay?" Pearl asked, putting a hand on AJ's shoulder.

"That's the idea, if I can find a job of course," Jackson replied.

Everyone congratulated them and babbled at the same time, and when it quietened a little Pearl spoke up.

"You got a job, don't worry about that," she said, and nudged Reg again.

Reg frowned. "How come I have to take in every stray that wanders by?"

"Hey now!" Carlos retorted and AJ chimed in, "Listen to you, you big meanie."

Reg winked at Jackson. "Well, you'll probably be more useful than the last few I've been saddled with."

To which the table booed and jeered him again, between laughs.

Frank arrived with a large plate of fish tacos made from AJ's lionfish catch that day, and three veggie tacos on a separate plate.

Pearl stood up. "I have to go back up, save me a taco," she said, and gave Reg a kiss.

As Pearl made her way back to the stage, the rest tucked into the tacos, and Jackson thanked AJ for his vegetarian dinner.

Reg finished chewing a bite of food and leaned over to AJ. "Has Gladstone made the authorities aware?"

AJ shook her head. "I doubt it, but we haven't found anything to report yet anyway."

"Just be careful – knowing Jonty he's already got a buyer and he ain't planning on reporting anything. You don't want to get caught up in that mess. Make sure anything you're a part of is by the book."

"I'm the one diving, so it's up to me what I bring out or leave alone." She smiled at Reg. "Priority will be to preserve the artefact, right?"

He looked at her sternly. "Wrong, the priority is the diver's safety, everything else comes second."

AJ felt embarrassed, she'd been called out, and he was right. Reg had been a diver for the British Navy and then worked salvage for years after that, all of which was dangerous work. He was still around because he dived smart, and he ran his own dive operation that way with an exemplary safety record to show for it. She didn't consider herself reckless or cavalier, but her sense of adventure sometimes led her to push the boundaries of good judgement, and she knew it.

"Yeah, I hear you. I promise I'll be careful," she responded, sheepishly.

He reached over and squeezed her shoulder as Pearl opened her second set with Kelly Clarkson's 'Because of You'.

32

FRIDAY EVENING

Jonty's hand throbbed so badly it made his head feel better. He'd sat in the waiting room of the hospital for almost an hour before they took him back for an X-ray. They verified his fingers were broken in multiple places. He explained in colourful language how abundantly aware he was of this fact. Next, he waited in a small room while they tracked down a surgeon to operate. Or more exactly, 'the' surgeon to operate. Apparently, there was only one orthopaedic surgeon who specialised in hands on Grand Cayman. It appeared he was somewhere enjoying his Friday evening and Jonty hoped the man wasn't too deep into the Scotch yet. Jules had told him she'd be right over when he'd called her, but she hadn't shown up for over an hour, blaming traffic. She'd fussed and smothered him with great sympathy but kept pestering him over which door he'd managed to shut his fingers in, the story he'd decided best suited the injury. He hadn't thoroughly thought through his story and she'd flustered him into contradicting himself, so now he could tell she didn't believe him. Fortunately, the nurse had made Jules wait out front so he was left in peace and quiet with his excruciating pain.

There was a knock on the door and Jonty groaned in relief that they could finally get on with it. The door opened and the nurse came in.

"Doing okay?" she asked. She was an older Caymanian woman with thick spectacles over which she liked to peer and inspect her victims.

"Not really, can't you give me some pain meds while I'm waiting, I've been sitting here for hours."

She made a huffing sound which he assumed was discontent. "Can't do no pain medications till the doctor sees you."

"Yeah, but he's gnawing on a T-bone right now, and I'm sitting here in agony, gotta be something you can give me?" Jonty pleaded.

He got a scowl over the glasses this time. "You should choose your timing better to shut your hand in places your hand didn't ought to be, ain't very convenient making all this trouble on a Friday night now."

He was about to lay into her but she kept going. "Besides, that insurance you gave the girl upfront don't seem to be no good. Card is two years expired and that number ain't active no more she say. So before you worry too much about getting your pain pills, best you think on how you gonna pay to have the good doctor fix you up."

Keep kicking me, he thought. He knew the insurance card had long ago expired – he'd spent about six weeks working for a dive outfit that actually provided health care, but it didn't work out. He couldn't remember why. Which was likely why it didn't work out. He had a habit of losing sections of time, and finding things had changed when he came around.

"Here," she said holding out two pills and a glass of water, "have some paracetamol for now."

He looked at her blankly. "Bit like a plaster on a severed limb, isn't it?"

She turned, opened the rubbish bin with her foot and tossed the two pills in, letting the lid slam behind them.

"Suit yourself," she said, poured the water out in the sink, and left.

"Bugger me," he whimpered, and moved from the chair to the examination bed. Carefully, he lay down, awkwardly trying to hold his broken hand with his good hand while lowering himself down. He ended up collapsing with a thud and a groan. The bed was rock hard and his hand seemed to hurt worse lying down. He levered himself back up with his elbows and swung his legs over the side. He looked at the rubbish bin. Sod it, he thought, I need something. He walked over and opened the bin with the foot pedal. It was full of latex gloves, paper towels and other stuff that shouldn't be touched. He poked about the paper towards the top and searched for the two pills. He saw something bounce down which looked like a small white pill and he dug deeper to try and grab it.

A knock came on the door, which instantly opened and an Indian man stepped in the room wearing a gaudy Hawaiian shirt and brown slacks.

"Mr. Gladstone, I have your X-rays and you've quite badly broken..." the man said in a heavy Indian accent before he stopped dead in his tracks. Jonty jumped back, banging his bad hand on the side of the counter and letting the bin slam closed.

"What are you doing?"

"Bollocks!" was all Jonty could come up with.

"Please sir, sit over here and stop hitting your hand on things, that will not be helping, you know."

Jonty complied, and breathed deeply as he was concerned he might pass out.

"I am Doctor Chandhok, and as you can see I was not expecting to be performing surgery this evening," he said as he reached for Jonty's broken hand.

"I'm Jonty Gladstone, and I wasn't planning on knackering up my hand this evening," he replied.

The doctor laughed. "Quite so, I'm sure. Well, despite our plans, it appears we will be spending the evening together. You will not remember much about it, but I'll do my best to stay awake." He laughed again, enjoying his own humour.

He carefully examined Jonty's hand, which was now all shades of purple and extremely swollen. He glanced up at the X-ray he'd pinned onto the light box on the wall.

"You shut your hand in a door?" the doctor asked.

"Yeah, stupid, eh?"

"Hmmm, well, yes, but this doesn't look like a door injury. I get door injuries all the time, very popular way to break fingers is a door. Usually inadvertently slammed by someone else. This looks like something was dropped on the top of your hand," he said and looked at Jonty.

"Okay, a door fell on my hand. Does that make you feel better?" Jonty replied, wincing every time the man wiggled or poked his hand.

Doctor Chandhok shrugged his shoulders. "Doesn't bother me how you choose to break your bones, I just take the mess you've made and do the best I can with it. You've done a good job making a mess, by the way."

"Thank you, Doc, I try not to do things half arsed. So how long will this take?" Jonty asked.

Doctor Chandhok stepped back and thought a moment.

"We need an anaesthesiologist. Actually, I don't need one, but you'll want one," he chuckled again, "so we have to see who's available. Once they're here and we get the room ready, the surgery itself will take two or three hours probably, depending on what I find once I get in there. An hour or so after that you'll come around in recovery and then I'll drop by tomorrow and check on you, let's say mid-morning. If all is good you'll be released tomorrow afternoon."

Jonty groaned. "That's not going to work, Doc, I gotta be outta here by first thing tomorrow morning. How about I come back in the afternoon and you check me out then?"

"Where do you have to be? If you have a piano solo I'd recommend cancelling it." He laughed again.

"It's a long story, but I have to be on a boat in the morning," Jonty said, and immediately wished he hadn't.

"No, no, no, that's a very bad idea. You cannot get your hand wet for the first week, especially sea water, very bad. I'm afraid no boats Mr. Gladstone," Doctor Chandhok said, and headed for the door. "Now, let me find an anaesthesiologist who's sober and we can get this party on the road."

Jonty decided not to correct his idiom, or debate his departure time. Doctor Luau will be tucked up in bed come six in the morning, he thought, I'll nip out then and be back after we get the cross. And if we don't get the cross, he reminded himself, a follow-up on the hand will be a waste of time. Birdie Boy had other plans for him, come Sunday.

33

1835

Cudjo ran to the hut he was born and raised in, the only home he'd ever known. Polly startled when he burst through the door, shocked to see her son covered in sweat and with fear in his eyes.

"Cudjo, what's wrong son, why you ain't in the fields?"

He threw his arms around his mother. "Mama, he's dead, I went to speak with him, but he was just lying there, dead."

"Who's dead son? What are you saying?"

"Mr. Ferguson. I saw him with my own eyes." He pulled back and looked at his mother. "There ain't nothing stopping his son now, Mama, nothin' gonna stop that man. What are we gonna do?"

He broke away from Polly's grasp and looked out the open shutter towards the plantation house. He couldn't see anyone coming.

"Oh my good Lord," Polly said in bewilderment, "Francis owns everything now. Everything, and everybody."

Cudjo turned back. "It's me he wants, Mama. If he has me, he'll leave you all alone. I shouldn't have run out of the house, I shoulda stayed and taken what's coming."

"Are you crazy? Look what he did to you yesterday, for no reason at all. He see you at the house?"

Cudjo nodded, trying to catch his breath. "Oh yeah, he saw me alright, he was waiting in Mr. Ferguson's room. I swear he was waiting for me. I don't know how, but he knew I were coming."

"You gotta go, son, you gotta get away from here," Polly said, and started gathering Cudjo's few possessions.

"Go where, Mama? There ain't nowhere to go." He tried to think of some place on the island he could hide out, but nothing came to mind. He'd spent nineteen years on the plantation and its boundaries had been the edge of his world. He'd been to George Town maybe a dozen times and to the neighbouring Eden plantation twice. He knew nobody outside his own tiny village of slaves. When he was a boy, the plantation seemed endless, a huge expanse of cotton plants in rows as far as the eye could see. But as he grew, and roamed the estate from dawn till dusk, he soon found familiarity in every shrub and tree, every crest and gully, and the 50 acres became no more mysterious than his own hut. He knew there was nowhere on this property to conceal himself from Francis.

"Go towards George Town, head north off the trail towards the shallow waters," she said. "There's fewer people and they won't know you if they do see you. Bodden Town too busy. I'll give you food, enough for a few days. Find somewhere you can make yourself a shelter, then come back at night and I'll get you more food."

"Mama, I can't leave you and the girls. No telling what he'll do. He could whip Phibba, till she tells."

"You don't worry 'bout that. You stay, and Lord knows he's coming for you. You don't stand no chance. This way we see what he does. If he takes the whip to my girl, it'll kill me to do it, but I'll tell him all I know. And what I know ain't where you'll be 'cos you ain't telling me, understand?" Polly said, with tears running down her cheeks.

Cudjo hugged her and took the bundle of clothes, along with some fruit and dried fish she shoved into his hands.

"Go on now, son." She held his face in her hands. "Find yourself somewhere to hide, away from here, you hear? Take that trail north, the one I say towards the shallow sound."

He turned and looked at the floor of the hut where the straw-stuffed bedding lay. He looked back at his mother.

"That ain't gonna do us no good, son, don't be thinking about that," Polly said and wiped the tears from her face.

"Papa say when we need it, we'd know, Mama. Sure seems like we need some help right now," Cudjo urged.

She shook her head. "What you gonna do, walk into the white man's town and hold up that cross? They cut you down and take it from you 'fore they give you nothing for it. Besides, Francis own you now, which means he own all you have, including that cross if he know it's there." She pushed him towards the door. "Best you forget you ever laid eyes upon it. Your Papa was a hopeful man, God rest his soul, today ain't the day he was speaking of."

Cudjo kissed her forehead and checked outside through the window again. He still couldn't see any activity, which puzzled him. Surely Francis would be coming for him? He prayed the man wasn't taking his anger out on Phibba or Sally.

"Leave out back of the huts, you hear? Then sneak along the coast to Eden's land before you head over to the trail." Polly told him. She grabbed a blanket from his bed and rolled it up.

"Here, you'll need this," she said, and piled it on top of his bundle.

She opened the door and they both looked around outside. A couple of the women were hanging out clothes to dry and the only baby in the village was playing in the dirt by the long table under the trees. Cudjo slipped out the door and quickly darted behind the hut to be hidden from view of the house. From there, he picked his way through the scrub and brush towards the shoreline, avoiding the trail as it was also open to view. When he made the bluffs, he knelt down and paused. The excitement and fear began to subside and the gravity of the situation fell upon him with a weight he'd never experienced before. Why had he decided to see Mr. Ferguson that morning? He berated himself for being so foolish, thinking he could somehow fix things. His father had always told him to do as they say. Before he died, he made it clear, their lives were owned by the Fergusons, to demand and use as they saw fit. For all these years, he'd not thought about his life as a possession of someone else. He worked hard and in return he had a roof over his head and food on the table. In one short day he'd become painfully aware of how fragile his life truly was. He touched the welts on his body from the whip of a man that could take away that life on a whim. Francis now owned his slave's existence. It was his to quash, without consequence or repercussion.

Cudjo thought about Phibba, his little sister he'd sworn to protect. What happened after he'd run from the house? Had the women continued about their chores? Had Francis simply let Cudjo run away? He looked around him and listened but the waves lapping against the ironshore was all he could hear. To the east were the woods. The woods in which Francis had terrified him as a small boy. He wasn't going in there. He hadn't set foot in those woods since that day, and didn't plan to now. He looked west. The bluffs meandered along the coastline for how long, he didn't know. He recalled seeing the cliffs continue beyond Pedro St. James. He'd been to the Eden plantation on one occasion when Mr. Ferguson traded supplies with them, but that was as far as he'd seen. He began walking west.

The trail along the bluff tops ended near the edge of the Ferguson property and from there it was tough hiking over the sharp and rugged ironshore. Stands of shrubs and bushes grew in clumps wherever dirt had gathered in the old limestone and he had to carefully pick his way around them. The sun was now climbing the eastern sky and the heat was rapidly rising with it. The ocean breeze kept the mosquitoes at bay, but his constant worry was being seen and questioned, now he was on Eden's land. It was slow going and he was just considering cutting inland towards the trail as his mother had urged, when he noticed a small curved bay at the base of the bluffs. He went to the edge and looked down. The circular inlet was small, maybe the height of four men across, but a ledge appeared to stay above the high-water mark, according to the colouration on the bluff wall. If he could figure a way down he might be able to hide there. Off the Ferguson property was a wooden ladder down to the water, but he saw no such easy access in this bay; Eden's fisherman must have another way to the water, he surmised.

He walked around to the far edge of the tiny bay and looked back at the ledge. Above it, the ocean had carved out a shallow cave, deep enough he thought he could be concealed. He needed a way down. As he scoured the bluff walls for a way to climb, he heard a voice from the brush behind him. He looked back but couldn't see anyone. The voice sounded like the accent of a slave speaking English, but he couldn't be sure. It didn't matter. A slave could turn him in as easily as a white man. He threw his bundle down and prayed it would land on the ledge and not roll into the water. The voice grew louder, joined by a second voice which sounded like an Englishman. Without further thought he took two steps to the end of the bluff and jumped, leaping as far away from the face as possible. It was farther down than he'd anticipated and he hit the water with a force that knocked the wind out of him. He gasped and clawed at the water as his feet hit the bottom and he felt the jagged surface of the ironshore. Despite the sharp pain in his feet, he pushed off the bottom and swam for the surface to get a breath. His head broke through and he sucked in air in huge gulps, shaking the water from his face and eyes. The waves hadn't looked very strong but he was surprised how much the surge lunged him towards the bluff before pulling him back out. He felt like a puppet having its strings pulled and dragged around. He couldn't hear the voices but knew he was making too much noise gasping and splashing. He kicked towards the bay and clung to the rocks on the corner while the waves shoved his body against them. He looked up but couldn't see anyone. He scanned the little bay and saw with relief his bundles of clothes, food and the blanket appeared to be strewn across the ledge.

"A pathway along here, you see, like Ferguson has," came a voice from above and a man stepped to the edge of the inlet. Cudjo ducked back around the corner and clung to the sharp rocks. If they looked down and saw his belongings on the ledge they'd surely raise the alarm or at least start a search. The sound of the man's voice was muffled from around the corner but grew louder again. They must be walking around the edge of the bay as he had just done. Had they seen his supplies and were now looking for the owner? From the head of the bay they'd have a better view of the ledge if they looked back. But if they looked down they'd see him, clinging to the base of the bluffs. As the voices grew louder above, Cudjo edged around the corner and prayed they were walking away down the coastline, back towards the plantation house. He looked up but couldn't see anyone peering over. The voices began to fade and he half swam, half crawled along the base of the bluff to the ledge and pulled himself up. He could no longer hear the voices. He sat back and breathed a sigh of relief. Well, I found a way down, he thought, as he surveyed the vertical bluffs surrounding the bay, but I've no idea how to climb back out.

34

SATURDAY MORNING

Reg's dock was busy at 7:30 in the morning. Thomas and Carlos were getting ready to take Hazel's Odyssey out with the Campbells and two other clients aboard, Reg had two full boats going out, and AJ idled Arthur's Odyssey, her RIB, up to the jetty. There was room for four boats, albeit a squeeze, and AJ tried to keep out of the way of the others who were loading paying customers. Jackson helped her tie up to the dock cleats, then she walked down the dock to say hi to Thomas. The Campbells greeted her enthusiastically and she introduced herself to the new couple who hadn't dived with Mermaid before.

"Where's Reg's buddy Jonty, I haven't seen him this morning?" Thomas asked.

"He's late, it appears," AJ replied, as she pulled her mobile out of her pocket to see if she'd missed a call or text. "I'll be really mad if I got up early for nothing. I did not want to get out of bed this morning."

Carlos and Thomas both looked at each other and grinned.

"Shut up you two," she said, slapping Thomas on the arm. "Take these people diving already, and quit picking on me."

She stepped off the boat and looked to the car park where the car she'd seen at Jonty's apartment the day before was just pulling in. She recognised Jules at the wheel. Coop scampered down the dock and wagged his whole body with his tail.

"Morning," Reg grunted as she met him halfway up the dock. "Where's Gladstone?"

"Looks like he's pulling in now," she replied. "What the bloody hell?" she mumbled as she watched Jonty get out of the car with what appeared to be a plastic bag over his left hand. Under the bag his hand was wrapped in something, but she couldn't tell what.

Reg laughed. "It gets better every time with this bloke."

Jonty and Jules made their way down the dock to the RIB where AJ met them, Reg in tow. Jules carried a long, metal tube of some sort in her hand.

"What on earth have you done to yourself now?" AJ asked.

Jonty stared at her from behind sunglasses and a baseball hat. "I'll explain on the way, let's get going."

"That a cast on your hand?" Reg asked.

Jonty barely glanced his way, carefully stepping aboard the RIB. "No, get the cast in a few days, once the swelling goes down, just a bandage for now."

"Best you don't fall in then," Reg said with obvious amusement, as Jonty struggled to make the step over the large inflatable sides of the RIB. Jackson took his arm and helped him as the boat rocked.

AJ grinned at Reg. "Bugger off and see to your own boats, you old goat. You're enjoying this too much."

Reg tapped his leg with his hand and Coop, who had been sitting waiting for permission to board the RIB, turned and looked up at him.

"Come on boy, you don't want to go with these scallywags." Coop reluctantly trotted over to him and Reg nodded to AJ.

"Be careful my girl," he said and walked away, Coop trotting alongside.

AJ stepped aboard and was surprised to see Jules was also on the boat. She looked at Jonty, who had sat himself in the same seat as before in front of the helm. He saw AJ look from Jules to him and shrugged his shoulders. Guess she's coming along, she thought, and stepped behind the helm, starting the twin outboards. Jackson cast the lines off and they idled away from the dock, following Hazel's Odyssey, which had just pulled away.

"So, what's the story on the hand, Jonty?" AJ asked.

Jules turned around from the seat next to him. "He had four pins and twelve screws put in last night, can you believe that?"

"Dang, okay. Why? I mean, how did he break it?" AJ asked, unsure why she was now discussing this with Jules rather than the hand owner.

"Oh, well, something about a door," Jules replied, looking a little confused.

"Door fell on it. According to the doctor," Jonty muttered without turning around.

AJ laughed. "And what happened to it according to you?"

"I thought you shut it in a door? That's what you told me," Jules asked, still looking confused.

Jonty reached in his pocket and retrieved a plastic prescription bottle of pills. He stared at the bottle, unsure how to remove the security lid one handed. Jules took the bottle and unscrewed the lid, tipped a pill out and handed it to him.

"How often are you supposed to take these?" she asked.

"When it hurts," Jonty grumbled back.

"Guess it must be bad 'cos that's the fourth one since we left the hospital, no wonder they didn't want you to leave."

"You're not supposed to be out of the hospital?" Jackson asked.

"Technicality," Jonty replied. "I'll drop by when we get back in."

Jackson and AJ looked at each other and both shrugged their shoulders. Jonty's head bobbed around as apparently the pain meds kicked in and he started nodding off to sleep.

"How long is it?" Jules asked.

"How long is what?" AJ asked, trying to remain polite but still not sure why she was aboard.

"How long until we get there?" Jules clarified.

"Oh, about forty-five minutes," AJ replied.

"Really? Are there bathrooms when we get there?" Jules asked.

AJ laughed. "Sure, it's unisex, we call it the Caribbean Sea."

AJ eased the throttles forward, bringing the RIB instantly up on plane as they cleared the shallows and headed for the edge of the wall where she'd run the length of Seven Mile Beach. Jules didn't seem to care for the answer, but turned and faced the front. Jonty's head bounced up and down as they skittered across the gentle waves of the sheltered west side. AJ winced at the idea of his concussed brain pinballing around in his skull, and wondered if they had bothered to check his head out while he was at the hospital.

35

____

SATURDAY MORNING

When they pulled up to the small inlet east of Pedro St. James, AJ was pleased to find the seas calmer than when they'd been there before. At least getting on and off the boat would be simpler. Jackson helped her set the anchor in the same manner, and Jonty didn't need to guide her this time, as she knew precisely where the entry to the cave was. Once the boat was moored securely, she began getting her gear ready to dive. Jonty had woken when they hit the rougher water across the south of the island, and now AJ could see his face, she could tell he was awake but not very lucid. Apparently popping Vicodin like sweets had caught up with him. On the bright side he did seem in better humour than normal.

"Take the lever with you," Jonty slurred.

"Okay," AJ replied. "How does it work exactly?"

Jonty fumbled for the steel tube with his one good hand and nearly fell out of his seat.

"Don't worry, I'll figure it out," she said, concerned he'd hurt himself even more.

Jackson picked up the tube and examined it. It had an arm bolted through the centre of the tube that pivoted up to perpendicular. A third of the way up the lever arm was an eyelet.

"Looks like you tie a line through the eyelet here, wedge the bar across the tunnel and then use the lever arm to pull whatever you tie the other end of the line to. Do you have some line?" Jackson surmised, and Jonty gave him a thumbs up.

"There's some cord in the cupboard under the helm," AJ said as she slipped into her BCD with the side-mount tank.

Jackson found the cord, handed it to her and she stuffed it into her BCD pocket. Jules had been quiet since they'd left the shallow waters of the west side and stood at the stern, looking at the water lapping against the hull of the boat.

"Jump in if you need to pee, we'll put the ladder down," AJ said.

Jules turned and seemed to be scowling at her but it melted into a smile. "That's okay, I can hold it, I don't have a bathing suit on."

AJ stood, waddled her way to the port side under the weight of her gear and sat on the large, rubber side of the boat. Jackson handed over her fins which she slipped on her feet. She did a final gear check, touching every piece of key equipment and looking at her computer on her wrist. She looked out across the open water off the bow, the clear blue sky touching the deeper blue of the ocean at the horizon, with a few wispy clouds soaring by high above. It was another beautiful day and she found herself forgetting the early morning and the lack of sleep. Instead she had the nervous anticipation of an exciting dive. They were the only ones on this stretch of water, except a small centre console she noticed to the east, undoubtedly a fisherman out of Bodden Town. She looked behind her and noted the tide was higher than the first dive she made a few days ago; it would probably reach high tide while she was in the caves and she wondered how full the cave she'd named the Tank would be. She might have to keep her scuba gear on today.

She smiled at Jackson as she pulled her mask down in place. "Hand me that contraption once I get in, please."

He nodded. "Be safe my love," he said softly.

She winked at him, and rolled backwards over the side into the water.

Surfacing, AJ reached up and took Jonty's levering device from Jackson. It weighed several pounds and she noted she would need to play with her BCD inflation to get her buoyancy neutral inside the caves. It would make things awkward if she had to pass the tube from hand to hand as it would act as ballast being shifted about. She gave Jackson an okay sign, and slipped below the surface with him and Jules watching her disappear. Once below, she found the surge greatly reduced from her first dive, allowing her to fin quickly to the entrance without having to time a scramble through the narrow gap. She was a little disappointed not to find the cave full of tarpon, but at least it made it easier to see where she was going. She pulled her torch from her BCD pocket and awkwardly slipped the tether over her wrist, hanging on to the cumbersome tube as she did so. She shone the light around the cavern and picked up the large crack that formed the tunnel heading north. She gently finned over and swept the light beam across the opening, spotting several lobster antennae probing the water, as she had before. She was about to kick her way into the tunnel when she noticed something missing. The turtle skull was no longer wedged in the crevice to her left. She shone her light around but couldn't see where it had shifted to, and wondered how it could have moved in the first place. Jonty had seen it several years ago, and likely it had been there for many years before that. What could have possibly moved it now? She waved her torch around the floor of the cave behind her, but couldn't see it anywhere. She backed up, suddenly feeling uneasy. It would be quite the coincidence if the regular rise and falls of the tide chose this day to dislodge the skull that had been securely wedged in place for who knows how long. Certainly enough time for storms and possibly even hurricanes to have left it be. She shone the light beam around the cave and back towards the entrance, finally spotting the skull staring at her from a crevice where the large rock had partially blocked the opening. She felt better having found the skull, but how could it have relocated itself there? You're wasting time, she berated herself, stuff moves all the time in the oceans. She shook it off, and turned back to the tunnel.

It was difficult to stay neutrally buoyant in the low tunnel with the weight of the tube, so she shuffled it along the floor and kicked gently to keep herself moving. With both hands occupied, one with the torch and one with the tube, she felt clumsy and was glad to reach the Tank. She shone the light up and could see surface water again so at least the room wasn't completely flooded. Rising up in the small cave, she carefully eased her head through the air pocket and expected to bump her head on the ceiling. Her mask actually cleared the surface before she felt her hair brushing the ceiling, and shining the torch into the next tunnel revealed the water was several inches deeper than the trickle it had been before, but easily passable. She laid the tube into the tunnel and began slipping out of her BCD, inflating it to keep it bobbing on top of the water. The drips and rivulets of water echoed around her like handbells playing out of time. To shove the BCD into the crevice she had used before required deflating it once it was supported on the narrow shelf, the higher water level pinning it against the ceiling until she did. She worried if it was secure enough, but the heavy tank seemed to anchor it, and she slipped herself into the tunnel with just her mask still in place, leaving her fins wedged behind her BCD. Just before she started down the tunnel she remembered the cord, retrieved it from her BCD pocket, and slid the coil over her arm. As soon as she started to shuffle along, she realised she'd forgotten to bring knee pads, and cursed herself. Keeping the torch above the deeper water in the tunnel was a chore and the light bounced around, dim when submerged and brightly illuminating her surroundings when not. Her eyes struggled to adjust to the changing conditions but she kept shuffling, feeling the neoprene wearing through at her knees and elbows. It was much harder sliding the heavy metal tube along now it wasn't buoyed somewhat, as it had been when completely submerged.

Finally, AJ reached the junction, where the sound of the waves from the south-facing branch sounded even louder than before.

Maybe because she'd convinced herself it led unabated to the ocean, she admitted. She really wanted to take a look down there and see, but not knowing how long it would take to shift the rocks, she decided to press on and investigate further on the way out. The last section was the part that she hadn't been looking forward to seeing again. The tunnel narrowed and funnelled towards the blocked end by the steps, making it feel even more claustrophobic than the tiny channels she'd already clambered through. The reel line that she'd left throughout the tunnel system was a welcome connection to the outside world; it was nothing more than a piece of string, but it represented a link to home. AJ pushed the tube ahead of her and started looking for somewhere she could wedge it to make use of the lever. The floor of the tunnel expanded wider like a low-lying crack and the walls went quickly vertical forming the space she could crawl through. If she could find rocks to wedge in the crack and set the tube behind them she'd have her lever system.

Leaving the tube in a good spot where she thought she could wedge it, AJ took the cord and shimmied her way forward towards the rocks blocking her path. Once close, her shoulders wedged against each side of the tunnel and her head kept banging against the low ceiling. To get her arms ahead of her, she shuffled back a few feet first, extended her arms forward and then crept forward again using her toes and elbows. Propping the torch to the side, shining ahead at the rocks, she tried to select one she might be able to tie the cord around. None looked particularly suited. Taking the torch she shone it between the rocks as she'd done before to see the steps. Behind the first two large stones was what appeared to be a piece of hardwood. It looked like a solid section of a branch and had to be tough to have survived all this time. She stretched her right hand through the narrow gap and touched the piece of wood. It felt smooth and rock hard. Something brushed against her hand and she yanked it back, smashing it against the rocks, and she yelped in pain. AJ felt trapped and vulnerable: her heart rate soared and she flicked the light around trying to see the culprit. She heard it first. A steady drip, drip, drip echoed around the confined space and in the light beam she saw the water droplets exploding as they landed next to the branch. She laughed, which eased away the fear and tension. Well, some of it. Reaching back through the gap with one end of the cord in hand, she slipped the line over the branch and fumbled around below it until she found the hanging line. Pulling it back through the gap she shuffled backwards again until she had room to work a slip knot.

Wriggling forward towards the rocks, she slid the knot down the line, pinning the coil of cord under her body to hold it in place. Reaching through the gap, she chased the knot to the branch until it was snugged up against it. Once more shuffling herself backwards a few feet, she pulled firmly on the cord and felt the branch move behind the rocks, pulling up to the backside of them. Feeling satisfied she had a set-up that might just work, she began the awkward crawl backwards to rig the tube and the lever. She hadn't gone but a few feet, when a sound caught her attention. It was similar to the waves she thought she could hear at the junction, but this was quite a bit louder. The rumbling echoed around her and with her head buried in the tunnel she felt helpless to see what it might be. A second later she didn't need to see to know. Sea water slapped around the sides of the tunnel and ran across her legs, splashing past her to the rocks ahead. The tunnel was flooding.

36

1835

Cudjo spent the rest of the morning making the shallow cave in the ironshore liveable. It was actually a ribbon of softer rock or compacted earth that had become sandwiched in the dead coral over time. The constant beating of the waves during storms over the centuries had hollowed out the erodible material, leaving a smooth indentation in the bluff face, four feet above the high tide mark. It was deep enough to shield him from the sun until mid-afternoon, and any rain, unless the winds carried the moisture from the south. Thinking about rain made him realise he had no provision for drinking water. He lacked water itself, but also the means of gathering or capturing the precious liquid he'd need to survive.

He set out the provisions he had brought in his hasty escape while he sat upon the blanket his mother had given him, and was grateful she'd thought to gather it. He had his second pair of pants, his two other cotton shirts, a cotton cloth he used to wash with, and the food his mother had provided. The last item he'd taken from beside his bed was the book he was currently reading from Mr. Ferguson's library. The novel was a leather-bound copy of book one of the two published under the name *Travels into Several Remote*

Nations of the World, better known as *Gulliver's Travels*. Tucked inside the cover was a piece of paper and a graphite pencil, both rare items on the island. Mr. Ferguson provided them with each book he loaned to Cudjo, and insisted he return the book only once Cudjo had made notes on the paper with his thoughts of the story. He stared at the book and thought about the old man who had taught him to read and write. Why Mr. Ferguson had chosen Cudjo to bestow the gifts of his time and knowledge he didn't know, and with his passing, would undoubtedly never know. When he'd asked his mother, she had told him to thank the Lord, and accept the man's graciousness. He felt an overwhelming sadness at the loss of the man. He was five years old when his own father had died, and while he recalled that night and the pain he felt, the peaks and valleys of a child's emotions couldn't be compared to the deep-seated sorrow he now experienced. This was the passing of a man he'd respected and admired, but it was also the passing of a way of life. Cudjo knew nothing in his family's world would be the same from this point forward.

He needed to figure out how to scale the bluff. His little cave was four feet above the water, but it was an additional twelve feet from the base of his ledge to the top of the bluff. The face was vertical, as the ocean's erosion undercut the cliff and the mass above would eventually collapse, leaving a flat face again. Most of it was jagged ironshore, with occasional ribbons of softer material where wisps of flora added a touch of green to the grey and brown. Cudjo felt he could climb the face as hand and foot holds appeared plentiful, albeit rather painful, but the risk of a fall if he had to repeatedly climb would be great. He began a mental list of items he needed. First priority was a leather costrel to carry water, and second would be a trowel to cut some better holds in the cliff. He feared scaling the cliff in the dark but he also had to climb back down or jump in the water again, neither of which seemed appealing at night. He couldn't risk hanging a rope over the side for fear of it being spotted during the day. He had no idea how long he'd be in hiding

– he presumed for the rest of his life, however short that may be in his precarious situation. But his main concern was still for his family. He drove himself into a frenzy worrying about what had happened to Phibba when he left the plantation house that morning. He'd expected to be chased and hunted by Francis, but he never saw the man set foot outside the house before he had fled. As the afternoon wore on, and the heat steadily rose, Cudjo became more agitated, and desperately thirsty.

The moment the sun dipped below the horizon, and the last vestiges of the day dimly lit the bluff, Cudjo carefully climbed the face and crawled over the edge into a low crouch. Seeing or hearing no one, he made his way to the low shrubs away from the bluffs, and headed east back towards the Ferguson plantation. As darkness fell Cudjo made his way from memories of nineteen years in the same 400 yard by 600 yard piece of the island that made up the 50 acres he knew so well. His first stop was along the borderline of Eden's property, where he took the steps down to the fresh water at the base of the well. After a full day in the tropical heat and humidity, he sat sipping the refreshing cool water for ten minutes before moving on. From the dark edge of the cotton fields he could see the fire glowing brightly by the long table near the half circle of huts. Everyone was gathered, finishing their supper. His heart sang when he saw Phibba sitting next to her mother, holding hands with her older sister, Pegg. Looking towards the plantation house he could see no one on the veranda where Mr. Ferguson had often sat during the evenings, under the light of the lanterns.

Cudjo waited and watched. The mosquitoes feasted on him and he welcomed the occasional flapping of bats' wings as they swooped on the vicious bugs. Around the supper table, there was no singing, no reading, and barely any conversation. When everyone had finished their fish stew, the women cleared the table, and one by one the group wandered to their huts for the night. The fire still burned, and it felt like hours before it died down enough for him to be comfortable making his way to the huts without being seen. Staying to the far end of his mother's wattle-and-daub shelter, hidden from the Ferguson house, he whispered through the open shutter.

"Mama, it's me, it's Cudjo."

He heard a scurrying inside the hut and his mother's voice.

"My boy, thank God you're alright, did you find somewhere to hide, son?"

"I did Mama, best I don't say where, but I'm fine," he replied.

"That Cudjo?" came Pegg's voice, and her hand reached through the window.

"It's me, sister," he said, squeezing her hand.

"I'll light a candle," he heard Phibba's voice say from the dark room.

"No, no," he said quickly, louder than he intended. "Don't make light, don't give the man no reason to suspect nothing." He breathed easier, it was good to hear her voice. "Are you alright, Phibba? What he do when I ran? He didn't fuss with you none did he?"

He heard her shuffle over to the window next to their mother. "No, he didn't come out of that room for a while so we went about our work. When he did he sent me to fetch the men from the fields to bury his Papa. He didn't have no one come for no services, not even a preacher from town. He made them dig a hole and threw the old man in like..." Her voice cracked and he could hear she was struggling not to cry, "Like he was an old dog, just buried so the critters wouldn't get at him."

"Since then he stayed at the house," Polly said. "Ain't seen him none."

"He ain't gonna let it lie, you know that Mama, he fixin' to do something," Cudjo replied.

"Messenger came to the house this afternoon. Sally heard him say there's some kind of gathering at Pedro St. James tomorrow. Francis told the man he'd be there," Phibba whispered through the window.

"She didn't hear what this meeting about?" Cudjo asked.

"She said there was words she don't understand, but she did hear him say the Governor of Jamaica had sent a man to have this meeting, said they gathering all the important white folks on the island."

"You stay clear of Eden's place, you hear me son, be a good time to be anywhere but there," Polly said firmly.

"I will, Mama, don't worry now. I need some water though, need something to hold some water."

He heard more shuffling inside the hut and then his mother's hands reached through the window with a costrel full of water, and a bundle wrapped in cloth.

"Here's some water and food, son, keep you going a few days," Polly said, as he took them both.

"Thank you, Mama, I'm gonna take one of them small spades from the tools 'round back too. I best be gettin' on now, I'll come back tomorrow when they all over at Eden's plantation."

"Maybe it's best you stay away for a few days, Cudjo," Polly said, quietly. "Let everything settle down some. He see you and it's gonna be bad, you know that."

Cudjo reached a hand through the window and his mother held it to her face. "I'm scared, Cudjo, I'm scared how things are gonna be now."

"I'm scared too, Mama," Cudjo stammered. "I wish Papa was here, he'd know what to do. I fear I made a mess of everything, not just for me, but for all of us. Nothing ain't gonna be the same now."

"You everything your Papa was, son, he'd be proud of the man you grown to be. But you right, ain't nothing gonna be the same. That Francis got evil in his blood, he all like his mother."

"Mama, we can't leave it there, we can't leave it just buried there. We need it somewhere we can get to it," Cudjo whispered.

"I told you forget about that thing, ain't no good to no one, we can't do nothing with it," Polly replied, clutching Cudjo's hand tightly.

"It may be no good to a Negro, Mama, but it would sure be

good in the hands of a white man, and Francis ain't gonna be that man. Too easy for him come searching through these huts, like his Papa never once did. Let me move it, Mama, somewhere he won't find it, somewhere we can, come that day Papa talked about," Cudjo urged.

"Damn it, son, pass me a shovel through the window. This foolish best I see it, but I'll do it," Polly replied.

Cudjo stepped around the back of the hut where they stacked the tools for working the fields. Careful not to knock anything over he picked out a full-sized spade and found a small trowel for himself to take. He passed the spade to his mother and heard her voice from inside.

"Move Cudjo's mattress aside and close the shutters all 'cept that one your brother's at. You'll have to light a candle now, but keep it low in this corner while I dig."

"What are you digging for?" Pegg asked as she quietly closed the shutters.

"Best you girls know nothing of it, safest that way. Gimme that candle and sit yourselves over there on my bed out the way," Polly instructed and began digging at the soil.

Cudjo hated to hear his mother doing the man's work of digging inside the hut, but he dare not risk them or him by going inside. He let her be, and apart from his two sisters whispering to each other, the only sound was dirt being moved for fifteen minutes or more. Breathing heavily, she finally shuffled back to the window.

"Here it is, reach in now, I can hardly lift this thing," Polly gasped.

Cudjo reached in and held the cross, still wrapped in the same cloth he had last seen the night his father died. He heaved the sturdy package through the window and set it at his feet.

"I love you Mama, girls, you take care of her now, you hear me?" Cudjo said.

Both his sisters replied they would and his mother reached out and caressed her son's face with her hands wet with sweat.

"Be careful, son," she said, stepped back into the hut, and let him go.

Cudjo gathered up the cross, his food and the leather water canteen, and quietly stepped behind the other huts, heading west. It wasn't far to where the old well had sat unused for five years. Shrubs and small trees had grown around the hole in the ground, well hydrated from the water below. The moon had risen and cast a faint light, but mainly he worked from memory to find the well, and he pushed thin branches aside to reach the stone steps leading down. Much debris and foliage had fallen down the opening, which he gathered up and set outside the well. After ten minutes of heaving stones, dirt and branches he dipped his hands into the stream of water at the bottom. He touched a finger to his lips. The water was still slightly salty. He climbed back up the steps and retrieved the cloth-covered cross. His curiosity urged him to unwrap it and see it for the second time in his life; although it was too dark to really make it out, he ran his fingers over the detailed features and precious stones. For a moment he let his mind wonder where this beautiful cross had come from, and what value it held. Value in a white man's hands, he thought in frustration. Wrapping it back up, he carried it down the steps and laid the package in the stream of water. Reaching down, he felt around to see how large an opening the stream had made down flow. It seemed like the package would fit, so he slid it away from the well opening into the cavity leading towards the ocean. Once it became wedged and would move no further, he began bringing as many rocks and stones as he could find down to fill the well. He started with the largest he could carry, chunks of ironshore cast aside when the well was originally dug. He couldn't fill it to the top, but he figured after a few weeks of weathering, it would appear that it hadn't been touched in years.

Cudjo stood above the well with his food, water and trowel in hand. He looked to the heavens and prayed his father would approve of what he'd just done. He felt lost and alone in a world that had turned from comfortably routine to hideously grim in such a short time. He wondered if he'd ever see the cross again or, for that matter, anyone would ever see the cross again. He considered it likely he'd just buried the precious emerald-encrusted silver treasure for eternity. Better lost forever than in the hands of Francis Ferguson, he reminded himself.

37

SATURDAY MORNING

AJ furiously shuffled backwards down the narrow tunnel with sea water careening around her. Almost back to the junction she felt her feet jam against something in her path. The only way she could turn her head was to look down and back, which dipped her face under the rapidly rising water. Even through her mask she couldn't see anything and her torch beam refracted and bounced off the turbulence, leaving her blind in the tight confines of the tunnel. She kicked at the obstruction and it moved, but not far. It felt smooth and stretched across the floor of the whole tunnel and she quickly realised it was the tube and lever she'd left there. Picking her feet up over it and sliding her legs across the metal tube hurt like hell, but she had to get out, and get out fast.

The water was surging every four or five seconds, about the timing between waves she realised. She made it to the junction and could finally turn around as more and more water surged from the fork she now knew for sure led back to the inlet. For a second she considered crawling down that tunnel, but having never been down there, she'd be gambling on it being passable, a gamble she couldn't take. She knew the way she'd come in, and furthermore her gear was that direction. At the rate the tunnels were filling, she needed an air tank and regulator any moment. Taking a lungful of air, she scrambled back down the crack towards the Tank with the surge now pushing her forward. With water splashing all around it was hard to pick out the turns back and forth to keep her in the higher, unobstructed part of the tunnel. She kept hitting her head on lower sections of the ceiling and several times she banged her mask straight into a rock and had to back up. The tunnel angled slightly down towards the Tank which accelerated the rise in water level, and she had to tilt her head sideways to grab some rapidly disappearing air. She took a long, smooth lungful and dove back under the water, shining her torch ahead. The water level was almost to the ceiling which reduced the turbulence and she could see a little more in the light beam. She thought she was over halfway to the Tank, but she needed to make it the rest of the way on one breath. Scrambling, clawing and pulling on the rock, she hauled herself along, dodging around the zigzag pattern of the crevice, and hoping at each turn she'd see her gear at the top of the Tank.

It felt like she'd been going forever, and she began to panic that she'd taken another exit from the junction, one she hadn't seen before. Her lungs burned, she desperately needed air and prayed the next turn would reveal the opening at the top of the Tank. It didn't. She was getting lightheaded and her lungs screamed for oxygen, she had to get air. Pinning her cheek against the ceiling she felt a tickle of air above the turbulent surface of the water. She exhaled the spent air and began drawing in a fresh breath. The fresh air felt like life being poured back into her body. As she drew in close to a full breath the air turned to salt water and she choked and spluttered, purging every precious molecule of oxygen she'd just taken in. Panic tried to seize her brain, but she consciously fought the body's instinct to inhale, and pressed her cheek back against the ceiling of the tunnel.

The water was surging with the wave action in the inlet; as long as the tunnel wasn't completely full, she just needed to time her intake of air with the lull in the surge. But all she could feel across her face was water, and she couldn't hold back the urge to gulp any longer. Despite her willing against it, her mouth opened, and air filled her lungs. She couldn't believe her luck, and inhaled as quickly as possible, closing her mouth before the surge brought more water. She dived back down and wrenched and pulled herself forward down the tunnel. After two more twists, she finally saw rock ahead and recognised the opening into the cave. But what she didn't see was her BCD, tank and fins. They were gone.

Half pushed by the rushing flow of water that now completely filled the tunnel and the room ahead, and half pulling herself forward, she reached the top of the Tank and swung her torch around looking for where her gear could be. Her brain hadn't had nearly the oxygen it needed in the past few minutes for rational thought, and all she could think about was making it to the precious air of the outside world. Her mind shot to the turtle skull in the first cave: did someone move it? Is there someone else in the cave system, another person who now had taken her scuba gear? The paranoia wrapped around her, closing in tighter than the tunnels she was trapped within.

She knew she didn't have enough breath to make the exit, but her only option was to try; turning back led to a flooded system of tunnels. She dropped into the tank and the depth change added pressure to her lungs and made her feel even more helpless. Shining the torch around the walls of the tank, she found the tunnel leading away to the skull cave. Her head felt dull and struggled to keep her thoughts in place; her limbs were already slowing and lacking strength. Shadows danced around her like the spectres who'd carried her gear away and her vision locked on whatever the small circle of light from her torch illuminated. Her feet hit the rock-strewn floor of the cave and she reached out to pull herself into the tunnel: she had to keep trying. Then her knee hit something smooth, hard and round. Confusing her, the distraction was enough for her mind to forget about making the exit; she would sit here a while and clear her head. There was no hurry now, she'd rest for a bit.

Consumed by delirium, she looked down and tried to focus her blurry vision on what she'd hit below. She recognised the object, it looked familiar, but she couldn't place it. Her heart rate had slowed to an occasion thump in her chest that seemed to pulse through her whole body, causing her lungs to convulse. Her lips began to part, she would breath in whatever the world had to offer, she had no choice. She reached down and rested her hand on the smooth round object and something registered in the far reaches of her oxygen-deprived mind. Her hand foraged amongst the debris and found a hose. As her mouth opened and water began to seep past her lips she pushed the regulator into her mouth and sucked in a mixture of water and air. It was enough to spark her mind awake, and she hit the purge valve as she coughed and choked. The next inhalation was clean, sweet air and the fog lifted.

AJ sat there in the base of the tank for several minutes, breathing evenly from the regulator, and wondering how she couldn't have figured out the only place her gear had to go was down. Of course it was lying at the bottom of the room; the surging water had dislodged it and pushed it over the edge. Finally, she wriggled into her BCD and glanced at her gauges. She had plenty of air but she'd been down in the caves for forty-five minutes. Jackson would be getting worried. Jonty was going to be mad, she'd lost his home-built tubular lever device and come out empty handed, but she was not coming back in these caves again. He'd have to wait until his various ailments healed, and if that meant the person who had stolen all his notes beat him to it, so be it. She could see Reg giving her that look. The 'I told you so' look. Well, she'd reached her threshold of safety that's for sure, she chuckled to herself.

She flashed the torch around the base of the cave and found one of her fins. She slipped it on and looked for the other one. Maybe I'm sitting on it, she thought, and raised up, moving to sit in the tunnel entry to the side. Shining the light beam around, she scoured the rubble. It was mainly chunks of limestone rock and a few small branches of wood, perhaps having washed in from the inlet when the system regularly flooded. From what she now knew, it appeared the whole system flooded every high tide, or perhaps when the high tide was above average; she'd check the tide charts when she made it back to dry land. It was possible there was a restriction in the tunnel from the inlet, maybe a barrier or simply the height of the tunnel above the water that stopped the water coming in until it was over a certain height. She found herself thinking about exploring that tunnel to ease her curiosity, then she reminded herself she'd just nearly drowned and was never coming back in here again. She saw her other fin, wedged down between two rocks the size of footballs, and reached down to pull it out. When she picked it up, something caught her eye below the rocks. It was dark but had a straight edge to it, an unnaturally straight edge. She figured it was just another tree branch and slipped her fin on her other foot, ready to leave.

AJ checked over her gear and made sure she had everything in place, before standing up on the rubble and shining her torch down the tunnel. She could see a faint glow at the end where the light trickled into the skull cave. It was a gorgeous hint of the outside world filled with sunshine and plenty of fresh air. She took a long inhalation through the regulator to remind herself she was safe now, with air to breath and a short swim out of the caves. She looked back one last time and shone her torch around making sure she was leaving nothing but bad memories and a reel line. There was that edge again, between the two large rocks. Her curiosity got the better of her and she dropped gently to her knees on the rubble and tried to move one of the rocks. The honeycombed limestone wasn't as heavy as it looked and she was able to roll it up and out the way. She shone the torch in the gap she'd created, and instantly stopped breathing. She reached down and pulled the second rock away to reveal the rest of the object laying on the floor of the cave. She brushed aside more debris and sand and stared at the perfect shape of a cross.

It was almost black with some kind of tarnish or material clinging to its surface. She tried lifting it and it was much heavier than the rocks. It took some effort to remove it from its nest in the rubble and set it down on the floor of the tunnel. The surface looked flat, the only texture from whatever the material was clinging to it. It was over a foot long and the crossbar maybe three-quarters of that wide. The vertical and crossbar were three inches broad and over an inch thick. With some effort she turned the cross over and saw straight away the other surface was not flat. Raised pieces like large buttons protruded as much as half an inch. She carefully rubbed one of the buttons and the material and dirt fell away to reveal a bright green stone. AJ could not believe she was holding the Cross of Potosí in her hands. The same flooding and surging water must have carried the cross down the tunnels years ago, and into the base of the Tank. Just the other day, she herself had unknowingly passed right over the top of it. Jonty had as well, for that matter: several years ago, he'd swum right over it. She couldn't believe her eyes. Here she held a piece of history, hand-crafted by Spanish artists in Bolivia 400 years ago, and last touched by slaves on Grand Cayman 200 years ago. Amazed, she asked herself, what should she do now?

The proper course of action was to leave it in place, contact the Cayman authorities and officially register the find. Well, she'd already screwed up step one as she'd moved it, but she had to check it out, it could've been two pieces of wood nailed together for all she knew. At least that's how she justified it, but was sure the folks at the Cayman Islands museum would throw their hands in the air. Her decision came from her desire to never come inside these caves again. She'd carry it out, call the authorities right away, with Jonty protesting she was sure, but he was in no position to stop her. She eased into the tunnel and carefully lifted the cross, but the weight of it pinned her to the floor. She pumped air into her BCD until she and the cross rose from the surface and hung in the water. If she dropped the cross she'd shoot to the ceiling like an escaping balloon.

Clinging tightly to the treasure, she finned down the tunnel that felt like a motorway compared to the other tunnels deeper in the system. She arrived at the skull cave and noted the turtle skull was in the same place she'd seen it when she entered. The spectres must have left it alone this time, she thought with amusement. Carefully, she kicked across to the opening and squeezed through the narrow gap. The surge was similar to when she'd gone in, gently moving back and forth and much calmer than the other day. She wondered how it would have been inside the caves if it had been that strong; the tunnels would probably have flooded more quickly and violently. She doubted she'd have made it out. She finned along the side of the submerged shelf and used breath control in her lungs to start rising up towards the hull of the RIB. Looking up and over, she noticed for the first time a second hull in the water. Someone was tied alongside Arthur's Odyssey. It would make life easier on her if that was a DOE or Joint Marine Police boat – Jonty wouldn't be able to argue about calling it in. She broke the surface by the ladder at the stern and looked up, ready to share the good news. It was then she realised the second boat did not belong to a government agency. Staring down at her was a dark-skinned man in loose pants and a form-fitting sleeveless shirt, with his hair braided in cornrows.

38

1835

It had been a struggle to descend the bluff in the dark, but Cudjo had managed without falling. He'd spent the night restless, with thoughts of his family, and Francis Ferguson, depriving him of sleep. In the early hours he'd lain on his side, looking out over the dark ocean with the sounds of water lapping against the rocks below. Stars filled the clear night sky and he wondered at the beauty of the island he'd called home his whole life. He'd grown accustomed, over the years, to feeling safe there, but now the fears around his father's death returned. He could barely picture his Papa, his memories faded and hazy after all the years. But he missed him all the same.

He recalled the strength he saw in the man – his giant – and how his giant was struck down, like any mortal could be. Clearer than a memory of the man's face, he could close his eyes and still feel his big, strong hand on his shoulder. Being swooped up and cradled against his father's broad chest. Everyone told him he was the image of his father, big and strong just like Solomon, but he didn't feel strong, not inside. He could work harder than anyone, carry heavier loads, but still he felt helpless and scared. He wanted to use his strength against Francis, he wanted to beat the little man down, but all it would bring would be misery for his family, and a noose for himself. He'd happily take the noose to rid their world of evil, but the retribution on his family he couldn't bear.

As dawn broke across the ocean and pale light shimmered off the gently ebbing water, Cudjo reached for the book he'd brought with him. He took the paper from inside the front cover, used the book as a rest, and began to write with the pencil. He didn't know why he was driven to put down the words, and expected to throw the paper away when he was finished, but the words fell from his mind, and the pencil kept moving. Mr. Ferguson had introduced Cudjo to poetry, reading Keats and Wordsworth to him, and although the young slave found the words hard to follow and understand, he enjoyed their rhythm. His own writing was much simpler, but a hint of Wordsworth's timing found its way in, whether Cudjo recognised it or not. When he was done, he tucked the paper back inside the front of the book, and set it aside. The sun was nearing its zenith, and he realised the landowners would probably be gathering at Pedro St. James. He took a long drink of water and ate some fruit, having altogether forgotten about food all morning. Taking the trowel, he examined the bluff face around the cove for a good spot to carve some steps. On the east face there was a continuation of the softer ribbon that formed his cave, and above it a smaller, second ribbon. He chiselled out small indentations with the point of the trowel, deep enough for his toes and the ball of his foot to gain purchase. He used his first steps to climb up and reach higher on the face to add a couple more notches. When he was done, he set the trowel back in his cave, took another drink of water, and climbed the bluff face.

Cudjo moved across the jagged ironshore to the brush line and squatted down. It was less than a quarter of a mile to William Eden's great three-storey, stone structure, where the meeting of landowners was taking place. A rare assembly of the powerful men who owned all the property on the island, and also owned the slaves who worked the land. The place his mother had specifically told him to avoid. Good sense told him she was right and that was the last place he should be as a slave on the run – Francis was likely telling every man there to watch for the fugitive. But, despite his misgivings, curiosity was too much, and he sensed something significant was happening. He started along the brush line at the bottom of the cotton fields and noticed no one working the land as far as he could see. The closer he moved towards the plantation house, the more he could hear raised voices. He stopped and hid further in the shrubs to listen. The voices weren't angry, they almost sounded like they were singing and cheering. Confused and wary, Cudjo stayed low and moved slowly closer to the slave quarters on the east side of the house. He could now see people dancing and clearly celebrating, not the white men he expected to see, but the slaves of the plantation. They were all gathered and jubilantly embracing and slapping each other on the back. Cudjo reached the huts and stayed hidden for several minutes watching the festivities in open view of the great house. One of the older slaves came near the hut Cudjo hid behind. He called to the man and the slave looked over curiously before smiling broadly.

"What are you doing hiding back there? You ain't from the Eden place, now?"

"No, I'm from Ferguson's, over yonder," Cudjo said, still crouched behind the hut and pointing east.

"Why you hiding back there?" the man asked, dubious to come too close.

"Why are you all dancing like fools in the middle of the day?" Cudjo asked in return.

"You not hear? We free men, the white man been told to set us free, we ain't slaves no more, or apprentices, or any other name they call us. We be free men and women," the man replied.

Cudjo didn't know what to say, he had no comprehension of what that even meant: free? Free to do what? Come and go as they pleased? Go where and do what? If they left Ferguson's where would they go?

"How you mean? We free to do what, you say?"

"Anything you wants," the old man replied with a broad smile.

"You wants to stay and work for your master, he gotta pay you now, or you tells him no."

The idea of telling Francis Ferguson no didn't seem like a realistic option to Cudjo, the whip marks still fresh across his body a stinging reminder of the man's disdain for Negroes. The old man turned to leave.

"Sir, what you all planning to do?" Cudjo asked.

The man turned around. "We gonna celebrate all night I reckon," he said with a laugh. "Then we see tomorrow how Mr. Eden gonna pay us before we go out in the fields." He laughed again. "Matter of fact, we see tonight what he say when he wants his supper made for him."

The old man re-joined the gathering and Cudjo sat back behind the hut and tried to understand what was happening. If he comprehended things correctly, he could go back to the plantation, gather up his family, and anyone else who wanted to join them, and leave. What he couldn't grasp was where they could go. They had no money and no property. Was there land they could live on somewhere on the island, or perhaps a different family that needed help and were willing to pay? Standing up, he decided he could ponder all this while he walked to his own village, where he would tell his mother the news.

As he strode across the edge of Eden's cotton fields, not worrying about staying hidden, Cudjo began to see the possibilities that lay ahead. The gloom and despair that had enveloped him for the past few days gradually lifted and hope took a firm hold of his disposition. He, his mother and his two sisters would leave the Ferguson plantation and seek employment with one of the other landowners. Surely they'd all be losing workers as slaves left to travel back to the lands they came from, or venture to new islands in search of opportunity. He figured the plantations would simply pay for the work now, instead of owning the slaves, and life would go on. Cudjo had no understanding of the finances and how slim the margins were for the cotton growers on Grand Cayman, the few that were left. Mr. Ferguson had always made it work, so surely others would continue to do so, he reasoned. The important part for him and his family was they'd be free of Francis Ferguson: the man had no hold or control over them now. By the time Francis returned from Pedro St. James, he, Polly and the girls would be gone, and there was nothing he could do about it. Cudjo stopped at the little bay and climbed down the steps he'd made. He gathered his few belongings and wrapped them neatly in the blanket, tying it up so he could carry it back up the face. He gave one last look to the sanctuary that had sheltered him for what turned out to be the most important two nights of his life. If he hadn't hidden from Francis, who knows what would have happened, and here, just a few days later, he was now a free man.

Cudjo crossed the property line and walked by the old well, where his thoughts wandered to the cross. With their new-found freedom he could take that treasure and sell it, surely it was worth a fortune. They could buy their own piece of land; he could grow cotton as well as any man with all he'd learnt under Mr. Ferguson. He walked on the clouds as he approached the half circle of huts, but was surprised to see no one was there. He looked up the fields and in the distance he could see the men working, just as they would be on any given day. He could also see several of the women helping, which wasn't altogether unusual. He walked to their hut to leave his things inside. He was thinking about how he would explain their new world to the others when he opened the door. Standing across the tiny room was Francis Ferguson.

Cudjo's first reaction was to run, but Francis spoke before he had a chance to bolt.

"Free man," he said, and Cudjo stopped in his tracks. "Free man, they say. But do you know what that really means?"

The shutters were all open and blocks of light streamed through the square openings, one block lighting the man's body, leaving his face still shaded. Cudjo couldn't make out his expression.

"Means you don't own me no more," he said firmly. "Means you don't own none of us."

Francis stepped forward slightly and the light moved across his face. He was smiling.

"True for them," he responded. "But you're a wanted felon, a runaway before emancipation was official. It doesn't apply to you."

Cudjo was taken aback, all he had was one old man's word that they were all free. What Francis was saying in words he didn't fully understand could well be true. He had run; if caught, it was up to the owner how he chose to deal with his possession. He could be whipped, or hanged, depending how strong a message the owner wanted to send.

Francis laughed. "No matter, I am not a man to concern myself over such details. The law says you're free, then free you shall be. As you seem to represent the slaves here, and you have the ability to read and write, come with me to the house and I'll sign your papers. You'll then be free to do as you choose."

"Papers?" Cudjo asked. "What papers is this, sir?"

"Papers showing you've been granted freedom by the word of the British government, of course. Not everywhere has agreed to the same – you need papers to prove you are free people."

Francis started towards the door and Cudjo backed out, keeping a safe distance from the man and, more importantly, his whip.

"Make haste, I have much to do," Francis said as he walked out of the hut and started towards the house. Cudjo desperately wanted to tell the others of their freedom as they seemed unaware, but maybe it would be even better if he was holding their official papers of freedom when he did. He pulled the door open to the hut and set his blanketed package on the floor inside, before taking after Francis, who strode towards the house.

They entered through the side door from which Cudjo had escaped just days before. In the main room Sally was making bread and turned in surprise when they entered.

"Sally, gather everyone from the fields, I'll address them by the huts when we're done here," Francis said.

Sally looked at Cudjo with concern in her eyes, but bowed her head to Francis.

"Yes, sir, Mr. Ferguson," she said quietly, wiped her hands on a cloth and left.

Francis continued through the house towards the study, where Cudjo had learnt so much from the man's father. The dividing walls within the house were thin woven wattle, supported by hardwood framing, but the exterior walls had a dense plaster covering which provided better insulation and protection. Heavy thatch roofing kept the rain at bay and ample shuttered windows allowed in light and breeze to cool the building. In the study, bookshelves lined the plastered outer walls and an ornate wooden desk imported from Jamaica sat in the centre of the room. Francis walked to one of the windows and looked out upon the fields.

"I suppose you spent many days in this study, with my father, more than I have I don't doubt," he said, without turning.

"I did, sir, your father was most kind to me, sir," Cudjo replied.

The study brought back a flood of memories. The patience Mr. Ferguson had shown as Cudjo had first learnt his letters and numbers, and later as he stumbled across the text of classic books such as *Robinson Crusoe* and *Ivanhoe*. How he so enjoyed the adventure tales, the world he could only imagine through the words on those pages. Many were set in far-off lands that sounded so different from the tropical island he knew. Castles and armies of men, gallant warriors, royalty and brave sailors, cities the size of which were unfathomable to the young slave boy.

"You knew my father better than I," Francis said quietly and turned to face the room. "Seems he preferred your presence over mine."

Cudjo didn't know what to say, his mother's words ringing in his head. Did Francis know Mr. Ferguson wasn't his father? Surely he couldn't know, unless the old man told him before he died.

"Something I found quite unacceptable," Francis said, staring coldly at Cudjo. "Shunned by my own father, and replaced by a slave."

Cudjo became more uneasy; the man's tone was becoming more severe and he wondered when they'd sign these papers so he could be on his way.

Francis's expression changed, and he laughed, almost to himself. "Funny thing, you know. It was your little sister who killed my father."

Cudjo froze. What could he possibly mean. "Sir? How could that be, sir?"

"She poisoned him," Francis said, waving a hand in the air. "She slowly poisoned him over several days." He laughed again. "Of course she didn't know that's what she was doing, but it was."

Francis leaned on the desk and looked at Cudjo. "I put the poison in the tea she made for him, unbeknown to her, then she administered the potion to him. Your own flesh and blood poisoned the man you admired so much."

"Why? Why would you do that?" Cudjo struggled to say. "This plantation would have been yours given time."

Francis stood upright and laughed again. "This place?" He waved his arms around the room. "You think I want or care for this place? I'd rather watch it burn to the ground than spend another night within these walls. These rooms that reek of the man who abandoned me, who discarded his son and allowed the wretched to take my place. A cotton plantation? The fool was damn near broke, the only value to this land is what another fool would pay." He stepped towards Cudjo, his words spitting from his lips. "I'll be home in Georgia, where my mother's family took me in, where they know how to treat their slaves and keep them in their place. This land can rot beneath its feeble crops, and you, you can rot with it."

Cudjo was stunned by the words, the venom spewing from the man's lips, the hatred he had for everything Cudjo had known and held dear in his nineteen years. He stood motionless and confused. The blade he hadn't seen since that terrifying evening in the forest flashed through the air in Francis's hand. Before Cudjo had time to realise or react, he felt a punch to his chest the same as he had as a five-year-old boy in the woods. But this time the pain came right away.

39

SATURDAY MORNING

AJ considered ducking back under the water, but where could she go? She had no idea who this man was on her boat, but she sure as hell hadn't invited him aboard, and alarm bells rang as soon as she saw him. The gun he pointed at her was the next sign. This wasn't the first time she'd had a gun pointed in her direction, but it didn't get any more comfortable with repetition. Having grown up in England, where guns were not prevalent, she had a distinct distaste for them; after all, they were intended for killing things, and right now she was the potential target.

"Get out of the water," the man said in a thick Jamaican accent.

AJ spat her reg out of her mouth. "You want to put that gun down and take this from me then?" She lifted the cross slightly higher.

The man looked back in the boat, where AJ couldn't see anything from the water. "Come get this, she got it," the man said excitedly.

Jules's face appeared next to the man's. "Well look at that." She reached down and with some effort managed to haul the cross from AJ's arms and lift it into the boat.

The man waved the gun at the steps hung between the

outboards at the stern of the RIB, and AJ moved over and climbed the ladder. As she stepped into the boat she could now see Jackson and Jonty at the bow, sitting on the deck with their backs against the inflatable sides. They both appeared unharmed. She dropped her BCD and tank and slipped her fins from her wrist where she'd carried them, stowing them with her gear. Jules and the man were studying the cross on the deck.

"So, what exactly is going on here?" AJ asked.

"This bitch played me, that's what's going on," Jonty blurted.

Jules looked up and smiled. "Wasn't difficult, he's not very smart. Go sit down in the front with them," she said and nodded towards the bow.

AJ complied, pulling her wetsuit off her shoulders as she went. She really didn't want to be held hostage in a bikini but she was cooking in the neoprene now she was out of the water.

"You two okay?" she asked as she sat on the deck next to Jackson.

"Yeah, we're fine. Sorry we had no idea what he was up to until he was alongside," Jackson replied.

"Shut up, all o' you up there," the man shouted.

Ignoring him, Jonty looked at Jules. "So, explains how Bo Derek here got into my place, you gave him your key. But why have him steal all my stuff, half of which you gave me, if you were going to nick the cross from me anyway?"

Jules stood and walked halfway to the three of them, careful to stay out of reach. "Frank got a little excited, and overestimated his diving capability," she said, looking back at her accomplice with some disdain. "Thought it better to get the cross ourselves so we didn't have to deal with you two. Or three, as it turns out. Trouble is he got in the cave and freaked out..."

"I did not freak out," Frank blurted. "And who da hell's Bo Derek anyway?"

Jules shook her head. "Whatever, he couldn't do it so we had to wait for you. Just worked out I got to tag along."

AJ looked at Jackson, who had shuffled away from Jonty a few feet. He winked at her.

"Hey," AJ said, looking back at Frank. "You move the turtle skull in there?"

Frank started to answer but Jules cut him off. "Idiot brought it up from the cave. I told him to put it back where he found it."

"Well, he didn't do what you said, it was right by the entrance," AJ replied. "Guess he was scared to go back in any farther."

Frank shot her a look and Jonty groaned, "Why don't you piss off the guy with the gun."

"You called him Bo Derek," AJ bit back. "And you're worried about me insulting him?"

Frank stood up and waved the gun towards the bow. "Who da hell's dis man, Bo Derek?"

"Shut up, all of you," Jules yelled. "They're just trying to get you riled up so you'll do something dumb," she said, turning to her partner. "Let's move the cross over to your boat, and get going."

"What about us?" Jonty asked, looking up at Jules.

"What do you think?" AJ answered before Jules. "They haven't hidden their identity in any way, we're a loose end."

Jules grinned. "Listen to Miss Know It All, got it all figured out, do you?"

"Seriously Jules?" Jonty said. "I mean a bang on the head is one thing, but murdering three people? That's not you, surely?"

"You don't know shit about me, you arrogant, ungrateful little excuse for a man," Jules hissed. "I had to put up with your petty, inconsiderate bullshit for months. You think you discovered the location of the cross? Who found and gave you the poem? Me, you imbecile, I did it all, I figured it out for you, all you were good for was diving and even then a girl had to do it for you."

"'Cos your idiotic lackey tried to knock my head off," Jonty retorted.

"This is just a waste of time, let's move it to the other boat," Jules snapped.

"Wait, are you saying you were looking for the cross before I met you?" Jonty asked.

"No," Jules replied, somewhat reluctantly. "I was researching my family, I wanted to see if I had any claim to the land."

"Your family?" Jonty said. "You're a descendant of the slaves, of Solomon?"

"No, of course not, the Fergusons. Francis Ferguson was my great, great, great, great-grandfather."

That seemed to silence everyone, and Jules helped Frank lift the cross, then he carried it over and sat it on the inflatable side of the RIB. AJ looked at Jackson, who'd been quiet since she sat down. He winked at her again. Frank set one foot over the gunwale of their centre console, straddling the two boats, while he picked the cross back up and shifted his weight to step over. Jackson released the line he had tucked under his arm and the two boats immediately began to separate, stretching Frank between them. Jackson had undone the line tethering the two together at the bow while everyone had been arguing and distracted. Frank pushing against both boats shoved the untethered bows apart. Doing the splits, Frank gamely hung on to the cross and the gun but to no avail. The harder he tried to keep a foot in each boat, the more he pushed them apart, held only by the stern line.

Jackson leapt to his feet as Frank plunged between the two boats with a loud crack, as he hit his head on the gunwale of the centre console on the way down. Jules lunged for anything she could grab from Frank as he fell but couldn't make it in time. Frank, the cross and the gun went underwater. Jackson hooked Jules out of the way as he dove over the side into the water, spinning Jules off balance towards the bow. AJ had jumped to her feet behind Jackson and met Jules coming towards her. A solid right hook sent Jules sprawling the other direction and AJ looked over the side to see what she could do for Jackson. He was surfacing with Frank in his arms, who had blood running from his forehead and was out cold. With Jackson's height allowing him to just stand on the ironshore shelf below with his head out of the water, they hauled, pushed and dragged Frank's limp body back into the boat.

Without a word, AJ stepped past Jules, still lying on the deck rubbing her jaw, grabbed her mask and tossed it to Jackson. He dived in search of the cross and AJ found her boat's toolbox from which she retrieved a bundle of industrial-sized Ty-Raps. She had Jules's wrists tied behind her back and her ankles tied together before Jackson surfaced with the cross in his arms. She heaved it over into the boat and Jackson dived under one more time. AJ zip-tied Frank's hands and legs before Jackson clambered up the ladder at the stern with the gun in his hand.

"Bloody hell," Jonty said, still sitting on the deck at the bow having not moved. "You two need a hand with anything?"

AJ smiled at Jackson. "No, I think we have it."

Jackson put his arms around her and pulled her close. "Thanks for the distractions. Once they got mad they stopped noticing anything."

She kissed him then reached for her mobile on the console.

"Who you calling?" Jonty asked, finally labouring to his feet.

"The police," AJ said flatly.

"But..." Jonty started, then thought better of it and shrugged his shoulders.

"Detective Whittaker, hi, it's AJ Bailey," she said into the phone when the man answered. AJ and Detective Roy Whittaker of the Royal Cayman Islands Police Service had become well acquainted over the past few years.

"Hello, AJ. I assume as you called me Detective instead of Roy, this is official business?" Whittaker replied in a light Caymanian accent.

"Afraid so, but good news is there's no dead bodies," she said. "Well," she nudged Frank's limp form with her foot, "pretty sure this one will wake up eventually."

AJ wrapped up her call with Whittaker after explaining what had happened and where they were. Whittaker said he'd dispatch a

Joint Marine Police boat right away and meet them there as soon as he could.

The three sat around and stared at the Cross of Potosí lying on the deck of the RIB. It looked a little forlorn, tarnished black and covered with remnants of some kind of material, only one shiny green spot gleaming where AJ had rubbed the debris away.

"Well that was all a little more dramatic than I'd hoped for," AJ said with a grin.

"Yeah, didn't quite go to plan," Jonty mumbled. "At least that wanker should have a good concussion, that makes me feel a bit better."

"It's going to the authorities, Jonty, it's gotta be by the book," AJ said sternly.

"Does now, police are on the way, don't have a choice," Jonty replied sullenly, and looked up at AJ. "Got a bigger problem now though."

"What do you mean?" she asked.

"A woman called Brenda, and more importantly, her pet Falcon," he replied.

"Who? What do a woman and bird have to do with this?" she asked.

"Long story, but did I mention the other bloke that broke into my place?" Jonty said sheepishly.

40

1835

Phibba sat at the long table under the mahogany trees by the half circle of huts with everyone else. Sally had fetched them from the fields and told everyone to gather at the table; the young Mr. Ferguson wished to address them. They'd all been told to work the fields that morning by the young master, all except Sally, who was requested at the house. As they'd walked back, Sally had told Phibba and her mother that Cudjo was with Francis, but he seemed fine and willing to be there. They all had a sense that something big was happening. Sally had told them all about the meeting she'd overheard was taking place at the neighbouring plantation. Phibba anxiously waited, holding her mother's hand, both of them lost in thoughts of Cudjo. She couldn't understand why he would have come back in daylight, or why he'd be with Francis. The man had whipped him just a few days back. A murmur went around the table and Phibba looked up to see Francis Ferguson walking down the veranda steps with a suitcase in his hand; the same case he'd arrived with one week ago. He walked clear of the house and set the suitcase down. He wiped his brow with a handkerchief, before wiping his hands and stuffing the cloth back in his pocket. Leaving the case where he'd set it down, he continued walking towards the small stand of mahoganies, and the slaves who still believed him to be their owner.

Phibba watched him approach. He was dressed in fine clothes and appeared relaxed, perhaps even satisfied, she thought. She searched behind him around the plantation house for her brother but couldn't see him.

"Sally," she whispered, "you said Cudjo was with him?"

Sally nodded her head. "He were, not but a short time back."

They both fell silent as Francis strode boldly up and stood below the shade of the trees. He looked slowly around the group and settled his gaze upon Phibba. She shivered as his cold stare seemed to bore through her and her heart began to race in fear. He grinned.

"I recently came from a meeting at Pedro St. James, the great house that neighbours this plantation, and hosts gatherings of government business," he said sternly. "It has come to my attention via a representative sent from the Governor of Jamaica that British law has declared emancipation for all slaves."

Dead silence remained amongst the group; a few looked around at each other. Phibba had no idea what that word meant and was sure no one else did either. Francis seemed amused and shook his head.

"You poor, ignorant creatures. It means slavery has been abolished. Done away with. You are no longer the property of this plantation."

Phibba looked at her mother. "He saying we're free?"

Polly put a hand on her shoulder. "Sir, we understanding you right, we all free to go as we please?"

Murmurs and whispers rumbled around the group as everyone started to understand what was happening.

Francis held his chin up. "That is correct, the fools in British government have seen fit to succumb to the Whigs, which is why I shall be returning to Georgia, where a man is left to run his business as he sees fit, and slaves are kept in their place. This foul situation will be the ruin of the plantations in all the islands."

A buzz ran through the people and quiet chatter soon gave way to excited cheer until Polly spoke up again.

"Sir, what of our homes here? Are we to leave?"

Phibba thought her mother brave to ask questions of their master, but maybe it was alright now he wasn't their master anymore. Francis glared at her.

"I don't give a damn what you do. I sold this land to Eden earlier today, it's his to do as he sees fit. I suggest you ask him if he minds you trespassing on his land."

Francis gave them all a look of disgust and turned to leave.

"Sir," Phibba called out loudly. "Where is my brother?"

Francis half turned, but continued walking. "In my father's precious study, last I saw him."

Phibba looked to the house and saw smoke wafting from the thatched roof.

"The house!" she screamed. "The house is on fire!"

Polly cried out and ran towards the Ferguson home as flames took hold and spread rapidly across the whole roof, the dry thatch acting like kindling. The men ran for pails of water and Phibba called out her brother's name as she ran behind her mother.

Francis Ferguson smiled and calmly collected his suitcase, on his way to the trail into town.

41

___

SATURDAY AFTERNOON

AJ and Jonty sat behind a cloth-covered table in a small conference room. Next to them, a well-presented older lady wearing a Cayman Islands National Museum button-down shirt anxiously shuffled some papers. Jackson stood off to the side leaning against the wall, watching the goings-on with amusement. On the wall of the room in large lettering were the words *Cayman Compass*, the name of the island's main newspaper, whose conference room they were using. Across the room, several people milled about, and a camera with a 'Cayman 27' logo was set facing the table. A microphone with the same logo sat on the table, next to a large plastic tub covered with a white towel.

Jonty leaned over to AJ. "I'd rather have a colonoscopy than do this," he said, nervously messing with the bandages on his hand, having yet to return to the hospital.

"We can knock it all on the head if you like; from what you said, Brenda's birdy man might take you up on the colonoscopy, among other things," AJ replied, unable to hide a grin.

"Sod you, let's just get on with it," Jonty grumbled and the museum lady scowled at the pair of them.

AJ looked at her watch: it was 3:00pm. She nodded to a lady

chatting with the cameraman who stepped forward and announced they were ready to start. She had a similarly badged microphone in her hand and looked at her cameraman, mouthing a countdown to him while holding up matching fingers to the group at the table.

"Today we have two treasure hunters with an amazing discovery in our home waters, right here on Grand Cayman. Jonty Gladstone and Annabelle Jayne Bailey are joined by the director of the Cayman Islands National Museum, Mrs. Gladys Wright, to reveal this incredible discovery, lost to the world for hundreds of years. Jonty, could you tell us what it is exactly you've discovered, and how did you come across this incredible find?"

AJ cringed at the use of her full name, but at least her mother would be pleased, she thought, if she ever saw this. Jonty cleared his throat, and sucked most of the anticipation out of the moment with an awkward delay.

"Uhh, so yeah, we uhh, well, I've been studying this particular artefact for a couple of years, and I got a break with some new information in the past week, so we took a look, and we found it."

The interviewer looked panicked at Jonty's bumbling response but managed to salvage some words.

"And can you now tell us, what it is you've discovered?"

"Oh, yeah, well it's the Cross of Potosí," he said flatly, and AJ pulled the towel from the tub to reveal the blackened cross barely visible in the murk, as residue from the artefact clouded the solution. The cameraman eased his tripod on wheels forward and focused on the tub.

The interviewer, desperate to turn this lacklustre unveiling around, moved on to the lady from the museum.

"Mrs. Wright, the Cayman Islands National Museum must be very excited to receive this new treasure. Do you plan to put in on display for the public?"

Mrs. Wright did not appear excited at all and spoke with a stern upper class, English accent. "We're a long way from displaying anything at this stage, there is much to do before that point. We are taking the lead on authentication and restoration of the artefact, as we have extensive experience in such matters. The Cayman govern-ment retains official custody, but we'll maintain possession and start our work immediately – it will take some time to verify the age and authenticity."

From the look on her face, that wasn't the drama the interviewer was hoping for. "But if this is indeed the famed Cross of Potosí, what value do you believe it to have?"

Mrs. Wright fidgeted uncomfortably in her seat. "I couldn't speculate at this stage, but if it's genuine, the cross itself is solid silver and the stones are Columbian emeralds. The materials alone are worth thousands of dollars."

The interviewer's patience began to run thin. "Surely the arte-fact is far more valuable than a few thousand dollars? Before we went on air you told me it was hand crafted in the 16th century, its historical value alone must be enormous."

"I told you if it was genuine it was quite valuable. We need to establish authenticity before we concern ourselves with ownership and value," Mrs. Wright snapped back. "The discovery and recovery were not handled in ideal circumstances, so we at the museum will tread carefully, and make sure we have all our ducks in a row before we make any further statements."

Exasperated, the interviewer turned to AJ. "Miss Bailey, you are the one that made the dive to recover the cross, what can you tell us about what must surely have been a harrowing, yet rewarding adventure?"

"Yeah, so Jonty here had a concussion, and then a bum hand, so he asked me to help out. We removed the artefact because the envi-ronment it was in was unstable, and I didn't think it was worth the risk to send anyone back in there," AJ said with Mrs. Wright looking down her nose at her.

"But yes, it was exhilarating to recover this amazing treasure that's been untouched, we believe, since 1835," AJ added unperturbed.

Apparently deciding that was the best she was going to get, the interviewer launched into her wrap-up and AJ gave Jonty a hard nudge.

"An amazing story indeed, brought to you exclusively by Cayman 27 on the day a 16th century Spanish treasure from Bolivia has been uncovered in the waters of Grand Cayman..."

"I had one other thing, if I may?" Jonty said, holding up his hand as though he was hoping for the teacher's attention. The interviewer sighed. "Of course, Mr. Gladstone."

"I just wanted to say, this was all possible through the generosity of local businesswoman Miss Brenda McGinnis, who kindly funded the research and exploration to uncover this lost treasure. It's in her name we proudly present the Cross of Potosí to the Cayman authorities and place it in the care of the Cayman Islands National Museum," Jonty said and nodded. "There, thanks, that was it."

"This is Shenice Westinghouse reporting, turning it back to the studio." The reporter quickly wrapped up before her pain could be prolonged any further, and she and her cameraman hurriedly packed up and left without a word. Mrs. Wright had a helper come carry the tub containing the cross out the door, and left with a policeman escorting them, after waving a half-hearted farewell to AJ and Jonty. Jackson joined them as they gathered up their bags and thanked the *Cayman Compass* reporter who had provided the room.

"No problem, I'll call you tomorrow morning and we'll meet to go over the full story. Remember, don't talk to anyone else, you gave me the exclusive," the man said as he shook hands with Jonty.

"Yup, call me on the number I gave you," Jonty replied, more cheerfully than normal.

"That the mobile that got nicked?" AJ whispered once they were out the door.

"Of course," Jonty smirked back. "So, can I get a lift to the hospital? My ride is in jail."

"Suppose we can kick you out as we drive by," AJ replied as they trotted down the outdoor stairs to the car park.

As they turned the corner of the building, they stopped dead in their tracks with their path blocked by a large man who'd clearly overdone the steroid use.

"Shit," mumbled Jonty.

"Shit is right," the man answered.

"Guys, meet Miss McGinnis' pet bird, Falcon," Jonty said.

"I'm very disappointed, Gladstone," Falcon said, flexing his arms and chest as he talked.

"That's good, I do hope I contributed to that," Jonty countered, clearly feeling brave.

"You did, you little shit. Miss McGinnis says thanks to your little dog and pony show here you're off the hook," Falcon snarled.

"That's mighty nice of her," Jonty said with a grin.

"For now." Falcon growled and swung his hand at Jonty's head, stopping just short before Jonty could even flinch. He slapped his cheek softly a couple of times, turned and walked away. "But one day Gladstone, one day, you and me are gonna spend some one-on-one time."

"Seems like a reasonable fellow," Jackson said, watching the huge man saunter across the car park to a lifted 4x4 Jeep.

"Yeah. Well, one day is better than tomorrow, so I guess it's a step in the right direction," AJ said.

"S'ppose," Jonty grumbled. "Are you taking me to the hospital or what?" he said, looking at his bandaged extremity. "If I'm gonna live a bit longer, I guess I'll get this hand fixed properly after all."

ACKNOWLEDGMENTS

My biggest supporters are my amazing wife Cheryl and my great friend James Guthrie, who offer their honest and invaluable feedback, as well as their unwavering encouragement.

I'm blessed with love and similar encouragement from my wonderful Mum, and my brother Michael, along with his family.

I've come to rely on and place enormous trust in my editor, Andrew Chapman; the final touch to my books is in his caring and capable hands. He can be found at PrepareToPublish.

Thanks to the incorrigible Jen Skrinska, and our lovely friend Casey Keller for their input and permissions. It's so much fun including these wonderful people in my stories.

Some fantastic authors; Wayne Stinnett, Cap Daniels and Nick Sullivan, have provided their help, guidance and friendship, for which they have my respect and everlasting gratitude.

I'm proud to have Drew McArthur's stunning photography gracing the cover of this book, and hopefully many more to come.

You may conclude some similarity between Sea Sentry and the marine conservation organisation Sea Shepherd… While Sea Shepherd are unable to license the use of their name in novels, they've been most kind in their interaction with me and I support their efforts.

Check them out at www.seashepherd.org

Thank you so much to my growing advanced reader copy (ARC) group, whose input and feedback is invaluable. It truly is a pleasure to work with all of you and my stories are better because of you.

Above all, I thank you, the readers: it is your kind words and loyal purchases that have opened the door to more adventures for AJ Bailey and allowed me to fulfil a lifelong goal of being an author.

LET'S STAY IN TOUCH!

To buy merchandise, find more info or join my Newsletter, visit my
website at
www.HarveyBooks.com

If you enjoyed this novel I'd be incredibly grateful if you'd consider
leaving a review on Amazon.com
Find eBook deals and follow me on BookBub.com

Visit Amazon.com for more books in the
AJ Bailey Adventure Series,
Nora Sommer Caribbean Suspense Series,
and collaborative works;
The Greene Wolfe Thriller Series
Tropical Authors Adventure Series

ABOUT THE AUTHOR

A *USA Today* Bestselling author, Nicholas Harvey's life has been anything but ordinary. Race car driver, adventurer, divemaster, and since 2020, a full-time novelist. Raised in England, Nick has dual US and British citizenship and now lives wherever he and his amazing wife, Cheryl, park their motorhome, or an aeroplane takes them. Warm oceans and tall mountains are their favourite places.

For more information, visit his website at HarveyBooks.com.

9 781959 627050